A FIERCE VENGEANCE

DOUG GIACOBBE

Dedication

For Gayle and Katie, with love.
Thanks as always for your patience.

Thank you for your idea for the cover, Katie.

I also dedicate this book to all the men and women in law
enforcement that I have known, both living and dead.
My other family.

Acknowledgment

I want to thank my good friend Doug Lockard for an interesting story that I borrowed in the creation of this book. We will meet again in paradise, my friend, where we will fish and drink good rum. I also want to thank Jeff Cochran, Miramar Fire Department, retired, for all the good information he provided to me about how trauma calls were handled in 1992.

"Everyone has a price."

Chapter 1

"I can't undo your bra!"

John Hessler laughed through his anger at himself for drinking as much champagne as he had in the last four hours. *What a fucking lousy time to lose motor skills*, he thought, lying at the ocean's edge behind a fancy hotel on Miami Beach trying his best to undress one of the bridesmaids from a friend's wedding. *Time for some wild beach sex*, was all that ran through his alcohol-laden head. Things were not going his way. The young lady, who he had met just one hour prior, was extremely willing to take part in his coital plans; however, she was as drunk and as clumsy as he. "Roll over on your side a second," he said.

Earlier in the evening, she boasted about how much she paid a plastic surgeon to create her huge boobs, and that they were perfect. Hessler was desperate to have his hands around them. She laughed, closed her eyes, and rolled on her left side, away from him. He began fiddling with the hooks on the bra, fumble-fingered from his consumption of so much of Moet's finest. Finally, he managed to unhook her bra and felt the weight of her massive breasts pulling the bra straps from his hands.

"Okay! Now we're in business. Roll back over, sweetheart," he said.

Suddenly he felt her body shiver and shake as her

breathing came in quick, breathy pants. *Wow! She's ready to go*, He thought, but only for a second. She let out a horrific scream, and then slammed him in the face with the back of her head as she came up off the sand like a coiled spring. He tried to hold on to her as she continued to scream. "What the hell is the matter with you? What's wrong?" he yelled as she ran up the beach, her bare breasts—Hessler only dimly registering that they were indeed quite perfect—bouncing in the night air. He tasted blood from his now smashed nose.

The beach lights from the hotel came on, signaling that the wedding party would be moving outside. Hessler rolled over to find out what had freaked her out and made her freeze. His eyes locked on the cold dead stare of a naked woman; her body partially submerged. He witnessed two things that stunned his mind and reactions to fear. The woman's throat was slit open from ear to ear, her tongue pulled out through the incision, and the word "PAYBACK" was written on her chest, right above her breasts.

He could now hear people yelling from the pool area of the hotel. He rolled over, trying to stand, sliding on the soft sand. When he gained his feet, he took a few steps back, staring at the dead woman, and then turned his head and observed two uniformed security officers from the hotel running toward him. As they approached, Hessler reached into the back pocket of his pants, pulling out his wallet and a handkerchief for his nose. Holding the fabric to his face, he held the wallet up, letting one end of it flop down, revealing a gold Miami Beach Police detective's badge. The two security officers didn't seem a bit concerned about the badge, or the man holding it, as they continued running towards the body at the water's edge. "Stop!" yelled Hessler, all Moet fuzz gone from his brain.

The two hotel officers froze.

"I'm Miami Beach Police Homicide, and this is a crime scene. Don't take another step."

"This is hotel property. We need to know what's going on, so we can write a report!" one of the security officers protested.

Angry already about missing his chance to screw the large-breasted bridesmaid and getting a headache as the champagne that leeched from his brain, and with blood still flowing from his nose, Hessler was in no mood to deal with the private security guys from the hotel. "I'm going to say this once. Take another step, and you'll be writing your report from a cell in the Dade County jail!" he yelled, getting angry.

The security officers held back at that. Hessler spun around towards the hotel and noticed a group from the wedding party walking towards him. Through the glaring lights of the hotel, he could see the groom, the best man, and all four of the groomsmen.

"What the hell, John? Please tell me you are not gonna fuck up my wedding day." said the groom, Sergeant Edgar Rodriguez.

Hessler grimaced. "I went looking for love but found a floater with a Colombian necktie," referring to the nickname for the dead woman's grotesque wound.

Rodriguez and the other members of the wedding party all reached into their back pockets and pulled out badge wallets, flashing the security guards as they walked toward Hessler. Each man folded them, badge out, and shoved them into the cummerbunds of their tuxedos. The wedding was now a crime scene. The detectives all turned toward the gathering crowd, deciding how best to secure the area.

3

"She one of your guests, Sarge?" Hessler asked, looking at Rodriguez.

Rodriguez stared at the woman's face for a couple of seconds before answering. "Not that I know of.," he replied. "Maybe one of my wife's friends, but I don't think so."

One of the detectives called MBPD on his cell phone, while another said something in Spanish to a curious hotel waiter hovering nearby, and the waiter ran to the pool deck and stripped a tablecloth from one of the wedding reception tables. Hessler draped the tablecloth across two beach chairs to block the crowd's view of the body.

The wail of approaching sirens got louder while uniformed Miami Beach officers arrived at the beach. The uniforms immediately began to disperse the crowd of onlookers that had gathered.

"Police officers! Get the hell out of the way," came a voice booming from behind the crowd. As if commanded by Moses himself, the crowd parted, allowing through three of the on-duty homicide detectives from the Miami Beach Police Department. Their supervisor, Lieutenant G.P. "Jeep" Little, stopped in his tracks when he noticed the rest of his squad facing the crowd in their wedding clothes.

"You know, I've been a cop in this department for forty-one years, but I've never seen a homicide scene so well guarded by such well-dressed men," he said smiling. His comment was directed at the groom, and Little's second-in-command, Sergeant Rodriguez, who was smiling a bit drunkenly back at his boss.

Little was only the third black officer hired to work for the Beach, as everyone in Miami-Dade law enforcement referred to his department. Even though there were other police departments along the coastline of Miami-

Dade County, there was always only one Beach. In 1951, when Little started his career, blacks weren't even allowed in the island city, unless they were there to work for the White Man as laborers or domestics. He was respected for being a stern, compassionate, and exceptionally thorough investigator. In the past ten years, he had solved every murder investigation assigned to him.

"Sergeant Rodriguez, I think we have enough officers here to keep this scene tight," he said. "Why don't you go back to your bride and enjoy the rest of this very memorable wedding?"

Rodriguez, who had just been promoted to sergeant the previous week, was a bit reluctant to leave the scene, allowing adrenalin to take over good sense. "Aw, c'mon Jeep, we want to work this one," Rodriguez replied. "This is the first murder of 1992! And the first since I got my stripes. We don't want to miss out on it."

Little leaned in close to his second-in-command. "Look, son, I am on wife number three because of this goddamned job," he said. "Now, you listen to old Jeep. If you want to make this your one and only wedding, you move your ass back inside with your bride. And take this drunken bunch of tuxedos with you. There'll be plenty more homicides this year, I'm sure of that. Detective Hessler is the on-call homicide investigator tonight anyway, and he even on-viewed the victim." Jeep leaned in close to Hessler, smelling his breath. "And I know you haven't been drinking tonight, since that would violate department policy for police personnel assigned to call-out, right, Detective Hessler?" he asked, smiling.

Hessler was busted. Staring down at his feet, he could tell this assignment was the penalty he would pay for bending, no, breaking, the rules. "No... No, Lieutenant, nothing but ginger ale," he said, hyper-aware of his unsteady stance and crooked grin.

Little smiled at the detective and patted him on the shoulder. "That's what I figured. A nice Jewish boy like you wouldn't be drinking on the Sabbath, anyway, right?" He said turning again to Rodriguez. "Edgar, why are you still here?"

Rodriguez smiled at his boss and motioned to his groomsmen to follow. Little followed them with his eyes as they walked through the crowd. "You boys be sure to give Edgar and his wife a toast for..." He stopped in mid-sentence when he caught sight of a man staring at him from the crowd. The gray-bearded man was, like Little, in his late fifties, not too tall, with a build like a lowland gorilla. The man was dressed in black pants and a traditional, white-colored Cuban guayabera shirt. Little yelled to Hessler, who was giving information to the other investigators. "Hey, John, keep an eye on the scene a minute, I gotta go take a leak," he said.

Everyone who entered or exited the crime scene would have his or her actions noted on the control sheet. Following protocol, Little checked out from the scene by signing out on a clipboard that was held by a uniformed officer. "Excuse me, excuse me," the lieutenant said as he pushed through the crowd that seemed to be growing by the minute. "Morbid mother-fuckers," he whispered as he bumped hard into the man wearing the guayabera.

That man waited about five seconds, and then walked through the crowd, following Little's footprints in the sand, up the steps to the pool deck, and proceeded to the men's room past the pool. He pulled open the door. Staring around the dim room, he couldn't find Little. He then heard someone urinating in one of the stalls.

"We're good, Juanito, we're alone in here," Little said from the stall. He flushed the toilet and came out, going to the sink to wash his hands, and then he wiped the sweat from his bald head. "So, what's the grand old man of the Miami-Dade Police Department's narcotics unit doing at a homicide scene on my island?"

Detective Juan Jimenez had worked in Miami-Dade PD's Organized Crime Division unit longer than anyone in that unit's storied history. Addicted to the rush of working undercover, he had passed up a promotion several times. He and Little had known each other since they started out in their respective departments as patrolmen. Jimenez leaned up against the sink counter and lit up a cigar. "Oh, I was just cruising around, and I couldn't help but notice a bunch of your patrol cars and a crime scene unit going Code-3 down Washington Street. I thought I'd come and check out whatever was going on. I'm bored tonight," he said with a grin on his face.

"Bullshit!" Little said, "I've known you too many years to believe that Hoss," Little replied. You might be able to B.S. your way around the dopers, but it don't work with me."

Jimenez laughed. "Okay, Jeep," he replied. "I had one of those mysterious messages on my office voice mail earlier that said something interesting was going to wash up on shore in this area tonight. I figured it would be a couple of keys of coke, so I thought I'd come down here and take a walk on your beautiful beach and put some sand in my shoes."

"Call came from Mr. Anonymous?" Little asked. "Oh yeah, usual shit," Jimenez said. "So, who found the body?"

Little chuckled and replied. "One of my homicide boys, John Hessler. He was trying to bang one of the

7

bridesmaids from Edgar Rodriguez's wedding when they realized they were trying to fuck next to a corpse."

Hernandez smiled as he took a drag from the cigar. "Man, that'll kill a hard-on real friggin' quick," he replied. "You got an I.D. on the victim?"

"Nope. White female, mid-thirties, blonde hair, and bare-assed naked," Little Replied. Cause of death, at least the obvious one, was a Colombian necktie. Any chance she's one of your informants or someone you flipped for information?"

"Anything's possible, amigo. Can you arrange for me to take a peek?" Jimenez said.

"Um, yeah. Walk down near the water's edge, and I'll have the uniforms shoo the crowd up towards the building," Little said as they exited the restroom.

Jimenez walked down the steps to the beach, and back down towards the crowd as Little signed back into the crime scene. Jimenez walked around the crowd and crouched down near the water's edge. Almost on cue, two of the uniformed Miami Beach officers began yelling at the crowd and the still frozen security guards to move up the beach toward the hotel. Lieutenant Little crouched down behind the body, and moved the tablecloth from the beach chair, just enough for Jimenez to see the dead woman's face. Under the white-hot glare of the Klieg lights that the crime scene people were using to do their work, Jimenez got a good view of the victim's face. His mouth dropped open.

Detective Hessler saw Jimenez stand up. "Hey, asshole! Hessler yelled. "The officers said move up the beach! Do it now!"

Jimenez started toward the hotel again at a very fast

pace. Little knew that Jimenez recognized the victim from his reaction. He quickly walked to the officer with the clipboard and signed out from the crime scene again, yelling at Hessler as he walked toward the hotel. "John, I gotta go piss again, I'll be right back," he yelled. "You know how it is with us old guys, right?"

Hessler nodded to him and continued writing notes on a legal pad. "Time to get that prostate checked, old man," he mumbled to himself.

Little entered the restroom and found Jimenez wiping his face with a wet paper towel. He was breathing hard, and Little saw an expression he had never seen on that face before: Fear.

"What's going on, Juan? Who the hell is she?" Little asked in a loud voice.

Jimenez fumbled with his lighter, trying to light another cigar. "You got a huge problem here, cabron! He replied. "Your victim is a DEA spook! Her name is Carrie Marvin."

Chapter 2

Goddammit! Little thought, as he ran back down to the beach. Out of breath, he began shouting commands to the uniformed officers guarding the scene. "I want everyone without a badge off of this beach, now!" he yelled. "Advise dispatch I need three more units out here and tell her to wake up the chief and have him call me ASAP!"

The uniforms quickly got loud with the crowd, telling the wedding guests to return to the hotel, and hustling the other hotel guests and beach riffraff away from the area. Little, after catching his breath, told the crime scene techs to erect a portable canopy over the body so people in their hotel rooms above couldn't see down at the dead woman or the crime scene. Little called all the police investigators and the techs together for a huddle. "Alright, guys, here's the deal. The deceased is an undercover agent from the DEA. I don't know what the circumstances are, but this night is gonna' suck something fierce if we don't get this right. Have dispatch call your families and tell them you're gonna be out here for a while." Looking at one of the uniforms, he continued to bark out orders like a man who had been through this too many times. "Go over to Sid's Deli on Collins Avenue and get sandwiches for fifteen, no make that twenty people," he commanded. "And lots of coffee, too. Just tell them it's for Little, he knows I'll take care of him later…" He was interrupted by a conversation between the officer with the clipboard, and what appeared to everyone but Little, to be a bystander. Hessler saw that it was the man in the white guayabera shirt that he had yelled at to move along, earlier. He was fuming mad that the interloper had returned. "Officer! Arrest that son-of-a-bitch and get him the hell out of here!" he shouted.

Little quickly overruled him. "Chill out, John, he's with me," he said as he waved Jimenez in. "This is Juan Jimenez from the Miami-Dade Organized Crime Division. He gave me the identity of the victim. What was her name again, Juan?"

Jimenez crouched next to the body. He made the sign of the cross and stood up. Little and Hessler were rattled to see the tears in his eyes.

"Last name is Marvin, first name Carrie," he replied. She's with… was with… The DEA for a long time. Did a lot of deep cover stuff. The real hard-core deep cover stuff. I met her at a couple of inter-agency task force meetings. I heard she got out of the game, though." Jimenez stared down at the body. He spoke quietly to the victim. "God, I hate seeing this kind of thing. Who did this to you, girl?"

Putting his hand on his old friend's shoulder, Little asked, "Any idea who her supervisor is, or was?" he asked.

Jimenez pulled a handkerchief from his pocket and wiped his eyes. "She was working for Al Cruz, when he was agent-in-charge down here, but Cruz got promoted to District Director," he answered. "The new guy in charge of the Miami office is named Howe, David Howe. I'd call him first and have him take it up the chain of command."

Little had not gotten this far in the Homicide Division without knowing that many a bastard could hide in plain sight in a law enforcement agency. He moved away from

11

Hessler, to speak to Jimenez in private. "Do you know this guy Howe, Juan?" he asked. "Is he a straight shooter?"

Jimenez hesitated a bit too long with his answer. "He's the new 'hot shot' with DEA. Jimenez responded. "About a year ago he was on the U.S. Customs interdiction boat Blue Thunder with Cruz when they got in a chase. Cruz caught a bullet, and one of the Customs guys shot up the smuggler's boat and blew it all to hell. Since then, Howe's been kicking ass. He started making busts right and left, and it got him promoted when Cruz was bumped up to District Director. I worked with Howe on a couple of cases. He gets massive scores of dope, but he has an attitude, that bad boy 'I was a Navy SEAL,' bullshit. And he's a real tight ass about where he gets his intel. It's almost like he's got someone inside some cartels."

Little got on his cell phone and called his dispatcher as the two men walked over to Hessler. "Get on the phone and call the DEA Miami Office," he said. "Tell them that Lieutenant Little from Miami Beach needs to speak to Special-Agent-In-Charge David Howe directly, and that it is an emergency. When you're done, call the chief again and tell him to call me, right now!" He turned to Jimenez and Hessler. "We may as well fuck up his night too, right?" he said.

It took about fifteen minutes before Little's cell phone rang. David Howe sounded like he just woke up. The connection on Little's analog phone was not good.

"I have some bad news for you, Agent Howe," he said. "It involves one of your people who just washed up on my beach, nude and dead. I need you to come down here right now." Little could not tell if Howe sounded skeptical or annoyed.

"What's the dead person's name, Lieutenant?"

Howe replied. "Do you have some identification on whoever it is?"

Little had not even met this guy, and he was already perturbed with him when he replied. "Look, Howe, the deceased is nude, like I said, with no I. D, but I have an investigator here from Dade County O.C.D. who knows this person. I'm not giving you any more information on an unsecured line. Now get your ass down here quick!"

Howe responded with a thick Tennessee accent. "All right, Lieutenant, I'll come down, and I'll even wake my District Director, Al Cruz, to come down there with me. But if this turns out to be bullshit, Cruz will be going to your chief, wanting your balls battered and fried on a plate, ya' hear?"

Little took a deep breath. No doubt, he was not going to like this guy at all. "Listen, son, I could have retired from this place ten years ago," Little answered. "If I'm wrong, you can go to the friggin' Governor and complain. Doesn't make any matter to me. So, get down here— now!" He said this as he hit the end button on the phone. "There is no satisfaction in hitting the 'end call' button the way there is in slamming down a receiver," he said. He turned to Jimenez, who was smiling slightly and shaking his head. "Interesting fellow," Little said. "I got two of my investigators on this squad that were Army Special Forces, and their attitude is way cooler than that ass wipe. What the hell is his problem?"

*****

At least one hour passed before a black Chevy Suburban pulled up in the parking lot of the hotel, near to the beach. Two men showed their credentials to the officer with the

13

guest list and signed in. Another officer notified Jeep Little of the new arrivals. Little motioned DEA District Director Alberto Cruz and Special Agent-in-Charge of the Miami DEA office David Howe into the crime scene. "I'm Lieutenant Little, Homicide, Little said in a formal voice. "Sorry to have to get you boys out of bed, but we need a positive I.D. on a homicide victim who may be one of your people."

The smaller of the two men reacted first. "Al Cruz, Lieutenant. This is David Howe. What makes you think your victim is one of our people?"

The voice that came from behind him caused Cruz to jump. "It's Carrie Marvin, Alberto!" Juan Jimenez said in almost a crying voice.

Cruz spun on the spot, his eyes wide open. "It can't be true. It can't be true," he chanted to himself, feeling his breath coming faster and heavier. He stared at Juan Jimenez for a couple of seconds, knowing this man never made mistakes, and then turned to Jeep Little. "May I see the victim, Lieutenant?" he asked.

Little recognized the strain on Cruz's face. Like Jimenez, Cruz's eyes were tearing up. Little thought, someone important is lying down there. "Sure, Cruz, come on." he said as compassionately as he could. The four men walked over to the body. Hessler was crouched down, digging around in the sand near a footprint that he found. He stood up quickly.

"What the hell is this?" he inquired, startled by the presence of the men. "It's okay, John," Little said. "They're here to make the I.D."

Al Cruz stared down at the woman in the sand and gasped. Tears began pouring down his face when he glanced into Carrie's lifeless eyes. His hot Cuban temper

14

kicked into high gear. "When I find the mother-fucker who did this, I swear I will cut him from his balls to his throat!" he said in a quiet but angry voice.

Howe stood to the side, showing no emotion, describing the wound on his cell phone, along with the word *Payback* written on her chest. "Hold on a minute," Howe said to the person on the phone. "There's something written on her belly. Looks like Spanish." He leaned over. "*Todas las casas se vienen cayendo*," he said in his thick southern accent. Looking up to the other three, he asked, "What's that mean?"

"It means, 'all of your houses will come falling down around you'," Cruz said, still wiping his eyes. Howe let out an emotionless, "Huh. All right, Lieutenant," said Howe, "you've got your positive ID, so what have you got so far?"

Little was starting to lose his patience. "Well, first I have some questions for you, Agent Howe. Was this woman working on an active case?"

Cruz answered the question. "She left the agency a year ago, Lieutenant. As a matter of fact, it was a year ago this week. But she's been under our protection in one of our safe-houses in Boca Raton for the past week."

Howe interrupted him. "Boca Raton P.D. has just arrived at the safe-house, Al. They found both of our protection agents there dead. They said there must have been a hell of a struggle, from the way the place looks. We need to get up there."

Jeep Little was far from satisfied. "Not so fast, gentlemen," he said. "I have a homicide here that I have lots of questions about. Why was Miss Marvin in your safe house?"

Cruz kept staring at Carrie's face as he answered. "She's, I mean, she was, a witness in a case we're building on a druggie named Derrick Drake. We received some intel from our snitches that a hit man, a real pro, had been hired to take her out. Nothing we could verify, but we had to take precautions. Hell, Lieutenant, she was one of our own."

"I understand how you feel, Mr. Cruz," Little replied. "My one and most important goal in this job, even before catching the bad guys, is that all my people go home alive, and in one piece, at the end of their shift. That's what matters most. How do you think this hitman found your safe house?"

Howe chimed in. "There weren't many people who knew about the house, or Marvin being there. We... Obviously have a leak in our agency. Someone may have gotten into our computer system. And when I find out who the bastard was that is leaking the info, I will personally break his or her neck. Again, Lieutenant, what have you got, so far? I mean, we'll work with you if you work with us."

Jeep looked at the man for a few long seconds and then replied, "Like I told you on the phone, we got a body. The Medical Examiner left just before you arrived. She told me that Ms. Marvin hadn't been dead very long. She didn't float up on the beach 'cause she's not bloated enough to be buoyant, yet. Clearly, she was placed here for someone to find. Based on what appears to be the cause of death, her throat being cut, and the writing on her chest, someone she knows must have really pissed off the person who hired the hitman. Any idea who the intended recipient is?"

Cruz and Howe stared at each other for a moment before they spoke in unison. "Callaway."

Howe stepped away as he took another phone call

from the Boca Raton police, followed by one from his own agents who had just reached the scene there. He then spoke to the FBI investigators who were on their way to the no longer safe house, eighty or so miles up the coast.

Cruz explained the situation of Carrie Marvin and Michael Callaway to the lieutenant.

"Mike Callaway is her fiancé. He's a former Customs Service Blue Thunder boat driver."

Jeep interrupted him. "I've heard the name. Wasn't he the one that blew up the drug boat you were talking about earlier?" he said, looking at Juan Jimenez.

Cruz immediately began rubbing the bullet-wound scar on his right side as he related the events of that night one year ago.

"Howe and I were with Callaway and his partner Hidalgo, because Howe had Intel on an in-bound drug boat," he said. "Carrie Marvin gave us the information while she was working a deep cover op on the late drug kingpin, Anton Drake. We chased a go-fast boat full of coke headed for Miami. One of the assholes on the drug boat opened up on us with a machine gun, and I took a bullet in the side. Callaway fired back, and must have hit their fuel tank or something, 'cause he blew them all to bits. Callaway got in a shit-sandwich with his Customs boss about blowing up the boat, and he resigned."

"I remember that night. We saw the fireball from the explosion here on the beach. Where is he now? Is he still on the job somewhere else?" Little asked, scribbling in his pocket-sized black book.

Cruz looked out to sea as he answered. "He's either at the 15th Street Marina in Fort Lauderdale, or on his boat, fishing in the Bahamas."

Little seemed surprised. "Sounds like comfortable

easy work for a guy who lost his job. How's he paying for all of that?"

Cruz gave Little a slight smile. "The man fell into a barrel of shit and came up smelling like money. He won $82 million on the Lotto a couple of nights before he was supposed to be terminated from his job. He bought a boat, and transits between here and the Bahamas quite a bit."

Jeep smiled. "Good for him, but was his and Miss Marvin's relationship, okay?" he asked, pointing at the body. "You don't think he had anything to do with this, do you?"

"No! No way!" Cruz almost shouted. "They were crazy in love with each other, they were supposed to get married soon. As a matter of fact, they just bought a very expensive condo on the beach in Fort Lauderdale."

"I have to ask, to cover all the angles," Jeep said in his most mellow voice. Jeep had been in this man's shoes and knew emotions were raw and ragged for him.

Cruz continued. "I know who is ultimately responsible for this, Lieutenant: Derrick Drake. Anton Drake's son. He's a sadistic little expatriated Brit with no other family since his father died, and no friends. If there is a hit man who did this, and Drake hired him, then he may not be done yet. He may come for Callaway, too. But yeah, my pensions on Drake as the person who set this up." He again glanced at Carrie, as if he did so long enough, the whole scene would go away, or he would wake from this bad dream or something, anything, but this horrible end. "Callaway and Carrie killed Drake's father, down in the Bahamas last year, purely self-defense, so I'm sure this is Derrick's idea of revenge," Cruz continued," It will be hard to pin it on him though, unless we find the hit man, or the." Cruz stopped short of saying what Jeep Little was already thinking.

"Mole?" Little said, looking deep into his eyes.

Cruz didn't respond.

"Look, Cruz, if I was in your position, I wouldn't admit it either," Little said. "But it appears you got someone inside who's spilling the beans to the wrong people. And those wrong people got this beautiful young woman dead in a horrible, horrible way, and then dumped her on my beach. Does your agency have an internal investigation going on that can find this person?"

Cruz just kept staring down, saying nothing, causing the normally calm Little to lose his temper.

"Jesus Christ!" Little yelled. "You haven't done anything to find the mole, have you? Have you gotten with any of the local agencies that work with you involved with this little problem?"

Startled by the outburst, Howe peeked up from his phone call.

Again, there was no answer from Cruz.

"Shit, man! You know how many people you're putting in danger this way?" Little continued. "If whoever this person is has enough access to find your god-dammed safe house, and your star witness, then sure as hell, he or she's got the names of every local cop assigned to working a task force with your agency. Goddamn! You're gonna get a lot more people killed. Some maybe from my department! I mean, what happened to the protocols? Did Boca Raton P.D. know about the safe house? Did they know it was being used? Did they know you had such a high-value witness staying there?

Cruz lashed out at Jeep. "Stand down, Lieutenant! We don't know who we can trust within our own agency, or where this person is, meaning we don't know if it's a field agent, or some goddamned secretary somewhere. We don't know if it's a man or a woman. I spoke to our bosses in Washington, and they wanted Howe and me to handle it. They've assigned some federal people, outside of the agency, to sniff around, covering it by calling it an agency audit. They will have clearance to dig deep into people's files and try to point us in the right direction, but you've got to help me, Lieutenant, by keeping your mouth shut about this. You know what gossips cops can be. You let this out to too many people, and eventually the investigation gets back to the Mole! And then we've got nothing." Cruz stopped abruptly and glanced back down at the body of Carrie Marvin. "We'll find the piece of crap who did this, Chiquita, and when we do, I'm going to filet him, or her, like a fucking fish."

"And what about her fiancé? What do you think he's gonna do when he hears what happened to his lover?" Little asked.

Cruz blew out a breath of air, hard, before he replied. "Thanks for reminding me of something that's going to be a huge problem. I know Michael Callaway. He's gonna want to set course for Drake's island and kill the little shit with his bare hands. The problem, as I said, is going to be keeping him under control while we do the investigation."

Little looked up and saw the usual members of the press congregating outside of the crime scene, setting up their cameras. "I gotta go talk to the vultures now, Cruz," Little said, shaking his head. "If you get any information that will help our investigation, call me. We will be communicating with each other, right?

Cruz nodded, and walked over to Howe, who was still talking on his cell phone. "Get off the damned phone, Howe, unless you are trying to track down Callaway. We have to get to him first with this news?"

"On it, Chief. Our people located Callaway," Howe replied. "He's in Eleuthera, in the Bahamas. His boat is tied up at Cape Eleuthera Marina. You wanna call him, or do you want me to do it?"

Cruz stared out at the first grayish light of the morning, that was peaking over the horizon. "No," he said. "Call Opa Locka Airport and tell our aviation guys to get the *Blackhawk* warmed up. I don't want to do this with a phone call. This will have to be a face-to-face moment. And make sure our people over there have a vehicle, and a boat for us to use. That island is slim, but it's one hundred and ten miles long, and Callaway could be just about anywhere on it or off the shore of it, fishing. It'd be better if we flew him back here, anyway. I know he's gonna want to see her. I know I would. We owe him that, and with the bonus that it will keep him from invading Derrick's island and causing an international incident. Let's roll. It's gonna be a long, lousy day."

Cruz and Howe stopped to listen to part of Jeep Little's conversation with the press people. "As of this time, we have no other information," he said. "Since this is an ongoing investigation, and we haven't notified the victim's next of kin, we will not release the victim's name, or anything else about the case. Thank you."

When the two DEA men left, Detective Hessler walked over to Jeep very confused about the situation.

"You heard the conversation I had with those two?" Little asked as he watched Cruz and Howe walk away.

Hessler cocked his head to one side and smiled. "Hell, Jeep, I think people heard you yelling all the way to Boca Raton," he responded. "This whole situation stinks. What do you figure is going on here?"

Little looked at Detective Jimenez, and both men

frowned and shook their heads. "Whatever it is, all we need to be concentrating on is figuring out who killed this pretty lady. Are you about done here?"

Hessler ran down his checklist and nodded.

Little let out a deep breath, as he saw his Chief walking toward the scene from the hotel. "Okay, are the removal people on the way to transport Ms. Marvin to the Medical Examiner's office?" Little said, holding out a container of Tic Tacs to his lead detective.

Hessler turned to see what his lieutenant was looking at. When he saw the chief walking their way, he quickly grabbed the container and popped five of the mints into his mouth. "Body snatchers are on the way, boss," he said, looking a bit guilty. "Thanks for the mints."

Let me talk to the chief, first," Little said. "You eat some more of those things before I bring you in. Like Mr. Cruz said, it's gonna be a long, lousy day."

Chapter 3

"C'mon baby, just give me a little more! You're almost there! Just a little more!"

Michael Callaway was breathing heavily as he pulled the trigger-throttle so hard it felt like it would break off the handlebars. He heard laughter coming from the radio headset built into his full-face helmet. A female voice with a British accent began giving him grief.

"Why does everything you Americans say have to sound sexual, Callaway?"

He laughed, as he watched the speed rise on the digital speedometer on top of the handlebars of one of the first Yamaha WaveRunner watercraft ever to be turbocharged. He flew over the glass-smooth bay near Governors Harbor in Eleuthera. The addition of the exhaust-driven supercharger, forcing thirteen pounds of air pressure into the intake of the watercraft's engine, bumped up the horsepower from awesome to freaky, and gave the little beast a top speed of over one hundred miles per hour. Or at least it was supposed to according to the builder. Just what a newly rich, speed-junkie like Michael Callaway needed to keep his boredom level down.

The woman taunting him over the radio was the builder of this water rocket. Mary Booker grew up around engines. For many years, her father was an aircraft engine mechanic in England's Royal Air Force. To earn more than his serviceman's pay, Warrant Officer Ralph Booker always ran an engine shop as a side job, wherever he was stationed, and even though he was an airplane specialist, his first love was boat engines. As Mary told Callaway in the past, it was a great departure to work on things that went fast on the earth instead of above it. Her childhood memories of her father were of them working on engines in whatever town, near whatever RAF airfield, where he was stationed. She earned a degree in mechanical engineering along the way, and it was no surprise when she began building and fine-tuning racing boats for a living. She settled on New Providence Island, in Nassau, with a small shop catering to people who had more money than brains when it came to going fast on the water. After moving to the island of Eleuthera, she constructed several boats that won the Miami to Nassau Powerboat Race, and then she got into building personal watercraft that ran at speeds absolutely frightening to most sane people. Michael Callaway wasn't one of those sane people.

"Hey, Mary. I thought you said this thing would bust a hundred. What happened to truth in advertising?" He breathed heavily into the microphone as he hunched his six foot one-inch frame down as he possibly could to make both man and machine as aerodynamic as possible.

"Relax, luv," Mary replied. "It takes time to get the motor and the hull to work together. You're a good-sized fella, so it will take a bit more adjusting. You Yanks are always in such a bloody hurry. Leave it to Mary. You know I'll get her running right!"

Callaway had no concerns. He met Mary when his last boat, Blue Thunder III, a United States Customs Service drug interdiction chase boat, developed engine problems on a patrol in the Bahamas. With one of its engines coughing and belching smoke from the exhausts, Callaway and his partner Jorge Hidalgo thought it the wiser move to tie it up at the nearest dock to try to make repairs. Callaway, having worked as a boat mechanic in his younger days, thought that they had taken on some bad fuel when they gassed up in the Bimini Island chain. He worried that perhaps the typical urine-quality Bahamian gasoline contained water and would soon affect the other of the two 580 cubic-inch "Rat Motors" powering the blue boat with the same malady, leaving them adrift at sea.

They limped the boat into New Providence harbor and radioed their base in Miami that they were out of service in Nassau.

Their then boss, Special-Agent-in-Charge Richard Todd, had his communications officer radio back that if he saw any activity on their agency credit card from Greasy Dick's bar, one of Callaway and Hidalgo's favorite hangouts on that island, they would both be fired.

Callaway asked around the local docks if there was a mechanic capable of working on the powerful Chevy boat motors, and only Mary Booker's name was mentioned. When the two met, they hit it off as if they were brother and sister. Both were military brats who loved to make boat motors run stronger. Callaway may have been the speed junkie, but Booker was the engine junkie. Within ten minutes, she diagnosed the problem as a case of overheated fuel mixture in one of the huge carburetors that fed fuel to the cast iron beasts that propelled the boat. Callaway was a little doubtful.

"Tell your mate to fire it up," she said.

Callaway whistled at Jorge, spinning his right index

finger in the air when his partner turned his way. The motor rumbled to life, running as rough as an alligator's back. Callaway watched as Mary, all of five-feet tall and as wide as a small barrel, walked over to the shop refrigerator and pulled two ice trays from the freezer. She dumped all the ice cubes on to a shop towel that was lying on a table, and then laid another shop towel on top of the cubes. Callaway's eyes widened when Mary grabbed a small sledgehammer and began pounding on the ice cubes, pulverizing them into little pieces. She then climbed up on the stern of the boat, leaning into the open motor compartment, with the ice chips in hand. With one hand, she unscrewed the wing nut holding the lid of the air filter housing and lifted the cover off, exposing the top of the carburetor. The Holly 800 cubic feet per minute Dominator carburetor sounded like it was trying to do its job of blending fuel with the giant whoosh of air that it was drawing in but was having trouble doing so.

"She sounds a bit constipated, don't ya think?" she yelled as she unfolded the shop towel, and to Callaway's amazement, began dropping chips of ice down into the sucking maw of the giant brass fuel mixer. The engine smoothed out almost immediately. Callahan thought for a second, and then shook his head and smiled.

"Water injection," he said as he rolled his eyes. She nodded affirmative and smiled back at him. By the time she was done playing with the engine's timing and the fuel jets on the carburetor, the Customs Service boat idled with a meaner sound then she ever had before.

"You probably had some crud on the exhaust valves, and that caused her to choke a bit. She should run fine now," Mary said.

Callaway pulled out his government credit card to

pay for the work, but Mary wouldn't hear of it. "I've heard from the locals that you boys are doing a great job out there. This one's on me."

Callaway smiled graciously, but he explained that without a bill to show why he and Jorge were out of service, their jerk of a boss would probably suspend them. She reluctantly complied, and an instant friendship was established between the boat mechanic from Liverpool, and the speed-junkie from Florida.

Bouncing along off Governor's Harbor, Callaway smiled, knowing that Mary would get the WaveRunner running right. He slowed down and turned back toward the dock. When he arrived, he gently cruised the little rocket up on to a davit and pulled off his helmet, allowing all the sweat in his military-style haircut to run down his face. He climbed up on to the dock, still buzzing with adrenalin from the ride, and flipped the switch that lifted the little craft up to dock level.

He was jogged back to earth with the sound of a vehicle driving up the dirt road leading to Mary's water's edge shop. The Chevy Tahoe had so much dark tint on the windows that Callaway couldn't see the occupants inside, even from the front. The passenger-side front door opened slightly, and a hand, holding a badge, poked out of the opening on top. He watched as Alberto Cruz climbed out and began walking toward him.

Oh shit, Callaway thought, *this couldn't be good. It's Carrie*.

"What's going on, Cruz?" he shouted as the driver's door opened and the tall, muscular frame of David Howe slid out of the truck. When neither answered immediately, Callaway began to feel his chest tightening up. Gut gripping feelings of panic set in. "God damn, it *is*

Carrie!" You fuckers let her get hurt," he said, not wanting to believe it could be anything worse. His breath began coming in strong and loud, snorting like the enraged bull he was about to become.

"What the hell happened, Cruz!" he yelled, causing Mary to come running to his side. Callaway started pacing toward the car.

There was nothing else that Cruz could say.

"She's dead, Mike. I'm so, so sorry, but Carrie's dead."

Chapter 4

Darkness closed in on Callaway as he collapsed to his knees the second Cruz finished the sentence. He was breathing short, fast, and panic-stricken, staring at the ground without seeing anything. Carrie was gone. Mary knelt and put her arm around him. Tears welling, Mary saw Callaway's eyes contort into an angry squint. His jaw clenched so hard that she thought she would hear his teeth cracking. He continued looking down.

"What happened, Cruz?" he growled again through clenched teeth. His fists were balled up with rage, and he could feel the shock and panic begin its consuming metamorphosis into cold rage.

Callaway and Cruz had become friends since the incident with Anton Drake. Carrie's friendship with Cruz was the glue that changed the two men from old competitors in the drug enforcement business to good friends. Of course, Callaway's shattering Drake's smuggling enterprise by sinking his drug-hauling submarine, and Carrie killing the man with a fishing lure, taking one of the world's biggest drug smugglers from this world, helped solidify the friendship, too. Now Callaway was mad as hell at the friend who brought him this terrible news.

Cruz couldn't look at Callaway. He stared up at the

roof of Mary's shop as he began to speak. "We... We had her in the safe house in Boca. I mean you know that God, I'm sorry I can't wrap my mind around all of this. Somehow, that information got out. Someone leaked the location. Both agents on guard were killed..."

"Al!" Callaway raged, finally looking up from the ground. "What happened to Carrie?"

"She... She washed up on South Beach, dead," Cruz mumbled with tears rolling down his cheeks.

"Leads?" Callaway questioned, still breathing in short, hard breaths, clenching his hands, he knew full well who was responsible for Carrie's death.

Howe spoke before Cruz could answer.

Howe spoke before Cruz could. "Miami Beach P.D. is handling' the homicide on Marvin. FBI and Boca Raton P.D. are handling' the killing of our two agents." Even with the drawl, his words were cold and emotionless as he continued. "She washed up on shore naked."

Cruz turned on Howe, angry beyond belief at the guy's callousness. He turned back to see Callaway, who was now up on his feet, and giving Howe an evil stare.

"You were the one guarding her, Howe. Who gave up the safe house? She told me you would be protecting her there! How did you fuck this up?"

Howe's cockiness came blasting out. "You were the one who fucked up, Callaway, when you got yourself involved in her undercover op on Anton Drake! She had a good undercover going on, but you just had to get involved. All you ended up with was Drake dead, and both of you damn near getting killed! Hell, you caused an international incident, Callaway! If you'd stayed out of it, both the Drakes would be in jail, and she'd be alive," referring to Callaway's unwanted entry into Carrie's deep cover DEA investigation of Drake's unknown method of smuggling drugs into the United States. In a period of one week, Callaway "accidentally" sank Drake's drug-smuggling submarine, and helped Carrie kill the man. Howe's words went through Callaway's brain like an ice pick.

Callaway stared at the man for a brief second. "Fuck you!" He bellowed as he ran straight for Howe. Futilely, Cruz tried to grab Callaway, but the bigger man shoved him aside. Howe stood perfectly still until Callaway's hands came up. He grabbed Callaway's right wrist with his right hand, with strength that felt like a vice grip, and spun around, pulling Callaway over his hip, and flipping him on to the ground on his back. Callaway groaned as he hit the ground. His anger overwhelmed him as he tried to get up to continue his attack when Cruz shoved him back down.

"Leave him be, Mike! He was a Navy SEAL, he'll hurt you bad."

Callaway struggled to get up, but this time Cruz had gravity to help him corral his angry friend.

"You're not thinking straight, man. You can't win this way!"

Callaway squinted his eyes at Cruz, blinked once, and realized he was right. He pulled himself up to a sitting position and exhaled like he had just surfaced from a very deep dive. Howe stood smirking in the background until his boss glared at him. Cruz was not pleased with his subordinate.

"You!" he said with a finger pointed at Howe. "Come with me!"

Smirk now gone; Howe followed Cruz around to the back of the Tahoe. Howe had seen the man's hot Cuban temper in the past. And even though he towered over his boss physically, Cruz, as a District Director, could crash and burn his recent upwardly mobile career in a heartbeat.

"Look Al…" Howe started to say before Cruz cut him off.

"You are a callous asshole, Howe!" Cruz yelled. "You think you're a hot shit since you got promoted? Well, get this good, *pinga*! I am a much hotter shit than you are. You ever talk like this to a friend of mine, or anyone in this kind of situation again, and I'll have you busted down walking a beagle, looking for contraband fruit at the airport in fucking Immokalee! Do you read me, dickhead?"

Howe closed his eyes, clenching his teeth hard, making it difficult to force the words out. "Yes, sir," he said, just louder than a whisper.

"What the hell happened to you, man?" Cruz asked. "You didn't have this cocky attitude before. You better cut it out if you know what's good for you."

Cruz, still fuming, walked back around the SUV, and said, "Callaway, I hate to do this, buddy, but I need your help. Carrie's mom is coming from Indiana to claim the body. You're the closest thing to a family she's got left. You up to it?"

Callaway had met Carrie's mother only once in the year since the run in with Anton Drake, and the announcement of their engagement. Cruz was right about Carrie's mom needing help, as the woman was alone and in bad health. Drake could wait. Seeing his dead fiancé on a steel table in the Medical Examiners' office would be really rough on him too, but he knew he owed this to Carrie. Arms crossed over his chest as if he was in terrible pain, Callaway turned toward Mary, but all he could say was, "Thanks."

Cruz, Callaway, and Howe got into the DEA vehicle, and drove to the airport. They climbed into the Blackhawk, with Howe taking the seat next to the pilot. Cruz and Callaway climbed into the rear compartment seats and put on the headsets that allowed them to speak in the very loud aircraft. The DEA chopper lifted off and headed for Miami.

Revenge. Retribution. Murder. Vengeance. These words formed the cadence of Callaway's very being, marching in time with the *whoosh-whoosh* of the chopper's blades. Callaway shot daggers of death into Howe's back for the first twenty minutes until Howe turned around in his seat and stared at him. Cruz motioned with his finger, telling Howe to face the windshield, kind of like a teacher would do to a little kid. The gesture was meant to be demeaning. Cruz leaned forward to the center console and switched the intercom system to Rear-Private e, allowing him to speak to Callaway without Howe or the pilot hearing them. "Pay no attention to him, Mike. He's an asshole!" he said.

Callaway glared at Cruz, but then his eyes changed to something different, something more primal. He glanced out the side window of the chopper.

He may be an asshole, Al, but he was probably right about me, he thought.

Silence engulfed the chopper for the rest of the flight.

Chapter 5

"Are you sure you want to do this, Mrs. Marvin?" Callaway asked.

With Cruz and Howe in the front seat, Callaway was in the back doing his best to keep his rage contained, trying to be as soft-spoken as he could be with Carrie's mom as they approached the office of the Miami-Dade County Medical Examiner. Callaway tried to be strong, thinking of all the autopsies he had witnessed, but also realizing that this poor woman had been through the experience of identifying a loved one in the past, too. He asked her again if she wanted him to make the official I.D. She smiled at him with tears in her eyes and nodded no.

"I've got to see my baby girl, Mike. One more time," she said.

He nodded, trying his best to smile, but his face stayed the same: hard, frightening, and brutal. Just as it was when Cruz told him of Carrie's death.

The vehicle rolled to a stop in front of the grim looking white building near Jackson Memorial Hospital that appeared like the entrance to a tunnel. Mike helped her out of the vehicle and down the ramp to the front door. Inside, it was ice-cold, as Cruz and Howe showed their identification to the woman at the reception desk. She used the telephone to alert the on-duty deputy medical examiner that a family was there to view and identify a body. They were then ushered down a hallway to a very substantial room that had numerous three-by-three-foot stainless-steel doors.

Callaway saw the strain on Mrs. Marvin's face. She did this before, with Carrie at her side, when drug dealers near the city of Gary, Indiana murdered her husband and Carrie's first fiancé. Mrs. Marvin clutched at Callaway's arm as she immediately remembered the smell of that horrible place when she walked into the autopsy room.

"I feel dizzy."

Callaway saw her eyes rolling back, and he grabbed her as her knees began to buckle. Cruz helped Callaway led her to a chair, while Howe stood there impassively watching.

Deputy Medical Examiner Dr. Barry Berman walked in from another autopsy room, and seeing Mrs. Marvin, went to a drawer and grabbed an ammonia inhalant. Breaking the glass vile in the inhalant, he gently held it under the grieving woman's nose, until her eyes opened, and her head snapped up.

"Are you alright, ma'am?" he said, turning and looking surprised, when he saw Callaway.

The two met many times, back when Callaway was a Ranger in Everglades National Park. Berman had the misfortune, it seemed, to be the on-call Medical Examiner on the midnight shift every time a body was found in the park. Because this happened so often, with all the drug turf wars that went on in the southern part of Miami-Dade County, he and Callaway crossed paths on more mosquito-packed nights than he wanted to think about.

Berman was a tall man, with long graying hair that he kept in a ponytail and a face that never showed any expression. He stood up straight as he eyed Callaway.

"Are you involved in this case, Callaway?" he asked. "I thought this was the Beach's homicide?"

Cruz pulled out his I.D. and showed it to Berman. "I'm District Director Alberto Cruz, DEA. This is Agent in Charge Howe of the Miami office. It is a Miami Beach homicide, sir. This is the victim's mother, Mrs. Marvin, and Mr. Callaway is the fiancé of the deceased."

Berman put one of his oversized hands on Mrs. Marvin's shoulder.

"I'm sorry for your loss, Ma'am," he said, as he stared at Callaway somewhat puzzled.

"Mr. Cruz, can I speak to you and Mr. Callaway for a minute, alone?"

Callaway and Cruz walked with Berman into the other autopsy room. As bad as the body storage room smelled, Callaway was taken aback, as he had when he attended autopsies in the past, by how much worse this room smelled.

"I'm sorry for your loss, Callaway, but what exactly is going on here?" he asked. "I mean, the DEA guy here called you mister. Are you still law enforcement?"

Callaway answered, looking at Berman with no expression. "No, Barry, I got out about a year ago. But I'm involved in this more than I really want to explain right now," he replied.

Berman looked up at the ceiling. "Do you know the physical condition of the victim, Callaway?" he asked. "Do you know how she died?"

Callaway thought for a brief second, before he realized that he had never asked how Carrie was murdered, and as he whirled around and locked eyes with Cruz, he realized he had never been told either. Cruz swallowed hard, as *he* realized that he was about to be in

36

a world of grief for not telling him. He opened his mouth to speak, but Berman beat him to it.

"Her throat was cut, and her tongue was pulled out through the wound," he said. "I won't know if that was the cause of death, though, until I complete the autopsy."

Callaway's eyes were burning a hole through Cruz's face, while the DEA Director babbled out his next sentence.

"I'm sorry, Mike! I... I just didn't have the heart to tell you."

Callaway's eyes blazed at Cruz, and he was about to burst with rage, when he thought of Carrie's mom.

"Doc, you've got to be real careful when you pull the sheet down for Mrs. Marvin to make the I.D." he pleaded. "She can't see Carrie's throat cut. Please, man, you've got to help me out. Her husband was murdered years ago, and she doesn't need to go through this crap again."

Berman had been a cold and careful son-of-a-bitch at every dead body scene that he had been called out to when Callaway was involved. But this time, when he saw how distraught Callaway was, his normally hard facial expression softened.

"She knows we have to do an autopsy, right?" Berman asked.

"Well, I'm sure that Indiana, where her husband was murdered, has the same requirements regarding a homicide that we do, so I'm guessing her husband had one," Callaway replied. "I just want to make this as easy as I can for her," Callaway said, almost pleading with the man.

"Okay, Callaway," Berman said, letting out a sigh. "But you still owe me a mummy."

He walked off to prepare Carrie for viewing.

"Mike, I can't tell you how bad I feel…" Cruz began to say.

Callaway interrupted him before he could finish. "Shut up, Cruz. Just shut up," he replied. "I get it. You were trying to help me out. I'm still pissed at you, and I will wring every last detail out of you before this day is done, but I get it."

Relief flooded Cruz's face. He was, however, confused by the last statement Berman made to Callaway. "What was the M.E. talking about when he said you owe him a *mummy*?"

Callaway sighed and said, "It's a running joke between us. One night on the midnight shift, back when I was a U.S. Park Police Officer in Everglades National Park, a snook fisherman anchored his boat in the Shark River, right next to a dead guy lying on the shore. He had to run his boat all the way back to where he launched, at Flamingo, to use a pay phone. When he called in from the phone booth there, he described the body as looking like a mummy. It turned out that the dead guy was wrapped in a bunch of sheets when he was dumped. Between the body decomposing and the buzzards working him over for a few days, he kinda appeared to be a mummy. Anyway, when I took Berman out there in my patrol boat, he got a little pissed off when he determined it was just another dead dope hauler. He wanted a mummy really badly."

He thought for a couple of seconds before he continued. "I guess he remembered the guy because the doper was killed the same way as Carrie. His throat was cut, and his tongue was pulled out through the wound, too. A Colombian Necktie."

Berman opened the door and motioned the two men into the body storage room, where Mrs. Marvin and

38

Howe waited. Hearing the door of the lobby open, he turned suddenly as another man walked into the body storage room.

"Detective Hessler!" Berman said. Hessler gave Berman an odd stare. "What's the matter Doc, you forget I was coming in for the…"

Berman cut him off in a loud, deep, voice. "Viewing!" he almost shouted, startling the detective, not wanting to hear the word *autopsy,* as he continued. "This is Mrs. Marvin, the victim's mother, and Mr. Callaway, the victim's fiancé. I don't know if you know these gentlemen from the DEA?"

"Yes, I do know them," Hessler said, extending his hand first to Mrs. Marvin. "Ma'am, please allow me to convey my sympathies, and that of the Miami Beach Police Department to you. I'm Detective John Hessler, the lead detective investigating your daughter's homicide case. From what I've learned about your Carrie, I know she was a true hero."

Mrs. Marvin smiled at the detective, looking totally wrung out while shaking his hand. Callaway couldn't help noticing a coolness that Hessler displayed towards him when they made eye contact. "Mr. Callaway?" Hessler said. "My condolences to you too, Sir. Uh… When we're through here today, I will need to speak with you."

From the tone of the detective's voice, Callaway understood this would not be a social conversation. He was to be questioned about Carrie's death. Standard operating procedure by whoever was investigating the crime. Callaway just nodded at the man.

Everyone then followed Dr. Berman into the viewing room. Carrie was on an examination table, with the sheet pulled tight up under her chin. Berman did a good job of securing the sheet under the stainless-steel table by using duct tape to hold it to the underside. Mrs. Marvin would not see the horrible things that were done to her daughter. Regardless, she began to weep, again burying her face in Callaway's shoulder.

Callaway stood there, staring at the face of the woman he loved. No tears in his eyes, just a twisting, painful knot of anger in the back of his head from the rage he was feeling. He had no way of knowing that his lover, before him on the examination table, had reacted the exact same way when she went with her mother and had to identify her father and first fiancé years before. He had yet to realize he was damaged, as brutally mutilated in the soul as Carrie's body had been in death. Damaged to a point where vengeance was not just the cadence in his brain, but his life from now on. All he could picture in his mind was the face of Derrick Drake. *Revenge. Vengeance.* A face he wanted to smash with his bare hands. He would have to find a way to get to Golgotha, Drake's private island in the Bahamas, to destroy the disgusting creature that killed her. *Think, Callaway, think. What do you need do to complete the act of revenge?* He needed information that would help him figure out who helped commit the murder. Drake wasn't the only one. He knew that. There had to be local people who were involved, along with some of Drake's hired scumbags from his private island, to take Carrie from a guarded safe house without anyone knowing of it until she washed up on that beach. He needed to figure it all out and make everyone involved pay the maximum price.

Dr. Berman had to ask Mrs. Marvin the question, the one that he had asked hundreds of mentally broken relatives, whose loved one's lay on one of these cold, stainless steel tables before them. "Ma'am, can you identify the woman on the table? Is she your daughter, Carrie Lynn Marvin?"

Mrs. Marvin sobbed loudly, gazing at her daughter, and then whispered, "Yes."

She turned and hugged Callaway, crying uncontrollably. He quickly walked her out of the room and sat her in a chair in the waiting room. Detective Hessler walked out and put his hand on the distraught woman's shoulder.

"Mrs. Marvin, again, I am very sorry for your loss," he said. Hessler stood up straight, and looking at Callaway, handed him, and Mrs. Marvin one of his business cards.

"Mr. Callaway, when you have a chance, fairly soon, I need you to contact me, so we can talk. Again, my condolences, sir."

Hessler turned around and walked down a hallway and through a door to the autopsy room, making sure the door locked behind him. He stopped about two steps into the room. Dr. Berman was preparing the tools he would use to take Carrie Marvin's body apart, so he could determine just how she died. He watched Berman adjust the microphone that hung from the ceiling, the one that he would use to verbally describe and record everything that he said and did, and found, during the autopsy. Hessler cautioned the man, before he did anything else.

"Hey, Doc. Why don't you give it a couple of minutes until Mrs. Marvin clears the building? Your voice kind of carries, and she doesn't need to hear what you're doing to her daughter."

Berman nodded his head, taking a deep breath and letting it out.

Hessler turned his head toward the door between the waiting room and the autopsy room, cocking his head to one side. "Something smells bad about this case, Doc. I mean it really smells shit bad."

There was a knock at the door to the autopsy room.

"Now what," Dr. Berman muttered, as he walked to the door and opened it just slightly. Alberto Cruz stood on the other side. He smiled at Doctor Berman and then peeked through the opening at Hessler.

"Detective, I would very much like to see a copy of the autopsy report after you get it. At the very least, I would like to know if the victim shows any indication of a struggle, and what her exact cause of death was, if there's anything other than the obvious. Can you help me out with this?"

Hessler turned toward Dr. Berman, and then back to Cruz. "Sure, Director Cruz. I will give you a call as soon as I know," he replied.

"Thanks," Cruz said, as he pulled the door closed, and walked down the hall to the waiting room.

Berman and Hessler heard his steps receding down the hall to the waiting room. Dr. Berman was still looking at the door as he confirmed Hessler's assessment. "Shit bad, and shit deep," was all he would say, until he began the autopsy.

Chapter 6

The day was sunny and mild. The kind of day that made Carrie Marvin fall in love with South Florida. A kind of day when she would drag Callaway to the beach, without his favorite fishing rod, and they would walk for miles just gazing at the ocean. Living through an early life of snow-drifts, and thirty-below zero Januarys in Indiana made the beach in Florida seem like heaven. Callaway would see it in her eyes back then, on a day like today, as he looked at the mile-long line of police cars outside of the cathedral. They all came to honor a hero, soon to be buried after a brutal death. And the cadence in his brain continued… *Vengeance*.

The ceremony at Saint Mary's Cathedral in Miami was short and to the point. The priest railed about drugs and corruption, and the mayhem they brought to South Florida. He blasted the news media for the way they treated the local law enforcement community, eliciting many nasty looks towards the few reporters that had slithered into the cathedral to report on the ceremony. Since there was a good chance any number of representatives from the local drug smuggling organizations would show up hoping to identify some agents from the multitude of agencies in attendance, Carrie's colleagues that worked undercover for the DEA didn't come to the ceremony. Only the administrators, the guys who sat behind desks instead of putting their lives on the line daily, attended the ceremony and the burial.

Callaway and Mrs. Marvin sat in the front row, flanked by DEA District Director Alberto Cruz, Callaway's old partner from the Customs Service, Jorge Hidalgo, and his good friend, Navy Commander David Eldridge. Callaway's head throbbed from the hangover that was playing soccer with his brain and the raging beat of revenge. As he rewound the day before, he tried to remember just how much Crown Royal he put away after seeing that Mrs. Marvin was comfortable in a hotel on the beach, and then met with Detective Hessler at his office in what was the old Miami Beach Police Department headquarters building. Everyone else in the police department worked in the new, sophisticated, and clean building at 1100 Washington Avenue. Hessler and all other MBPD detectives were given the honor of working out of the earlier police building that had been there since Al Capone had a residence on Palm Island, in the bay on the west side of the city. The Criminal Investigations Unit had to put up with mold, mildew, and some of the biggest cockroaches to be found anywhere above the equator.

After his visit to the morgue, Callaway settled Mrs. Marvin into the Fontainebleau Hotel, north of the police department on the beach. He knew that placing her in the nicest hotel in town would have no effect on the emotionally beaten woman, but he felt good that he could control dealing with all her needs without having to be present. He had made a point of speaking to the on-duty manager, a conversation that ended with an assurance that she would be the best cared for guest in the hotel. This service was boosted by Callaway's pledge to the manager that he would receive two one-hundred-dollar bills to match the ones he had just given the man. Then he went to the downstairs bar.

When he arrived at the Miami Beach police station late the next afternoon, after a short stop at Duncan Donuts, Callaway walked into the large room that housed the homicide detectives. Sitting on a chair in front of Hessler's desk, he placed one of two cups of coffee and a large bag of glazed jellies in front of the detective. Hessler stared at him for about twenty seconds.

"Is this a bribe, or are you just trying to enforce a really aggravating stereotype, Mr. Callaway?" Hessler asked with no emotion in his voice.

Callaway pried the plastic lid off his coffee cup and took a long sip before tilting his head back and rubbing his temples. He struggled to keep his voice and demeanor neutral, no emotion, no tell.

"No," he replied. "I figured you could use some caffeine and a bunch of sugar carbohydrates, because you're putting in a lot of hours on this case. Stuff like this was my salvation when I worked the boats on the midnight shift. I want to complement you about your palatial police station, too." He said, not trying to hide his sarcasm as a way of lightening up the situation. He noticed that Hessler's facial expression did not change. Callaway cleared his throat. "So, what's on your mind, Detective Hessler?"

Hessler had made his bones as a cop by being ultra-observant on the job. He was known as a detail man, checking the most minuscule connections in a case, puzzling out who did what. Right now, he saw a disheveled man sitting in front of him looking like he was barely holding it together, appearing sad, pissed off, and wrung out to dry. A guy who looked like someone who just lost the love of his life.

Having only met Callaway at the office of the Miami-Dade Medical Examiner a couple of days prior, Hessler did not know if this was the way that Callaway normally presented himself, but he could smell a slight hint of alcohol on the man's breath.

Hessler began, "Since you were a cop, I'm not going to talk to you like I would to *Joe Average* homicide survivor. You get what I'm saying?"

Callaway nodded, trying to determine if the look of concern on Hessler's face was in fact genuine, or if the man had learned a new interrogation method that he wanted to try out. The "proceed with caution" sign began flashing in his booze-saturated brain, warning him not to get diarrhea of the mouth. Hessler leaned back in his chair, trying to look like he was in charge.

"Been to the bar, have you?" Hessler asked.

Callaway grimaced with embarrassment. "Yeah, I had a few last night, Hessler. What about it?"

Hessler stared hard at the man. "I've worked in homicide for two years now, Callaway. We get a bunch of homicides on the Beach. It's tough on the people who work them. Hell, our Victim Advocate gets called out from home so much that she should be allowed to retire with a pension after only five years of service."

Hessler looked around the room and pointed at a man standing by the copier. "You see the guy in the light blue shirt?" he asked. "That's Edgar Rodriguez. He's my sergeant. I was at his wedding on the night when I found your fiancée on the beach. Given how much bad shit he and every other cop in this unit sees, how much chance is there that his marriage will survive?"

Callaway was getting a bit pissed off. *What the hell? Where is he going with this? I don't know how to deal with this shit?* he thought. "What are you trying to say, Hessler?" he asked. " I thought you wanted to see if I was involved in my fiancée's death. What is this bullshit?"

Hessler shook his head. "I've pretty much ruled you out from any direct involvement, given where you were and where Ms. Marvin was on the night of the murder," he replied. "Still, I guess you could have hired someone to kill her, but what would be the point? Your buddy Cruz has me pretty much convinced that this was a set up by Derrick Drake, and he vouched for you, big time. What I'm telling you is that I've seen so many people destroy themselves after suffering a tragedy like this. You look like you've already crawled into a bottle. Watch yourself that you haven't gotten in too deep, and you won't be able to get back out."

Callaway was beyond angry. The cadence increased to a crescendo now. He looked around the room, trying not to look at this man, who was, in fact, reading him like a book. Jeep Little walked over, having noticed the tense situation occurring at Hessler's desk.

"Is there a problem here, Detective Hessler?" he said, eyeballing Callaway.

"No, Lieutenant, everything's fine," Hessler replied. "This is Mr. Callaway, Carrie Marvin's fiancé. He came in, so I could speak to him about the investigation. He brought me some delicious donuts, too. Want one, boss?"

Little gave his detective a nasty look, and then turned to Callaway. "Jeep Little, Mr. Callaway," he said, extending his hand. "I run this nut-house that we call the homicide unit."

Callaway shook the man's hand, and nodded, nervously feeling like he was in a car dealership, and the salesman just called in the sales manager to close the deal.

"I'm sorry for your loss," Little continued. "You, as a former law enforcement officer, realize that we have to interrogate anyone connected with the crime, or the victim. My detective has advised me that you look clean in this case. The two gentlemen from the DEA that came to the scene the other night is sure that Ms. Marvin was killed by Derrick Drake, or one of his associates. What's your take on that statement?"

Callaway closed his eyes as he began to speak. The vengeance was boiling inside of him.

"Derrick wouldn't do it himself," he said. "He wouldn't have the balls to do it. At least he wouldn't unless he was on his island, and that would be physically impossible, I would think. Carrie called me from the safe house at about 8:30 pm on the night she was killed. So, it would be tough to get her to his island and back in that short time." It had to be some scumbags that work for him."

Little continued questioning. "How did Ms. Marvin sound on the phone?"

Callaway thought for a second.

"You know, she said she felt kind of groggy, like she wanted to go to sleep. She was talking about the incident we had with Derrick's father, Anton, a year ago, and then she said she wanted to go to bed, and she hung up. She's not… I mean, she wasn't the type to go to bed early," he said, his emotions going crazy with sadness and anger.

Lieutenant Little could see that the man was on the verge of breaking down.

"Um… I think we have all we need from you, Mr. Callaway," Little said. "Again, I'm sorry for your loss. Please let us know if there's anything we can do to help you, okay?" Little went back to his office, as Callaway tried his best not to lose control.

"Can I go now, Hessler? Is there anything else?" Callaway asked.

The detective went back to writing the report he had been working on when Callaway arrived.

"Just let me know if you're leaving town. I'll be attending the funeral out of respect for Ms. Marvin," he said, not making eye contact with Callaway. When Hessler heard Callaway open the door to the hallway, he looked up. "Thanks for the donuts," he whispered.

Callaway walked out the door, heading back to his condo, with a side trip to the liquor store.

*****

The cathedral was filled with uniformed police officers, most of them Honor Guard members, from departments and agencies as far away as the City of LaPorte, Indiana, where Carrie was born and raised. Four deputies from the LaPorte County Sheriff's Office, all high school classmates of Carrie's, made the long trip south to pay homage to their friend and sister with a badge and to act as pallbearers. When the Mass ended, the packed cathedral emptied out, with every member of the law enforcement community finding a place to line up in rows in front of the building, standing at parade rest waiting for the casket and Mrs. Marvin to appear. When they came out, Callaway held tight to Mrs. Marvin, as he knew what was going to happen next.

A sergeant from the Miami-Dade Police Department Honor Guard called all personnel to attention in a loud voice. Mrs. Marvin stood wide-eyed, staring out at the thousands of uniformed people awaiting them. They slowly moved forward between the rows of people on either side of the walkway.

"Present arms!" commanded the Sergeant, as all in uniform saluted their fallen comrade. The casket was placed in the hearse, and Callaway helped Mrs. Marvin into the limousine.

The funeral procession meandered through downtown Miami, past the U.S. Federal Courthouse, where so many people Carrie had investigated faced trial, and then prison, and then continued out, west of Miami International Airport to the cemetery. At the grave site, Callaway sat next to Mrs. Marvin, next to the coffin. The poor woman held tight to his left hand, just to keep from falling out of the chair, shaking in anguish. Callaway looked at the crowd assembling about fifty feet away on the other side of the coffin. He recognized Al Cruz, who was looking down and mouthing Hail Mary's as he fingered the beads of a Rosary, while Jorge Hidalgo was next to David Eldridge, who stood tall in his Navy dress white uniform. Detective Hessler was standing next to Cruz. Callaway wasn't surprised that David Howe wasn't there. *Maybe he's out handling something from the investigation, he thought. It doesn't matter, he is still an asshole,* Callaway thought.

But then he saw two people that momentarily surprised him. Richard Todd stood in the first row, Old Major Dick himself, Callaway's former boss at the U.S. Customs Service. The man who tried his best to fire Callaway, and consequently the man that Callaway got removed from the Agent-In-Charge position at the Miami office of that fine agency. Callaway sent an in-depth dossier of Todd's continuous screw-ups to the Commissioner of the Customs Service in Washington D.C. The Commissioner was there as well, standing about ten feet from the end of the casket next to the head of the Drug Enforcement Agency, Carrie's former boss. The Commissioner of Customs seemed to have aged since Callaway last saw him. He concluded that it was incidents like this that contributed to all the wrinkles on the man's face, and the white hair on his head.

Even stranger still was the presence of Todd's former secretary, Donna Kendall, standing about five people away from her former boss. *No surprise, there,* he thought. *She hates every molecule of that man's body.* Callaway knew that she had been transferred to the DEA, so she and the rest of the Miami District Office staff were there, too. *But why the hell is that prick Todd here?*

The priest commenced saying the usual prayers, the ones Callaway had heard so many times at so many police funerals.

United States Marines, in their crisp dress-blue uniforms, marched perfectly to the center of the grave, one on each side of the coffin.

Damn right, Carrie deserves the full ceremony. A fitting tribute for a federal agent, he thought.

"Present, arms!" came the command again. Every man and woman in a uniform snapped to salute, while everyone else, including Callaway, placed their hand over their heart. Callaway had yet to shed a tear since his life changed, and he managed to hold fast as another Marine played "Taps" on a bugle. He steadied himself for what he knew would come next, as he heard the Honor Guard sergeant bellow again.

"Red-dy!"

Seven officers in front of him raised the barrels of their brushed-nickel plated Remington 870 shotguns to the sky.

"Fire!"

Seven 12-gauge blanks exploded through the quiet of the ceremony, causing Mrs. Marvin, and most of the cop-funeral uninitiated, to jump, while all the police, unfortunately so familiar with this part of the ceremony, did not flinch a bit. On command, the officers fired two more volleys of seven from the weapon affectionately known to police as "the long-arm of the law." Callaway stood silent, not reacting, until he heard that first note. The one note that always got to him, at every police funeral he ever attended. A piper from a pipe-and-drum band that came down from Broward County commenced playing "Amazing Grace."

When the first note subsided, a lump formed in Callaway's throat, threatening to take what little breath he had left. *Why did you take her from me, Lord?* he thought.

Finally, tears began to roll down his face as he stared at the flag on the coffin. He couldn't handle the song because it meant a law enforcement officer, and in this case, his love was dead. Callaway's right hand was over his heart, but his left was at his side, clenched in a tight fist.

Cruz looked up from the casket to see Callaway's tear-streaked face. He elbowed Hessler and whispered, "Look," wanting to remove any doubt from the detective's mind about Callaway's love for Carrie.

The two Marines, with their practiced precision, grabbed the ends of the American flag that covered Carrie's casket, and began to fold the piece of cloth that everyone at the funeral found so sacred at absolute correct angles. The corporal, the higher ranking of the two, tucked the last end into the flag that was now a perfectly folded triangle.

Clutching it to his chest, he spun to right face, and marched to the Director of the DEA, and slowly presented him the flag. The director, who had been a Marine Corps officer and knew the drill perfectly, pulled the flag tightly to his chest as the corporal, looking him directly in the eyes, raised his right hand in an exaggeratedly slow salute, then lowering his hand in the same fashion. The corporal then marched to the other Marine and made an about face. Almost imperceptibly, he whispered, "Forward march," and the two were back among the ranks.

Both the Director of the DEA and the Commissioner of Customs walked to where Mrs. Marvin was sitting, and then bent down, presenting her the flag. "Mrs. Marvin, on behalf of the United States Drug Enforcement Administration, and a grateful nation, please accept this flag as a symbol of your daughter's incredible courage and service. She is a true hero, ma'am. We are *all* extremely sorry for your loss," the DEA director said, trying his best to keep his composure.

Mrs. Marvin extended her trembling hands, and taking the flag, she held it to her chest. The commissioner of the Customs Service turned toward Callaway. "Michael…" was all he could say as he extended his hand, which Callaway clasped and held, but did not shake. Mike saw tears welling up in the commissioner's eyes as the man returned to his place in the crowd.

Mrs. Marvin grabbed Callaway's hand again, holding the flag to her chest with the other as the ceremony ended.

People walked up to say goodbye to Carrie, some placing flowers on top of the casket. Once again dry-eyed, Callaway stood and watched, and took note of those people he knew, nodding to them as they passed. He watched as Donna Kendall walked by the coffin and made the sign of the cross. She then made eye contact with Callaway and gave him a slight smile. She walked over to him and, strangely, gave him a hug. During the time that they both worked for the Customs Service, they had spoken maybe twice. The only time that Callaway ever saw her smile was the day Callaway told her about sending that file of information about Todd's screw-up's while working as Agent-in Charge of the Miami Customs Service office. The same file that would eventually result in that hated man's removal from that position, to be exiled to the boring position of auditing federal agencies in Florida. Donna ended up transferring to the DEA office in Miami soon after Todd got bumped out of the Customs position.

"I'm sorry for your loss, Mr. Callaway," Kendall said quietly. I've heard a lot about Agent Marvin since I'm working at DEA now. She was pretty special to our agents." She leaned forward and hugged him, again surprising Callaway. What she whispered to him next floored him.

"There's a mole in the agency that gave her up to Drake. There are those among us who want to see the killer punished. Painfully, if at all possible. We want revenge, a fierce vengeance, brought down on *him* or *her*. Keep an eye on your email." She kissed him on the cheek and walked away. Callaway just stood there, shocked, when he heard a voice behind him.

"Callaway?" The man had a Hispanic accent. Callaway turned and saw a bearded man with a stocky build.

"I know you, but I can't remember your name," Callaway said.

"I'm Juan Jimenez, Miami-Dade O.C.D. We met a long time ago. I also worked with your girlfriend a couple of times," he said, looking at the coffin. "I was the one who identified her on the beach where they found her. I got a voicemail at my office telling me that something I would find interesting was gonna wash up on the shore that night. I thought it would be some dope, and I was down there poking around, trying to poach from my good friends from the Beach Police, and I saw the commotion when they found her."

Callaway remembered the man considered a legend in Miami-Dade's undercover unit.

"I appreciate you coming here, today, Detective Jimenez, he said. "But aren't you taking a chance, showing up here, and… Talking to me? What if the druggies sent their people here to try to ID the people who hunt them?"

Jimenez frowned, while taking off his Ray Ban sunglasses. He looked down at the ground, shuffling his feet. "That is precisely why I'm here, aside from paying my respects to Agent Marvin. I figured that the killer might get cocky and show up "

He smiled now, looking up at Callaway. "I didn't get where I am by not taking chances, *hermano*. I want to see the piece of shit that killed her punished. DEA Miami is compromised. I have no way of working on that, but if I get anything from my contacts, or informants, I'll be in touch. Do you have an email address, yet?"

Callaway was new at the recent innovation called email. He gave Hernandez his address but was curious about one thing. "The voicemail. Any hints from the caller?" Callaway asked.

Always on guard, Hernandez looked around at the crowd, and looked back at Callaway. "Not really. Sounded like a white male. He muffled his voice. He was on a pay phone, I'm guessing, from all the background noise I could hear. Weird. Kind of talked like he was reciting poetry," he said, shaking his head.

He put his hand on Callaway's arm. "You and I are

alike, you know. We like to see bad people punished. I think you will see to it that the scum that did this is punished hard. It is what they deserve. Make sure you give Herrera my regards. I hear he's dying of lung cancer from all the cigars he smokes. Still trying to look like his buddy Fidel, huh? I'll be in touch." He walked away.

Callaway tried to process what he had just heard from Donna Kendall and Detective Jimenez. Clearly, Juan knew all about Drake's Chief of Security, Martino Herrera, a former member of the Cuban Intelligence Directorate, or DGI, with close, personal ties to Fidel Castro, and Kendall sounded like she was part of some vigilante cadre within the DEA.

Callaway knew that Jimenez had informants all over Cuba and the Caribbean. He also knew of Herrera's reputation for being a ruthless killer. He flashed back to hearing about the cave that was found on the island of Golgotha, when the Bahamian Defense Force and police, aided by U.S. federal law enforcement and the Navy, invaded that terrible island one year ago. Commander Eldridge had described in great detail what he saw in the tomb, the cave full of the remains of anyone who got in the Drake's way. Callaway had always wondered how many of the dead in that cave were killed by Herrera himself.

As Jimenez walked away, Callaway saw his three friends, Jorge Hidalgo, Commander David Eldridge, and Al Cruz approaching him. Cruz's eyes darted towards Jimenez as they passed each other, but no other contact was made, out of respect for the Miami-Dade detective's safety.

"How ya holding up, Mike?" Eldridge said, patting him on the shoulder.

Callaway kept looking at the coffin, just nodding his

head. The cadence had begun again, marching in quick time now. He wanted to fly to Golgotha right now, with guns blazing, to kill Derrick Drake, and Martino Herrera, not worrying if he lived or died in the process.

"I'm okay, skipper," he said, not being truthful.

Cruz looked at him with red, puffy eyes, still holding the rosary in his hand. "We're working really hard to find the mole, Mike," he said. We will find him or her, and I will beat a confession out of whoever it is. I know you want to kill Drake, but you need to let us do the work, and do it right. Don't go rogue, don't do this alone, man."

Again, Callaway just looked down and nodded. Finally, Jorge came up to him, and grabbed him in a bear hug. "Hey partner, let's go fishing," he whispered.

Callaway planted his face on his old partner's shoulder and sighed. "Yeah, we'll do that for sure, bro."

Commander Eldridge smiled at the three men. "I got an idea. I've got a case of Coronas in my refrigerator back at my house. Why don't we meet up over there and watch some hoops. We can order pizza and kill that case of beer." He was trying his best to get Callaway's mind off Carrie. A task that he knew was impossible. Jorge and Cruz jumped in.

"Come on, Mike. It'll do you good," Jorge said, with his arm around Callaway's shoulder.

"All right." Callaway replied, glancing at Mrs. Marvin, who was still sitting, and looking at the coffin. "I need to stay with Mrs. Marvin, and then take her to the airport. Then I'll come to your house."

They all gave him a look of disbelief that Callaway couldn't help but notice.

"No, no, I mean it. I'll come by as soon as I see her off. Give me a couple of hours," he said.

Callaway and Mrs. Marvin walked towards the limousine, only to see a group of reporters standing near the vehicle, waiting to get an interview. Callaway managed to keep them away from him and Mrs. Marvin prior to the funeral. He was a ghost to them, since, like any smart cop, he had his residence and other information removed from public access, but now here they were, waiting like a pack of hyenas. Just before Callaway and Mrs. Marvin reached the limo, a group of State Troopers from the Florida Highway Patrol Honor Guard circled the reporters and camera people, while the driver of the limo drove around the group and picked up the grieving duo. The limo sped away, as the press people screamed that they would report the troopers for what they did. The troopers walked away nonchalantly.

Hidalgo, Cruz, and Eldridge left, clueless that they were being watched by a man, hunched down in a beat-up, white, Dodge panel van parked on the other side of the cemetery. Looking through a long eye-relief Burris telescopic sight, mounted on a Thompson Contender single shot pistol. He watched the men enter their vehicles and drive towards the exit. He started the dilapidated old van and began to follow them.

"Now, which one should I follow this time," he said to himself. The man followed them out on to the road that would take them to the Dolphin Expressway.

"I guess I'll stick with the Navy guy," he said, and then fell in about five cars back from Commander Eldridge's car. Much to his surprise, Hidalgo and Cruz fell in right behind Eldridge, and drove up the on ramp to the Dolphin. Knowing already that the other two men lived in different directions from where Eldridge lived, he chuckled, realizing that all three of his targets were probably heading to the same place.

"Well, thank you, gentlemen," the man said. "You may have just saved me some gasoline."

*****

Neither Callaway nor Mrs. Marvin said a lot on the way to Miami International Airport, which was only five miles from the cemetery. Callaway carried her bags to check in, and then walked her to security. He gave her a hug, knowing that the likelihood of them ever seeing each other again was slim. His new life was now like walking into a tunnel of vengeance, and he did not expect to make it out of the other end.

"Be careful, Mike. I mean when you go to that terrible island. Be careful," she said.

Callaway was stunned by her words. "Mrs. Marvin, why would you say that?"

She looked him in the eyes, slightly shaking her head. "There's no need to lie. I know you will avenge our girl. I just don't want anything to happen to you."

He looked at her trying to force himself to smile and lied at the same time. "What makes you think I would do such a thing?"

She smiled at him, as she turned to walk down the jetway ramp. He could barely hear the tear-choked words that she said next. "Because she would do it for you."

Chapter 7

Callaway waited until Mrs. Marvin's flight took off before having the limo take him to retrieve his car, so he could drive to Commander Eldridge's house in Miami Beach. While the island city had some of the most expensive houses in the country, Eldridge lived in a much cheaper area that still had some wooded sand dunes that were as high as his house. He drove into the slightly run-down neighborhood and right past the nondescript white Dodge panel van parked a few houses down from Eldridge's place. Callaway began to pull his Mustang off the road near the Commander's house and on to the grass swale that was between the sidewalk and the road. He slammed on the brakes when, in the glow of the vehicle's fog lamps, he saw a big pile of junk directly in front of his car. Backing up, he put the shift lever in neutral, and shut the engine off. The headlights delay kept the lights on long enough for him to study the stuff on Eldridge's swale. There were numerous pieces of rotten wood, both beams and old four-by-eight sheets of plywood, along with several nasty pieces of drywall that looked like they had gone through a flood. There was a multitude of nails sticking out of just about every piece of lumber in the pile. Callaway knew that Eldridge was doing a self-remodeling of the beat-up old house that he had bought, but he was amazed there was any of the structure still standing by the size of the pile of stuff on the swale.

"Glad I didn't pull up any closer, or I probably would have lost both of my front tires, and maybe my oil pan, too," he muttered as he climbed out of the car.

He didn't realize that the man sitting comfortably in the white van down the street in front of a house for sale, was monitoring every step he took. He watched Callaway through a monocular range finder, with the aid of the streetlight glowing in front of Eldridge's house. The monocular was a single-tube device, normally used by golfers and hunters, that had just a slight amount of magnification, and was meant to give a rough estimate of the range between the user and his target. The man in the Dodge had no intention of shooting anyone this evening. He was just sizing up his prey. He had a legal pad on top of his thighs, and he was taking notes on Michael Callaway. The man began writing below the information he had already taken on Alberto Cruz, Jorge Hidalgo, and David Eldridge.

"Okay, Mr. Callaway," he said in a tone just above a whisper. "Height, a little over six-feet. Weight, about two hundred. Build, muscular. You're walking like a civilian, so it doesn't appear that you're carrying a gun, at least on one of your ankles or hips, but maybe in your waistband up front? You walk a little faster than normal, but not much." The man chuckled, adding, "You look a bit tense, Mr. Callaway. I wonder why?"

He watched Callaway walk up the porch of Eldridge's house and ring the doorbell. "And you're right-handed." the man said.

As Callaway entered the house, the man in the van finished writing his statistics on Callaway, under the information of the other three men, and put the note pad in a nylon range bag, being careful not to bump the two Thompson Contender single shot pistols within.

"I could have taken you out with one shot, tonight, Callaway, but that's not what my employer wants. If possible, your friends all must die first. Boy, you really must have pissed somebody off." He buckled his seat belt and started the engine. Pulling out onto the street, he gave one more look at Callaway's car.

"He keeps that Mustang GT nice and shiny. That'll be a good place for him to die." He grabbed the notepad and made an entry, with an asterisk next to it to buy a floor jack, since Callaway's car sat so low on the ground. Seeing his face in the rear-view mirror, he smiled. "I love my job!" he yelled, as he headed for his home.

*****

Commander David Eldridge opened the front door of his beat-up little home, delighted to see that Callaway, in fact, had shown up. He suspected that his good friend might have retreated to his condo in Fort Lauderdale, to empty another bottle of Crown Royal before passing out on his couch. Eldridge's concern for Michael Callaway was obvious from the look he gave him as he stepped into his living room.

"Mike!" Said Eldridge. "Everyone is in the back room. Glad you decided to join us."

The two men walked through the living room, which looked like a construction site, and through a sliding glass door that Eldridge closed behind them. Entering the back room of the house, the only room with air conditioning, he saw his other two friends. Alberto Cruz and Jorge

Hidalgo stood when Callaway walked in. Jorge, his friend, and former partner from the days gone by in the Customs Service, was the first to speak.

"How you holding up, partner?" he said, grabbing Callaway by the arm, and giving him a hug. "Did you get Mrs. Marvin on the plane, okay?"

Callaway nodded yes. Al Cruz was next, shaking Callaway's hand.

"You want a drink, man?" he asked. Cruz looked up at Eldridge, who was standing behind Callaway, and saw the big man shaking his head "No." But it was too late.

"Sure. What kind of whiskey do you have, David?" Callaway responded.

Eldridge gave Cruz a frown. "Yeah. Let me go look in the kitchen. There may be some in there," he said, trying to keep Callaway from getting too drunk to function. *Hell, I would drink myself to death if I were him, so how can I judge?* He thought.

Cruz and Hidalgo sat down and continued drinking their beer quietly. Cruz tried his best to make Callaway feel better. "We'll get the son-of-a-bitch mole that did this to Carrie, Mike. I promise you that. And if I can find a way to get you alone with him or her, I will do so!"

Callaway knew this was the beer talking, since Cruz had already sworn this vendetta to him half-a-dozen times. Cruz, and DEA Miami, were in a major dilemma. *If they can't figure out who the mole in their office is*, he thought, t*hey are a non-functional entity. Short of transferring every single person in that office to different locations around the world, they are done*.

Callaway looked at the man, who was well wasted from the beer, and wondered for a second if Cruz could be the mole. His head was pounding from the day's events and the relentless cadence. He kept seeing Carrie's face. *Nah, couldn't have been him*, he decided. *He would have given up Carrie to Anton Drake the minute she started working her undercover operation on Drake's island a year ago.*

"So, Al, what's going on with the investigation? he asked. "Does Miami Beach P.D. have any leads? I saw Detective Hessler at the funeral. The newspaper said that the FBI isn't releasing any information on the killing of your two agents in the safe house in Boca. That usually means they have nothing, right?" Callaway figured now would be a good time to pick Cruz's brain, since it was saturated with alcohol.

Cruz gave him a blank stare for a moment before answering. "Mike, I talked to Lieutenant Little this morning. He said his detectives are shaking the trees, trying to get anything they can about Carrie's murder, but so far, no luck."

That's because none of what has happened involved any of the local scumbags. This was all planned and paid for by Derrick Drake, and most likely executed by Martino Herrera and the DEA mole. Callaway thought. "I didn't see your boy Howe at the burial. Is Mr. Bad Ass that angry at me that he couldn't show up at Carrie's funeral?" Callaway asked, trying to get a reaction.

Cruz tried to give Callaway a stern look while fighting the effects of the beer, "Look Mike," Cruz answered. "I know you hate Howe, but he's really a stand-up guy when it comes to work. He's also a cocky prick, I'll be the first to admit that. But I have to overlook that a lot because he gets the job done."

Callaway really needed that drink to drown out the

words marching through his brain. "Hey, David," he yelled, "you making that whiskey yourself? How about that drink?"

Eldridge was in the kitchen staring at the only bottle of whiskey in the house. It was a bottle of Canadian Club that he bought to celebrate the purchase of the small, dilapidated house he was trying to rebuild, a little at a time. Not being much of a drinker, he had only poured two drinks for himself, leaving the bottle almost full. Letting out a deep sigh, he removed the cap, and poured all but enough for about two shots from the bottle into the kitchen sink. "The things we do for our friends," he whispered, shaking his head.

He carried the bottle and a short glass full of ice into the room and handed them to Callaway, telling him, "Sorry this isn't up to your usual standards, but this is all the whiskey I have."

Callaway took the bottle and the glass from his friend with a smile. The house smelled of that musty, mildew smell that only old homes in South Florida had. He had to raise his voice a little to talk above the loud *window-shaker* air conditioning unit that sort of kept the back room cool. "Nice Florida room," he said, again looking around the rectangular shaped room at the rear of the house.

Eldridge looked at him kind of befuddled and asked, "What does that mean, Mike?"

Callaway and Hidalgo both laughed a little. Callaway realized that he and Jorge were the only native Floridians in the room, since Cruz, though Cuban, was from New York City, and Eldridge was from Boston. Callaway smiled.

"Down here, when you close in your screened-in porch, it becomes a Florida Room. Don't try to understand it—it's just what we do down here, David. My parents did the same thing with our house where I grew up. The only thing they did differently was to put a ceiling under the rafters to make it look better and keep the cool air from the air conditioner in."

Eldridge looked around the room, and at the rafters. "I don't know," he answered. "I kind of like the rafters showing. It makes it look like the inside of an old sailing ship. God knows, it's probably the closest thing to being at sea I'll ever have again."

Callaway thought about how Eldridge lost his sea command, after a Navy board of inquiry beat him up for firing on boats in international waters to save him and Carrie from an attack by the late Anton Drake's henchmen. He raised his glass to toast his friend's former command. "To the *USS Pegasus*!"

Cruz and Hidalgo raised their Coronas high. "To the *Pegasus*!"

Eldridge smiled, "To the only sea battle I ever participated in during my long career in the navy," he said.

Jorge tried to lighten the conversation up. "Speaking of boats," he said. "Where's that floating bingo parlor of yours, Mike? What island is she nesting at now?" he said, referring to Callaway's live-aboard shrimp boat turned yacht.

Callaway thought for a second about how Carrie once referred to his boat as a floating whorehouse and then he looked at his watch. "Well, right now she should be just about ready to untie from the dock in Elethuria. I hired a couple of Mary's guys to cruise her over here."

Hidalgo laughed, "How is sweet little Mary?"

She still building those rocket boats for the very rich?"

Callaway poured the last of the Club into his glass.

"Oh yeah," he answered. "Matter of fact, I had her working on a little project for me, before"… He looked down at the floor for a couple of seconds, and then he continued. "She was building me a turbocharged WaveRunner that she guaranteed me would break one hundred miles per hour."

Hidalgo shook his head. "You rich guys!" he said laughing. "I need to win me a lottery. I don't even need it to be eighty-two million, like you won. I'm not picky!"

They all laughed, as Jorge continued, "You still have that speed need, partner. One hundred miles an hour, on a freaking WaveRunner? Man, one wrong move and you're busted all to hell. Water feels like concrete when you hit it at that speed. I thought your little flats boat with the nitrous injection kept you going fast enough. By the way, did you ever get it fixed after Anton Drake's men shot it up last year?

Callaway smiled at his partner, realizing that all this small talk was meant to get his mind off Carrie. *Not working, amigo*, he thought.

"Yeah, Jorge," he answered. "Took me awhile to get it over to the Hewes Factory, but it's getting done. Matter of fact, it should be delivered to the marina in Miami Beach in a couple of days. All the damage will be fixed, and I'm having a couple of other things installed. I guess they like me at the factory, because they threw in a remote starter for the outboard. I'll be able to start it from the dock with a little push-button fob on the key ring."

Jorge's eyes opened wide, "Perfect!" he said. "You can take me fishing again."

Callaway gave him a strange look and laughed, "You are still the only Cuban I've ever met that hates to fish," he said. "You don't have to go fishing to keep an eye on me, man."

"No, partner. I've been fishing a lot over the last year," Jorge replied. I even went out and bought a *gringo* rod and reel. No more Cuban Yo-Yo for me. Let's go out to Biscayne National Park, and you can teach me how to catch bonefish."

Callaway suddenly became silent, thinking about the day he had taken Carrie fishing, and how they made love on a tiny island in the middle of nowhere. He put his hand to his chest and touched half of the globe pendant that he had made for Carrie. He told her that they would share the world. *I told her, and now she's dead.*

His anger began to build, bringing that pain to the back of his head again, as he stood up quickly, "I gotta go, guys," he announced. "It's getting late, and I'm not feeling too well."

His friends all stood up. "Mike, did I say something wrong, man?" Jorge blurted out.

"No, bro, I just feel like crap, and I need to go home," Callaway responded, sounding totally depressed. Commander Eldridge put his hand on Callaway's shoulder.

"Why don't you stay here tonight, Mike?" asked Eldridge. "You can sleep out here in the back, I mean, in the Florida room, where it's nice and cool. It isn't your fancy condo, but this recliner is really comfy. We can go out and get breakfast before I go in to work in the morning."

Callaway smiled. "Thanks, David, but I'll be okay."

He shook hands with the three of them and started for the front door.

"Hey, Mike, I'm gonna come by your place to see you in the next couple of days. You wanted to know what the medical examiner's report had to say, and I should have it tomorrow or the next day," said Cruz, in a somewhat drunken slur.

Eldridge and Hidalgo both gave him the *shut-up* look. "I'm sorry, man" was all Cruz could say.

Callaway stopped and turned his head slightly. "No, Al. It's okay. Please take it over when you get it. I told you I wanted to see it. Just don't come by too early, okay?" he asked, knowing he would be drinking himself to sleep when he got to his condo.

"Thanks, guys." And with that, he walked out the front door.

Callaway climbed into the Mustang and started the motor. All he could think about was how he would get revenge on Derrick Drake. It was time to start doing some digging to figure out how. He just hoped he could stay clear-headed enough to do that tonight.

Chapter 8

Callaway was like a child with a new toy when it came to the new technology called the World Wide Web. Even though it had only been in existence for a short time, by 1992 it was already an amazing place to go, to learn things, and communicate with people. When he arrived home from Commander Eldridge's house, he poured himself a tall glass of Crown Royal with a little water and sat down at the computer, ready to do some research. There weren't a lot of people on the Web yet, but most government agencies were already there, along with those who could afford a decent computer system. Going through the ritual of DOS codes, he was able to get on the Web, to see if he'd received any emails over the last few days. He saw one sent by someone called "avengeher229. "

"Who the hell is this?" he mumbled to himself. "Stupid ass can't even spell." He was shocked when he opened the mail and found a case file and information from the sender that made his eyes open wide. "Here is some information that may help you, regarding the death of I.D. # 229," he read out loud. "More to come. Avengeher." It all clicked even though he was trying to think through the buzz he was starting to get from the Crown. Number 229 was Carrie's DEA identification number, something pretty much everyone in law enforcement was issued in some way, shape or form.

Callaway was intrigued by the information he received from Avengeher 229. The case file was all about Carrie's working with an informant, a member of the Seminole Tribe of Florida who had also wound-up dead. By the dates on the file, this had all taken place before Carrie went under deep cover to infiltrate and join the criminal organization of the then living Anton Drake. There was just too much coincidence between Carrie's murder and that of the Seminole informant, Melinda Eagle, who's picture was included in the email. The poetic words written on Melinda's abdomen, the method of execution, and the fact that both women were involved with Drake's organization, one fighting it and one with an unknown connection, tied them together too tightly.

"How did they get their hands on this stuff?" Callaway mumbled as he read through the case file. One part of the file consisted of notes handwritten by Carrie. When Callaway read her signature at the bottom of the last page, his eyes began to tear up, and the rage in his brain began to bang around again. He took a couple of deep breaths and continued to study the document. Carrie's last contact with Melinda had been rather intense, for the young Seminole woman was convinced she had been compromised, and that Anton Drake would have her killed. She had refused federal protection, stating that she thought her tribe would be better at protecting her. As he continued to read, Callaway saw a reference to the investigation conducted by Seminole Tribal Police officers assigned to enforce the law on Native American reservations. There was also a reference to the fact that the tribe had ultimate jurisdiction on reservation land when it came to enforcing the law. Callaway had dealt with some members of the Miccosukee Tribe, which had separated from the Seminole

71

tribe in the mid twentieth century, while he worked as an armed Federal Parks Service Ranger, assigned to Everglades National Park. As he continued to read, he kept finding references to the victim's brother, Joseph Eagle, who was listed in the report as a police officer with the Seminole Tribal Police Department. Joseph Eagle found his sister's body after she had been listed as missing, in the northern part of the Everglades near where it meets the Big Cypress National Preserve. While the federal officers and deputies from the Broward and Collier County Sheriff's Office searched the roads and some larger canals that snaked through the area, Joseph Eagle and other members of the tribe were out on horseback, in canoes and airboats, searching all the places that a white man would never think to look. The Collier County medical examiner's report, also included in the attachment, stated, "The victim suffered a laceration wound to the throat, through which her tongue was pulled." It also stated that this *Colombian Necktie,* like the one that Carrie suffered, was not the cause of death. It was listed in a separate box in the form as *Drowning,* making Callaway wonder if Dr. Berman's report would state that this was how Carrie had been killed. The other item in the Medical Examiner's report that startled Callaway was the fact that Melinda Eagle was found with writing on her abdomen, same as Carrie. The message written on Melinda's body was also in Spanish and apparently a marker pen of some type had been used on her, too, to write "*Cuyos miembros insepulto en la costa desnuda, los perros y los buitres hambrientos devornado rasgo.*" He translated, "whose limbs unburied on the naked shore, devouring dogs and hungry vultures tore, " as he took a long drink from the glass.

Avengeher stated that he or she would follow up on

this, and the poems written on Carrie's and Melinda's bodies, to see if anything could be determined about the killer from the words written on both women. The writer also included detailed drawings of Drake's island home, and other items of importance on his island.

Callaway read the information over and over, stumped about what Melinda Eagle's connection to the Drake smuggling operation had been. *Were you a mule, carrying the drugs into the country?* he thought, taking another sip of Crown. *Were you his distribution connection in Florida? You were murdered when Anton Drake was using his submarine to move the drugs off his island and out to the pick-up boats. What the hell were you doing with this low-life scumbag, girl?* He figured money was probably not the reason, since those born into the Seminole tribe were given a check for many thousands of dollars every year, proceeds from the tribe's lucrative gambling enterprises in Florida. Callaway remembered how the tribes survived when he was a child, prior to their involvement in the gambling business. "You guys have come a long way from selling trinkets and wrestling alligators for a living," he said, laughing. "Good. Revenge against the government for trying to throw you out of Florida a hundred years ago was appropriate. I guess I need to pay Joseph Eagle a visit." He closed the file and shut down the computer. Downing the last of the Crown, he walked to the kitchen to pour another. There would, again, not be much sleep for him that night. He sat down on the living room couch and turned on the television, thinking about the grand scheme he was concocting to kill Derrick Drake. Callaway smiled when he thought about the email from Avenger 229. "How 'bout that Derrick," he said. "Now you have a mole in the DEA, and so do I." He turned

73

off the television and fell into a restless sleep. He woke up three times that night, thinking about Carrie and wondering about the Melinda Eagle connection. The contents of the file kept bouncing around in his head. He kept thinking through all the information, which only led to more questions. It seemed like Carrie was missing the important information about how, or with whom, Melinda had been connected to the late Anton Drake's drug smuggling operation. *Melinda was killed when Anton was smuggling the stuff from the island on the submarine. The one that I destroyed,* he thought again, as a slight smile came to his face. He remembered the picture Avengeher included with the file. Melinda was a tiny, and very attractive, twenty-five-year-old woman—not the type Drake would use as a bodyguard, as he did with Carrie. He considered the obvious option. Maybe she was one of Derrick's sex toys. He did have a habit of killing them off, but their bodies usually ended up in that horrible cave full of bones on Golgotha. This was too different and, at the same time, just too coincidental.

When he awoke at nine the next morning, his head was throbbing. Still, Callaway called the Seminole Tribal Police Department to arrange a meeting with Officer Joseph Eagle. The department Desk Officer was neither informative nor polite.

"Mr. Eagle is no longer employed by the Seminole Tribe as a police officer, sir," she said in a monotone voice. He was surprised to hear this. When he asked why, and if she knew where he could be located, he was given a firm "No," to both questions. Callaway was a firm believer that when you can't get an answer, kick it up a notch. "May I speak to the Chief of Police, please?" he asked. He was transferred to the office of Chief Victor Cummings, who at first gave him the same answers. Callaway was persistent, guessing why the man wouldn't answer his questions. "Look, Chief," he said. "I'm not a reporter or a lawyer. I'm a former federal agent. U.S. Customs, to be exact. My fiancée was killed the same way that Melinda Eagle was, and in connection with the same bad people. I'm just trying to bring a little closure to my loss, that's all, Sir." He looked up and mouthed, *"I'm sorry,"* for lying to the man.

Chief Cummings let out a big sigh before he replied. "Tell you what, Callaway, why don't you come to my police station, and we'll talk some more. How about it? Can you be up here at 4:00 pm?"

Callaway agreed immediately. Since he didn't know where he would be going to meet with Joseph Eagle, he made a mental note to throw his Smith &Wesson Model 60 in a holster and place it in the glove compartment of his Mustang. *Don't want to get myself arrested for carrying a concealed firearm, since I'm not a cop anymore,* he thought.

Between the Fort Lauderdale traffic and the drive up U.S. 27 to the little town of Clewiston, it took almost an hour and a half to cover the distance to the police station. As he drove around the southwest corner of Lake Okeechobee, to get to the town of seven thousand residents, he could smell smoke in the area. "Must be harvest time," he mumbled, referring to the process of burning a sugarcane field before harvesting to clear out the weeds, while everything else would be harvested. "Big Sugar" occupied a large portion of land around the south side of the big lake that fed the Everglades its water. Callaway pulled into the Jimmy Cypress Public Safety Complex and parked in a visitor space. Entering the lobby of the Police Department, he spoke to the desk officer seated behind an inch of bulletproof glass. She sounded like the same person he had spoken to when he first called the station seeking information about Officer Joseph Eagle. The woman was clearly a tribal member, and she gave him the same cold shoulder she'd given him on the telephone that morning. She called the Chief's Office, and within a minute, Chief Cummings appeared to let him through the locked door to the administrative offices of the department. Cummings was white, and he was just as suspicious of Callaway as the Seminole woman at the front desk.

"May I see some identification please, Mr. Callaway?" Cummings asked.

Callaway pulled out his wallet and produced his driver's license.

"And how long has it been since you were with the Customs Service?" the Chief asked.

"It's been a little over a year since I quit," Callaway answered.

The Chief smiled and said, "Just needed to make sure, Mr. Callaway. I called the Customs Service and checked you out. The people I talked to said you're a stand-up guy. Come with me, and we'll talk in my office."

Callaway followed him down the hall and into his office. The wood-paneled wall behind the Chief's desk was the usual shrine of pictures on plaques, news articles mounted on plaques, and letters of commendation mounted on more plaques that most police officials above the rank of lieutenant displayed. Callaway was impressed by the quality of the man's resume on the wall, as it was, even though it was *much* smaller than those of other chiefs he had met.

"So, you were the Chief of Police in Bakersfield, California?" Callaway asked, trying to break the ice and get a conversation going. "That had to be an interesting gig."

Cummings gave him a slight grin and shrugged. "It paid the mortgage," he answered.

Callaway didn't know what to make of the short answer. Most police chiefs he'd met in the past were happy to tell you so much of their life story you just wanted to tell them to shut up, but this man displayed something he had never seen before: humility. And the items on the wall all appeared to be credible, and not a mass of bullshit like he experienced in other offices. He tried to open the chief up a little more, since he wasn't feeling comfortable around the man. He was sweating from all the liquor he'd consumed the previous evening, and Cummings' attitude wasn't helping the situation one bit, either.

"And I see you went to the FBI National Academy. Very impressive," he said, gesturing at the framed certificate hanging on the wall.

Again, he got the slight grin from the chief. "You said on the phone you wanted to speak to me about Officer, uh, former Officer Eagle, Mr. Callaway?" Cummings asked.

Wow. A police chief who really doesn't like to talk about himself. Again, *how refreshing,* Callaway thought as the Chief continued.

"You must understand that this is a very tough issue for both the department and the tribe as well," the Chief continued. "I mean, there are only seven hundred actual tribal members, so everybody knew Miss Eagle, and of course, they all know Joseph."

Callaway sat back in his chair, tensing at what he would have to tell the Chief next. "This is close to home for me too, Chief," he said. "I believe that whoever killed Melinda Eagle killed my fiancée too. Her name was Carrie Marvin. She was a DEA deep-cover agent. She and I fought a battle with a big-time drug smuggler named Anton Drake about a year ago. In the process, we killed Drake, and thought that we put his smuggling operation out of business. I guess we were wrong. Obviously, Drake's son Derrick got their cocaine business up and running again. And I think Derrick ordered Carrie's death because she was about to testify to a grand jury with information that would have indicted Derrick. Or maybe it was just a revenge thing. I don't think it was that, or he would have come after me, too." He took a deep breath, trying to keep from losing control.

Cummings looked at him, and Callaway noticed that his facial expression had softened somewhat. "I'm sorry for your loss, Mr. Callaway," he said. "Your fiancée washed up on shore in Miami Beach?"

Callaway nodded yes.

The Chief continued. "I got a call from the homicide detective from Miami Beach who's working the case. Detective…"

"Hessler," Callaway responded, realizing that this man had much of the information Callaway just gave him well in advance.

Cummings saw the look on Callaway's face. "Sorry, Callaway. I was an interrogator in the military, Cummings said. "I like to know where a person's coming from when I talk to him. So, we have two women who were murdered by the same method? Are there any other clues to link the crimes together?"

Callaway figured it was time to go over the line, a little. "I'm going to have to trust you a bit, I guess," he answered. "Lately, that's been tough for me to do with almost everyone, since the one person I absolutely trusted is dead. Melinda Eagle was a confidential informant that my fiancée was working with. She was somehow connected with Anton Drake's operation. For some reason, she came in, and decided to work for Carrie as a CI, but again, I don't know why. That's what I need to find out. I'm looking for any connection I can find."

"And your girlfriend gave you this information?" Cummings asked, with no discernible emotion.

Callaway knew he had to be careful. *I don't know this guy. I can't give him too much, so I don't blow in my source,* he thought before he replied. "No, I got this somewhere else," he answered. "And no, I'm not going to tell you who. Now, if you could just tell me where I can find Joseph Eagle, I will get out of your office and not bother you again."

The Chief sat back in his chair, looking a little perturbed. "Oh, I'll tell you where he is," he said. "He's somewhere in the fucking Everglades, camped out, and falling down drunk on his ass! He was the best cop in this department, with the best record of keeping the peace around here, and he was very good at keeping the assholes off this reservation. He was my best conduit to the members of the tribe, and I had to fire him!"

Callaway was taken aback by Cummings' sudden anger. "Man, when you go off, it happens quick," Callaway said. "Look, Chief, I am just trying to find out what happened to my fiancée, and who was involved. That's it! Now, why did you fire Joseph Eagle?"

Cummings gave Callaway a good long look before he answered. "He climbed into a bottle after his sister was murdered. Clearly, you've done the same thing!"

79

Callaway looked at the man, frozen, because this was the second time someone had said this to him. Callaway made a feeble attempt to disregard this warning, just as he had with the first one from Detective Hessler, but the Chief continued.

"Look at you, Callaway," he said in a slightly raised voice. "Your eyes are watery, your face is flushed, and I'll bet that you would kill me for a cup of water right about now. I could smell the booze on you as soon as I opened the door to the lobby!" The Chief paused, looking up at the ceiling, while taking a breath to compose himself. "I fired Joseph Eagle because he wrecked a police car."

Callaway considered that statement for a moment. *Jesus! This guy is tough. If every department ran off every cop who wrecked a police car, we'd have nobody protecting us,* he thought. He was about to question the Chief's actions, but he didn't get the chance.

"His blood alcohol level was .31,"Cummings continued. "Seriously drunk. I had no choice in the matter because he ended up losing his right leg from the wreck. The Tribal Elders told me to do it, to fire him, because they saw him falling apart. They're a very close-knit group, the Indians. They said they would take care of him, but after he got a prosthetic leg, he disappeared into the swamp somewhere. I don't know where he is, but I can point you to a couple of his family members, who know me, and trust me, and they may be able to help you out."

Callaway didn't know what to say. He could see himself falling into the same rabbit hole as Joseph, but it was like he was standing off to the side, watching his own destruction take place. He waited patiently while Cummings wrote down a couple of names and addresses of people close to Joseph Eagle. Cummings told Callaway that he shouldn't get his hopes up about getting any help from them, as they would protect another tribal member no matter what, since they were all family. Callaway shook Cummings' hand and headed out the door to his car.

It took him an hour to reach the first of Joseph Eagle's relatives, when he pulled into the dirt parking lot of a boat ramp and bait store off Alligator Alley. The road was given its name for the insane number of alligators that seemed to thrive on either side of it, and sometimes on it. He knew from reading the police report supplied to him by Avengeher229 that he was near the place where Melinda Eagle's body had been found. Callaway looked around at a broken-down old shack of a building, with a dilapidated old barn next to it. *Looks like it's closed,* he thought as he got out of his car. There was a noise, like someone hammering on metal, coming from behind the structure. Callaway walked around the building and found a man with long gray hair beating the living hell out of a dent in the hull of an aluminum jon boat. He was holding an almost square block of cast iron on the other side of the dent and pounding the twisted metal as hard as he could to flatten it.

"Hi!" Callaway blurted out.

The old man didn't turn around. "Took you awhile to get out here, Callaway," he said, still tending to his work on the damaged Jon boat.

"Traffic was a little heavy on the Alley," Callaway said. "What did you run over that put the dent in your boat?"

The old man was tapping lightly now, trying to smooth out the ripples in the hull.

"Gator. Damn big one, too," he replied. "Why do you want to find my nephew, Joseph Eagle?"

81

Callaway wasn't expecting the conversation to turn quite so quickly. "Uh, I guess you are Mr. Fred Eagle, if you know who I am?" Callaway asked with some apprehension. "Did Chief Cummings call you to let you know I was driving out here to meet you?"

The old man finally turned around to look at him. His dark eyes seemed to look right through Callaway's eyes, and into his brain. "The police chief didn't need to call me to let me know you were coming," he replied. "And before you start thinking that I knew you were coming, from some kind of mystic Indian ESP bullshit, let me put your mind at ease. The Chief's desk officer is one of my nieces. She heard your entire conversation when you were sitting in his office. When she heard that you were going to see Fred Eagle, she gave me a call. So why do you want to talk to my nephew, Joseph Eagle?"

Callaway relayed the whole story about the similarities in the death of Melinda Eagle and Carrie Marvin. He also explained the DEA connection between the two deceased women. The old man put down his sledgehammer and wiped the sweat from his forehead with the sleeve of his shirt. He sat down on a cinder block and stared out at the expanse of the Everglades.

"All right, Callaway, I'll help you as best I can," he said, reaching into a nearby cooler to pull out a bottle of Coca-Cola. "You want one?" he asked. He pulled another bottle from the cooler. Callaway was so dehydrated from his previous evening's alcohol binge that he would have gladly consumed the nasty Everglades canal water that ran along the rear of the shop. He took the ice-cold bottle and sat on a rusty fifty-gallon oil drum, downing the soda in one long drink.

"The last time I saw Joseph was two days ago," the

old man said. "He made a camp along the bank of one of the canals near the Big Cypress Preserve. It's pretty close to where he found his sister's body. God, what a horrible way for my poor niece to die. Joseph found her on a canal bank, naked, with her throat cut and her tongue pulled out through the cut. They even wrote some crap all over her belly. Some garbage about arms and vultures." He suddenly picked up the sledgehammer and threw it twenty feet, striking a large coral boulder, startling Callaway. "I'm eighty-five years old, Callaway," he said. "If this happened twenty years ago, I would have already found the son-of-a-bitch that killed Melinda, and I would have fed him to the gators."

The old man seemed to calm down as he, again, looked out at the River of Grass, which is the Everglades. "I can draw you a map to Joseph's camp. Come on inside."

He led Callaway into the bait shop through the back door, and then pulled a sheet of loose-leaf paper from a binder. He started scribbling the makeshift map with a pencil, then stopped and looked up at Callaway with a concerned look. "You better be really careful how you approach Joseph, Callaway," he warned. "When I saw him two days ago, he was pretty loaded up with whiskey, and he was in an awful mood. He gets that way a lot since his baby sister was killed. Oh, and he's got a shotgun with him, too, so like I said, be real up front with him. Don't make him guess what you're doing out there. He may have lost a leg, but he's still strong as hell."

Callaway thanked Fred Eagle for the information and the map. "How long do you think it'll take me to get out there? It's starting to get dark," he asked.

Fred Eagle looked out the window at Callaway's Mustang GT. "You won't get there at all in that thing," he answered smiling slightly. "You'll rip the oil pan and the suspension right out of it on those paths that go through the woods." He reached into his pants pocket and pulled out a set of keys as he continued. "Take my truck. He knows it, so it may keep him from shooting at you when you pull up. It's in the barn next door."

Callaway shook hands with the man and walked over to the other building. When he opened the door, he was not that awfully surprised to find that the old man's truck was a two-year-old Ford F-150 four-wheel drive, all jacked up with heavy- duty suspension, off-road tires, and big exhaust pipes. It seemed that pretty much every male member of the Seminole tribe, and a few of the women, too, had a jacked-up F-150 or Silverado that could stomp its way through the swamp trails with no problem. He laughed at the paint job, which was maroon with gold stripes that ran up the hood, over the cab, and down the tailgate. "FSU. What a surprise," he said, smiling. He put the key in the ignition and fired up the motor.

Hearing the distinct whine of a supercharger coming from under the hood, he laughed again. Looking at the map, he put the truck in gear, and drove out onto Alligator Alley once again, heading west to search for Joseph Eagle as the day came to an end.

Chapter 9

The maze of dirt roads was rather tough to follow, after Callaway left the relative straightness of Alligator Alley. The crude map drawn by Fred Eagle was not much help when he attempted to read it in the dim interior light in the Ford. It was close to 11:00 PM when he finally rolled up on a cleared area near a canal bank. He could see a fire burning in the middle of the site, providing the only light on this moonless night.

Callaway kept thinking about what Chief Cummings said about Joseph Eagle going bad, and what Fred Eagle said about the man's demeanor. *The last thing I want to do is try to sneak up on a full-blooded Seminole Indian, who's pissed drunk, pissed off, and armed with a shotgun,* he thought as he opened the truck's glove compartment and removed his Smith & Wesson Chief's Special revolver that he'd transferred from the Mustang. He shoved the little revolver inside the front of his pants and pulled his shirt down over it. Sliding down out of the elevated cab of the F-150, he hit the ground and froze. "I know you're watching me, Joseph Eagle," he whispered to himself. He decided to play it safe and announced himself. "Joseph Eagle! My name is Michael Callaway. I mean you no harm. I just want to talk to you."

He could hear nothing but the crackling wood fire and

crickets chirping all around him. Slowly, Callaway walked forward towards the fire with his arms spread and his hands wide open, trying his best not to look like any kind of threat to the man. When he got within ten feet or so of the small blaze, he could see something lying directly on top of a burning branch. He moved a little closer and could make out the outline of a large fish. A couple of steps closer, and he could see that the item was a large garfish, with the flames licking at its armor-like skin. Callaway knew of the old-school Seminole method of cooking these nasty-looking creatures with their billed mouths full of long, sharp teeth. The Seminoles would catch them on a line, or gig them with a spear, and then throw the live fish directly into the fire to cook. With their leather-like hide, their flesh would cook inside as if in an oven, and when they were done, there would be an audible "pop," as the skin would burst open.

Callaway was completely entranced by this when he realized that he had been sucked into standing in the light, making himself a perfect target. He turned slowly towards the woods, bumping something with his right foot. He glanced down, keeping his arms away from his body, and his hands still open, trying to look as non-aggressive as possible. Callaway could see that the object he bumped into was a half-empty bottle of J&B whiskey. Callaway could also see footprints leading away from the bottle and that the right footprint was deeper in the dirt, indicating somebody with a severe limp. *Well, I guess I'm in the right place, but I don't care much about the situation. A drunk, angry man could be difficult to reason with*, Callaway thought. He stared at the woods in the direction where the footprints led. He could see nothing, but he froze when he heard the mechanical click of the safety being disengaged on a firearm.

"What do you want?" a deep voice boomed from the woods.

"Joseph, I was U.S. Customs Enforcement," Callaway said. "We unfortunately have something in common. My fiancée was killed the same way your sister was, and I believe, by the same people. I need to talk to you about Melinda, and I need information, man. I need your help. Please!"

Callaway stared at the woods and saw a large shape emerge. Joseph Eagle was an easy six- foot two and about three hundred pounds. He limped towards Callaway slowly with a pump- action shotgun mounted to his right shoulder. When he got to within ten or so feet, he stood staring at Callaway as though he was sizing him up. Callaway didn't know what to do during this tense moment, and then from the fire came a loud "pop!"

"Your dinner's ready," was all Callaway could say.

"You Signal-Zero?" the large man asked, trying to determine if Callaway was in fact a former federal agent who would know the Ten-Code term for "armed with a weapon."

"Yes," Callaway said.

"What and where?" Joseph Eagle asked.

"Chief's Special, in my waist band, front," Callaway replied.

Joseph Eagle raised his right thumb to the upper rear of the shotgun frame and pushed the safety on his shotgun to the "On" position. He lowered the muzzle, and motioned Callaway to a log that was half-buried. "Sit down, Callaway," he said.

Callaway quickly complied.

Joseph Eagle leaned the shotgun against a cypress knee, the local name for the cypress roots that stuck straight up out of the ground, and then he limped to the campfire. He picked up a three-foot long sharpened wooden stick and stuck it into the gills of the equally long fish cooking on the fire. Hefting it out of the flames, he placed the sizzling creature on a wooden plank on a nearby folding table. He pulled what appeared to be a Marine Corps KBAR knife from a scabbard on his hip, and with one chop, decapitated the fish. Eagle then slit the creature's belly open and removed its entrails. He continued to cut the fish lengthwise until he had two halves. Eagle stuck the tip of the knife under the front of the skeleton and pried it out in one piece.

"I see Uncle Fred loaned you his truck. You like gar?" he asked as Callaway watched him work.

"Uh, I don't know. Never had it before. But I love fish. I'll eat with you," Callaway answered.

Joseph Eagle grabbed another plank and slid one half of the steaming fish onto it with his knife, and with one hand, gave the plank to Callaway, who placed it on his lap. Joseph Eagle limped over, his plank and half of the fish in hand, and sat on the same log, hard enough to bounce Callaway a couple of inches up in the air. Callaway watched as the Seminole pulled some fish out of half of the carcass with his knife and gobbled it down. He looked at Callaway for a couple of seconds. "You came out into the swamp with no knife? No wonder we beat you guys so bad," he said, referring to both Seminole Wars that occurred during the nineteenth century.

Callaway got the reference and smiled as he watched Joseph Eagle reach into his pocket and retrieve an old Buck folding knife. "You might want to stick the blade in the fire for a few seconds. I can't remember what I gutted with that knife last," Joseph Eagle said.

Callaway leaned forward and let the flames at the edge of the fire touch one side of the blade, and then turned it over to sterilize the other side. Joseph Eagle handed him a canteen that was hanging under the folding table, and Callaway poured a little water over the blade to cool it off. He sliced a hunk of fish from half of the gar and put it in his mouth. Callaway had fished and eaten his catch since he was five years old, but he never experienced anything as vile and horrible tasting as the hunk of garfish residing in his mouth at that moment. Feeling a need to compliment his host, he chewed and swallowed the fish, and nodded. "This is great!" he said, forcing himself to smile.

Joseph Eagle looked at him for a few seconds, and then he smiled. "You are so full of shit, Callaway! We only eat these frigging things when we can't catch any bass or bream. This is Seminole survival food. An Indian MRE. Period!" He picked up the bottle of J&B and handed it to Callaway. "Here. It helps to wash that shit down with this."

Callaway took the bottle, unscrewed the cap, and took a swig, thinking, *Joseph Eagle, you are dead right about all facets of this meal!*

"Your fiancée was the one who washed up on the beach in Miami, Callaway?"

Callaway figured this was as good a time as any to put his plank and the rest of his delicious fish down to talk. "Yeah. Her name was Carrie Marvin, and she was an agent with the DEA. I know someone from Derrick Drake's drug organization from the Bahamas murdered her. I received some information that Melinda was acting as a confidential informant for Carrie. They were both murdered the same way. I'm trying to find the connection between the two murders."

Joseph Eagle gave Callaway a hard stare. "I know who Anton Drake was, Callaway. Melinda talked about him a little, he said. "I also know he got killed last year. Who's Derrick Drake?"

Callaway sat up a little straighter on the log before he answered. "He's Anton's son," he said.

"Carrie and I, actually Carrie, killed Anton Drake. And you're one of a few people in this world who knows that fact."

Joseph Eagle looked at his guest, and Callaway saw the man's eyes tearing up. "Thank you," was all the big Seminole could say.

"I read the case file on Carrie's work with Melinda," Callaway continued. "It's not very complete. I just don't understand how she got tied up with Drake and his organization. I mean, and *please* don't get upset when I ask this question, but was your sister a drug user?"

Now Joseph Eagle sat up straight on the log. "My baby sister never, ever used drugs!" he yelled. "I would have kicked her ass if she ever did!"

Callaway slid a couple of inches along the log from Joseph Eagle, trying to give himself a little edge if he had to get away from the man, just in case he lost it. "Well then, what was she doing, hanging around Drake?" Callaway asked. "Was she smuggling, or selling his stuff over here? Look, I'm not trying to piss you off, or insult your sister, I'm trying to find out what the hell was going on."

Joseph Eagle looked around at the canal and took a deep breath. He reached down and slid his prosthetic leg off, revealing the pointed stump of his right leg, below the knee. He laid the prosthetic on its side, and rested his leg on it, trying to get comfortable. Callaway felt a bit relieved at seeing this, knowing he could at least get away from this angry mountain of a man, if need be. He watched Joseph Eagle as he took a long hit from the bottle of whiskey and then handed it back to him. Callaway was in the middle of taking a sip when the man spoke. "She was in love with Drake's head of security."

His words caused Callaway to choke on the brown liquor. Callaway coughed out the name, "Herrera?! How in hell did that happen?"

Joseph Eagle looked down at the ground now, speaking in a softer tone. "She went to Nassau on vacation for a week. From what she told me, she and one of her friends wandered into this dump of a local bar. What the hell did she call it? Greasy——"

"——Dick's," said Callaway, completing the name of the scuzzy bar where he saw Carrie for the first time in years, apparently working as one of Anton Drake's bodyguards, when in fact she was working a deep cover narcotics investigation on Anton himself.

Joseph Eagle continued, as Callaway took a long hit from the bottle. "Well, in walks this Cuban guy, all dressed nice, and smelling good, and he introduces himself as Marty, and he starts buying Melinda and her friend drinks," he said. "The next night they had dinner, and the night after that they were in the rack together. Know this, Callaway. My sister was no slut. She legitimately fell in love with this guy, and from what she told me, he was in love with her, too. I mean, he bought her all kinds of expensive shit, and then he gives her keys to this fancy condo that he has on Paradise Island. She started going over there every weekend to see the guy, on his dime. We, my family, kept telling her to quit seeing him. I mean we didn't know what he did for a living or anything. Our tribe likes to keep the blood pure. It's a traditional thing. But she wouldn't listen. You know, love is blind, and sometimes it's very stupid."

Callaway could tell that Joseph Eagle knew nothing about Martino Herrera's past. "So, Melinda never said what *Marty* did for a living before he went to work for the Drake's?" he asked.

The big Seminole shook his head.

"Martino Herrera was a high-ranking officer in the DGI, the Cuban Intelligence Directorate," explained Callaway. "Kinda like Fidel Castro's version of the Russian KGB. He left that job to become Anton's head of security. The man was a spy who, from what I know, slipped in and out of the United States several times to infiltrate the anti-Castro groups in Miami. He's suspected of killing several people in the U.S. God only knows how many more on Drake's island. When the Bahamian Police and our federal people invaded Golgotha, Drake's two private islands, they found a cave full of human remains."

Joseph Eagle looked at Callaway. "She knew too much, didn't she?" he said in a quiet voice. "That piece of shit Herrera killed her because she knew too much about him!"

Callaway nodded. "I'm guessing that she found out something about his association with Anton Drake, or Derrick Drake found out that old *Marty* had taken a lover, and they ordered her death." Callaway took a deep breath before he told Joseph Eagle another piece of secret information. "Drake knew that Melinda went to Carrie, because… Well, there's a mole in the DEA Miami office." He could see the rage build quickly on Joseph Eagle's face. The man looked like he was about to explode, when he suddenly put his hands to his face and began to cry.

"Oh God!" he yelled, sobbing. "I told her to go to the DEA! I thought they could keep her safe. I thought they would arrest Drake and Herrera! I got my sister killed!"

Callaway put his hand on the man's shoulder. "You didn't know. Nobody knew until Carrie was killed. She left Miami to go deep cover into Drake's organization. She wouldn't be able to even contact Melinda. Did she hand Melinda off to another agent?"

Joseph Eagle rubbed the tears from his eyes and looked at Callaway. "Yeah. Her case got turned over to some hillbilly named Howe," he said, trying to regain his composure.

Callaway tensed up just hearing the man's name as Joseph Eagle continued. "He suggested she would be better protected if she came back to the tribe. The elders thought she would be fine on reservation land, because, as you probably found out today, we'd know it if some white guys came sneakin' around. Whoever took her was skilled, because she was snatched right out of her bed, in my house, in the middle of the night. Bastard even killed my pit bull that was guarding the yard."

Callaway was curious about that statement, inquiring how the dog was killed.

"Shot," Joseph Eagle said. "Nine-millimeter, right through the head. Must have been a suppressed weapon, cause I didn't hear a thing."

He began sobbing again. "I didn't hear them take her, either!"

Callaway tried to console the man. "You're lucky to be alive, Joseph. Carrie was taken from a DEA safehouse, and the agents guarding her were killed. Callaway figured he had gotten as much as he could from Joseph

Eagle. The man put on his prosthetic leg and limped over to his tent. He turned and looked at Callaway before he entered.

"*Sho Na Bish*, Callaway," he said.

Callaway had heard those words of thanks from Miccosukee that he helped him, out in Everglades National Park many years ago.

You're welcome, Joseph Eagle, he thought, his head buzzing from the whiskey, the cadence began pounding full beat as Callaway pulled himself up into the cab of Fred Eagle's truck and somehow found his way back to the owner's bait store. He slept off the J&B in the truck until he awoke to someone pounding on the window. Fred Eagle stood there with a cup of coffee in his hand, having arrived at 5:30 am to begin his workday. Callaway drank the strong brew, talked to the old man for a while, and then poured his hung-over self into the Mustang for the ride back to his condo in Fort Lauderdale. He realized something, as the loud exhaust sounds coming from the long-tube headers and barely-nothing mufflers gave him a massive headache: *Chief Cummings was right. I've climbed into a bottle, too. I just wonder how far?*

Chapter 10

Callaway awoke to the telephone ringing like a pounding gong in his head. He wondered why his head hurt even worse than normal from all the whiskey. He arrived home from his trip to the Everglades covered in mosquito bites, at about 9:00 am, and crawled into bed. "I hope the damn mosquitoes feel as bad as I do from drinking my blood," he mumbled as he grabbed the phone next to the bed.

"Hello," he answered, trying to make his bone-dry mouth function.

"Hey, Mr. Callaway, it's Manny, down in the lobby. There's a Mr. Cruz down here who wants to see you. He says you're expecting him."

Manny Perez worked security in Callaway's condominium building, and the two had become friends in the year since Callaway moved in. He wanted desperately to become a police officer. Callaway took a liking to the man because of his "it's all good" attitude, and his devotion to his work. Manny made sure the building was secure and had personally intervened in several attempted car burglaries in the building's underground parking garage. He didn't stand very tall, and he was a little overweight, but he was tough enough to wrestle down one burglar and hold him for the police. Callaway tried to help Manny prepare for the entrance exams for the various police departments that he applied to, but he knew that he would never get hired: he just didn't have the mental capacity to do well in the tests. Callaway didn't have the heart to destroy the man's dreams. "It's okay, Manny. You can send Cruz up," Callaway mumbled.

"You okay, Mr. Callaway? Manny asked. "You don't sound so good."

Callaway rolled his legs off the bed and sat up. Immediately, the room began to spin. "Yeah... Yeah, I'm fine, Manny," he said, trying to fight off the wave of nausea that came over him. "Just tell Cruz to give me ten minutes, and then send him up. I need to get dressed."

Manny acknowledged, and Callaway hung up the telephone. He closed his eyes, trying to get his balance back, but it didn't work. He stood up and lost his balance, falling back to a sitting position on the bed. Callaway could feel the vomit coming up. Standing again, he ran to the master bathroom, bouncing off of the door frame as he ran through, and sliding to his knees in front of the bowl, heaving his guts out for two minutes straight, Callaway felt extremely weak, and fell back to a sitting position on the floor. "God damned garfish," he mumbled as he staggered to his feet. "Seminole survival food, my ass!" He brushed his teeth, but the foul taste of bile still lingered. He slowly walked back into the bedroom and pulled a t-shirt out of a drawer. Callaway grabbed a pair of shorts he had left on a chair three days before and was pulling up the zipper when he heard a knock at the door. "Give me a second, Cruz!" he shouted, looking at himself in the mirror.

He didn't like what he saw. He ran a brush through his hair and then walked to the front door, checking through the peephole to make sure it was his friend from the DEA. Callaway opened the door and saw the smile quickly disappear from Cruz's face.

"Jesus, Callaway! You look like shit." Cruz said as he walked through the door. "And you don't smell much better, either!" Cruz was dressed in a pair of blue cargo shorts, sandals, and a yellow golf shirt. Callaway tried to change the subject by ragging on his friend's wardrobe.

"Good to see you, too, asshole," he said. "You're dressed a little casual today aren't you, *District Director*?

Cruz looked at him and laughed. "You realize that it's Saturday, don't you?" he said in a condescending tone. "I don't work on Saturdays anymore because I am a District Director. I was all dressed up yesterday, when I came by to see you, but you weren't home."

Callaway realized that he had lost track of the days since Carrie's funeral. *Way too much booze,* he thought, trying his best not to get sick again.

Cruz plopped down in a chair near the sliding glass door that led to the condominium's terrace. The curtain in front of the glass door was closed, and the lighting in the room was dim, even with the lights on. "You mind if I open the curtains?" Cruz asked as he looked around for the cord to do so. "It looks like a cave in here. Smells kind of like one, too."

"Yeah, I do mind!" Callaway said.

Cruz looked at Callaway and shook his head before he replied. "For a guy who won $82 million dollars, you look like you live under a freeway overpass, Callaway," he said, smiling.

Callaway tried to act like the words didn't bother him, as his stomach began to rumble again. "Why are you here, fucking up my morning, Cruz?" Callaway said scornfully, sitting on the couch across the room.

Again, Cruz smiled. "Well first of all, *culo,* its two o-clock in the afternoon," he answered. His facial expression changed quickly to a frown. "And secondly, I told you over at Eldridge's house that I would come by when I found out Carrie's cause of death." He stopped cold when he saw the expression on Callaway's face.

"Well?" Callaway said, forcing the word out.

Cruz looked at his friend for a long couple of seconds before answering. "She was drowned, Mike. Whoever the scumbags were that did this drowned her first, and then they cut her throat." Seeing that Callaway began breathing heavily, Cruz stood up. "Mike! Are you okay?" he asked.

Callaway jumped up and ran into the guest bathroom, slamming himself to the floor on his knees, not even bothering to close the door. Once again, he began vomiting, trying to keep himself steady in the bowl.

Cruz was starting to get sick from the sound and the smell. "You okay, Mike? Can I get you anything?" he asked as he turned and opened the curtain. "We need to get some fresh air in here, man."

Callaway stopped vomiting for a second when he heard a strange noise in the living room that sounded like ice cracking. He heard a gasp, and then a hard thud.

"Cruz? You okay?" he said, trying to slow his breathing down. He grabbed some toilet paper and cleaned his face up before getting up and walking into the living room. He froze when he saw his friend piled up on the floor, motionless. "Al!" he screamed. He knelt quickly and rolled the man over on his back. Callaway saw blood all over the front of the yellow golf shirt. He could see a tiny hole in the shirt, at about the level of the man's heart. He stuck the index and middle fingers of his right hand hard into the side of Cruz's throat, trying to find a pulse. He found none. Grabbing the telephone, he dialed 911. The operator at the Broward Sheriff's Office Communications Center answered calmly, only to hear a terrified Michael Callaway screaming at her. "I need rescue here, now!" he yelled. "Police officer shot! I'm doing CPR! Get them here quick!"

He dropped the telephone receiver and pulled Cruz's head back, forcing the man's mouth open. He gave the bleeding man four quick breathes, and then began chest compression. Blood pumped from the wound with every compression. At every fifteenth compression he gave him four more breaths. Callaway was sweating profusely as he worked to try to keep his friend alive. About eight minutes of desperately hard work had gone by when the front door of the condo opened. Manny Perez used his master key to open the door and let Fort Lauderdale Fire Rescue personnel into the room. They immediately went to work on Cruz, letting Callaway rest. The intense strain of giving CPR had taken everything out of him, and he collapsed unconscious on the floor.

Manny sat Callaway up and started talking to him until he woke up. When he did, he saw that the medics were packing up their equipment, and two uniformed Fort Lauderdale police officers were staring at him. He looked at Cruz, and almost passed out again when he saw that his friend was dead. His body laid there, shirt torn off by the medics, with what appeared to be a small entry wound in his upper chest. There were IV needles sticking out of both arms where the medics pumped him full of saline, trying to sustain him while giving him CPR. The medics had also tried using a pair of Military Anti Shock Trousers that inflated around his legs to force blood up to his heart and brain. Callaway knew the medics had tried everything, but his friend was dead. The anger that he felt before, when Cruz told him how Carrie had been murdered, came back. He felt the same knot of pain twisting in the back of his skull as he stared into Cruz's dead, open eyes, until he was shocked back to reality.

"Mr. Callaway?!"

He looked up to see one of the Fort Lauderdale police officers talking to him.

"Can you understand what I'm saying, sir?" the officer asked.

Callaway slowly nodded.

The officer continued. "Sir, you have the right to remain silent," the officer said in a monotone voice. "You have the right to an attorney."

Callaway interrupted him. "You think I did this?" he said in disbelief.

The officer continued. "It's procedure, Sir. We're conducting a homicide investigation," he said, not skipping a beat. "If you cannot afford an attorney, one will be appointed for you by the state. Should you decide to make a statement, you may stop talking at any time. Anything you say can be used against you in a court of law."

A man wearing a suit walked in just as the officer finished giving Callaway his Miranda rights. Callaway could see a badge on the man's belt.

"Mr. Callaway. I'm Detective Harkins, Fort Lauderdale P.D. Homicide." He turned to the police officer nearest to Callaway. "Has he been Mirandized?"

The officer nodded.

"Can you tell me what happened here, sir?" Harkins asked in a polite tone.

Callaway looked at both of them, confused, and dazed. "I was in the bathroom when I heard a noise," he answered. "I came out and found Al lying on the floor, covered in blood. I gave him CPR. I tried to save him."

Detective Harkins' facial expression didn't change. "Because of the location of the wound, you could have worked on him for a week, and it wouldn't have helped him one bit," he said. "We looked at his I.D. He's a federal agent. How do you know each other, Mr. Callaway?

Callaway struggled to stay on his feet. "I was with U.S. Customs," he answered. "I resigned last year. We worked together a few times and became friends. My fiancée was a DEA agent. She was killed last week. He came over to see how I was doing."

A crime scene technician took pictures of the sliding glass door a few feet away from Cruz. Callaway's eyes focused on a small hole in the glass, just under five feet above the floor. "That's where the bullet came through?" he asked. "How can that be?" He sat down, looking out of the sliding glass door. He could see the balcony floor extended five feet from the side of the building, where it was bordered by a railing made of three- inch diameter aluminum tubing. The distance between each of the four rails was only about ten inches. From the angle where he was standing, he couldn't see any part of the beach. He could only see the ocean.

"The shooter was out on the water," Detective Harkins said as he stood next to him. "That's the way it appears, Mr. Callaway. Your fiancée was the one who washed up on the beach in Miami?"

Callaway nodded.

The detective continued, "We are five stories up, with a balcony floor, and a railing in between the shooter

101

and the victim." he said. "How far out would the shooter have to be to connect with the victim?"

A voice from behind them spoke. "About five-hundred and fifty yards to get the right angle, I'm guessing."

Callaway and Harkins turned to see another uniformed Fort Lauderdale officer who had just arrived.

"Is that your expert opinion, Officer Klauser?" Harkins asked with a slight grin.

"Mr. Callaway, this is Officer Steve Klauser. He works on patrol now, but he used to be one of our SWAT guys. Did you just come on shift, Klauser?"

The tall, thin officer with gray hair walked over to look at Cruz before he answered, "Yes sir. Charlie-shift afternoons, as always," he said. He stared at the bullet wound and then at the hole in the sliding glass door. Glancing out at the ocean, he shook his head as he continued. "Whoever did this is a pro. Definitely master sniper material. He must have been on a boat, which made the shot even more difficult. I mean, it's calm out there, but boats tend to move. And the fact that it was made at an upward angle makes it even more impressive. Up or down angles have a tendency to make a shot go high."

Callaway thought of the night one-year prior, when he accidentally blew up one of Anton Drake's drug boats with one badly placed shot out on the water. He stood up and looked at Cruz, who was shot and wounded by the druggies during that crazy chase at sea off of Miami Beach as the medics were busy removing all of their equipment from him. "Yes, it is hard to shoot from a boat," was all he could say to the officer.

Klauser gave Callaway a surprised look. Detective Harkins's cell phone rang. Harkins listened to the caller for about a minute before hanging up. "That was one of my guys down on the beach," he said. "He canvassed all the people who have been down there for the past two or three hours. Nobody heard anything, which means the shooter must have used a suppressed weapon. They said there were some boats in the area, but the only one they remember was a personal watercraft with a single rider that went hauling ass north around the time of the shooting. No description on the rider other than a white male."

Callaway kept looking at Cruz, as the body removal service arrived and unceremoniously loaded him into a body bag. The sound of the zipper was horrifying in the quiet apartment. Cruz was loaded on to a gurney and wheeled out the door. All that remained was a bloodstain on the carpet. "Oh, Jesus Christ!" Callaway yelled, as his legs got wobbly, and he fell backwards on to the couch. "That bullet was obviously meant for me." He began to sweat, trying to keep from going into shock.

Detective Harkins looked at him, tapping his pen on his notepad. "Why would you think that Mr. Callaway?" he said.

Callaway put his hands over his eyes, breathing hard. "Nobody would have known that Cruz was coming over here today," he answered. "He just opened the curtain to get some light in the room, so he was standing in front of the glass. The shooter must have thought it was me."

"Which means, Callaway, there is probably a price on your head," Harkins responded. "Whoever killed your girlfriend is trying to get you, too."

Officer Klauser jumped into the conversation. "Someone obviously paid a lot of money to have you killed. A hit man with a skill set like this doesn't come cheap," he said without any emotion.

Callaway looked at the window and the blood stain on the floor, feeling vulnerable and guilty at the same time.

Detective Harkins closed his notebook and stared at the water, five floors below as he spoke.

"Look, Callaway. We'll get this clown. I don't care how good he is," he said with authority. "But… Keeping you alive? That's going to be the tricky part." He looked at Klauser, continuing, "You have this zone on the afternoon shift, right, Klauser?"

The officer nodded.

"Okay. Mr. Callaway, I want you to stay in your apartment," Harkins said. "Keep the curtains closed, and don't answer the door, unless you absolutely know who's out there. Don't stand in front of the door unless you're sure it's someone you know. If you order anything to be delivered, you call our dispatcher, and we'll have a unit come by to make sure everything is as advertised. Do not go out unless you absolutely have to. Klauser's a good man. I'll make a call to see if we can get an extra unit assigned to this zone, so he can hang out close by. We want to make you as small of a target as possible. I will keep you advised of everything we learn about this case as a professional courtesy." Callaway nodded that he would comply, while thinking about something else. *If I stay here, this asshole hit man knows just where to find me. I've got to arm-up and make it as difficult for him as I can.*

Chapter 11

All policemen know the dangers they face on the job, from the moment they walk out of the front door of their house to the moment they shut their car off in their driveway when they return home. They prepare for as many eventualities as possible. Sometimes they get it right, and sometimes they don't; in that case, there is a less than happy ending. It's different, though, knowing the danger is out there. Training and preparation as much as possible for that particular threat is all they have to fall back upon. They also understand that over the course of their career, they will piss a few people off— criminals— by arresting them, knocking them around, and sometimes even shooting them. These "*acquaintances* tend to carry a grudge, one that can manifest into a violent encounter, by chance, or an intended meeting. For this reason, cops tend to be selective when it comes to friends, gravitating towards other heavily armed members of the profession, who don't think it odd to always sit in the rear of a restaurant, with their back to the wall, watching everyone who comes to the front door.

Michael Callaway knew there was someone out there gunning for him. The hit man that killed Alberto Cruz displayed tremendous skill when he shot the man from some kind of small boat rolling in the Atlantic Ocean at least 550 yards away from Callaway's balcony railing. The fact that the shot was made at an upward angle, to a target in the living room of Callaway's fifth floor beachfront condominium, was equally amazing. This was no minor drug smuggler he'd arrested when he was with Customs, or some guy holding an undersized lobster when Callaway was working for the Federal Parks Service many years ago. The person looking to kill him is a pro.

Detective Harkins told Callaway that his best bet to stay alive was to stay home, in the condo, but *away* from the balcony. He tried this for one day, sitting in his living room all alone, with his Remington 870 shotgun across his lap. He couldn't sleep, and every time he heard a noise in the hallway, he broke into a cold sweat. "No way in hell I'm doing this anymore," he said aloud as he loaded all his handguns into the black ballistic nylon range bag. *Gotta move. Cabin fever is getting to me. Can't let the son-of-a-bitch have an easy time finding me. Gotta be a hard target that can fight back. And I gotta stay sober,* he thought. His mind was going one hundred miles an hour. When the guns, ammunition and targets were packed, he loaded his Smith & Wesson Model 60 Chiefs Special with five rounds of Remington 158 grain lead hollow points, the ones that were known in law enforcement circles as the FBI Load, since they were standard issue for enforcement personnel of that federal agency. He shoved the little 1 7/8-inch barreled revolver into the front of his pants and pulled his t-shirt down over it. Callaway touched the knob on the door to the hallway, and suddenly felt a chill. *That bastard could be waiting for me anywhere. Even down the hallway or in the parking garage,* he thought, his palms drenched in sweat. Fear, a previously seldom-known emotion for him, gripped him so much that he put the bag on the floor, and with his right hand, he pulled the revolver from his belt. He then took his ball cap off and carefully placed it over the gun and his hand. He looked down the hallway, as far as he could, through the peephole in the door, and then slowly turned the doorknob. Callaway pulled the door open and did a quick "Israeli peep," a maneuver he learned at the Federal Training Center in Georgia, swiftly ducking his head out, and in, giving him a look down the hallway to his right. Before doing it again to the left, he grabbed the ball cap from his right hand, flashing it out into the hallway and back to see if he drew fire. Nothing.

Callaway placed the hat back over his gun, picked up the range bag with his left hand and walked down the hallway, swiveling his head around like an owl. When he reached the elevator door, he realized he was soaked with sweat. A painful knot throbbed in the back of his head, and he heard his heart beating in his ears. He was reaching for the down button when the door opened before he could touch it. He stepped back. A figure stood in the elevator. Callaway dropped the range bag and raised his hat-covered revolver toward the black-clad person, eliciting a slight scream from the woman standing in front of him. He lowered his hand quickly, taking his finger off the trigger. "Mrs. Markowitz! I'm sorry, ma'am, I didn't mean to scare you," he said apologetically.

The old woman, who had fled Germany as a child to avoid the certain death that awaited six million other Jews, looked at the hat covering his hand.

"There damn sure better be a gun under that hat, Mr. Callaway, after what happened in your apartment. I know I slept with mine under my pillow last night. Can't be too careful since my husband died, you know." She walked past him slowly as she continued talking. "I thought I would be safe here, with an ex-cop living next door. Clearly, I was wrong—that poor man getting killed at your place, and everything. I'll keep an eye on your apartment, honey, and I'll call the cops if any suspicious characters show up while you're gone." Callaway was stunned by the old lady's demeanor. "You sure you don't mind, Mrs. Markowitz?" he asked. "I mean don't put yourself in any danger, okay?"

She smiled at him as she put the key in the lock on her door. "Don't worry, honey, I'm a tough old broad. I know what to do."

Callaway smiled at her. "Mrs. Markowitz, do you really have a gun in your apartment?" he asked.

"Of course, honey," she replied. "After what the Nazis did to my family, I am a firm believer in the preaching of Rabbi Meyer Kahane. He said 'for every Jew, a .22, never forget' or something like that. And he was right! And besides, this is South Florida. Everybody has a gun here. You be safe out there, honey. Shoot first and ask questions later."

He watched her disappear into her condo, and then he entered the elevator, pushing the button for the garage floor. Callaway was breathing short, tense breaths as he rode down. He felt the cold sweat soaking him when he reached the underground parking garage. Bursting out the door, gun in hand, he pressed his back against the wall and crab-walked to his car. He stopped at the rear of the Mustang, looked in all directions, and stood to one side of the vehicle, opening the trunk with the remote alarm button on his key chain. Callaway stared into the empty trunk like he expected the killer to be hiding inside. Placing the range bag in the trunk, he opened the driver's door, stuck the revolver back in the front of his pants, and slid into the seat. He inserted the key into the ignition switch and was about to turn it when he froze. *If this guy is hunting me, and he could make a shot like that to kill Cruz, he may have been military. And if that's the case, he might also know how to use explosives!* he thought, going deeper into panic. He carefully pulled the key out of the ignition switch, feeling the sting of sweat in his eyes. Slowly he leaned out of the open driver's door, bending until the top of his head was almost touching the garage floor, and looked underneath the car. At first glance, everything looked fine. He was about to sit up, when he saw a single wire hanging down over the left exhaust header. *There shouldn't be any wires up there, except for the oxygen sensors, and those have two wires!* Callaway climbed out of the Mustang as if he were crawling over a carton of eggs and began backing away from the vehicle. He had moved about ten feet when he heard a voice behind him.

"You all right, Mr. Callaway?" The voice had a heavy Spanish accent.

Callaway spun around, his hand going for the revolver, when he saw Manny. The man jumped back about five feet when he saw Callaway's reaction.

"Manny, I need you to go back to your office and call the police. Tell them that I think there's a bomb in my car, and that they need to send the bomb squad out here fast!" Callaway said about as quickly as a human being could speak.

Manny's tan face became decidedly pale.

"Manny! Come on dude, I need your help!" Callaway said. Callaway continued. "I'll stay here and make sure that nobody gets near the car. Go back to your office and call the police on the telephone!"

Finally, Manny stopped looking at the car, and stared into Callaway's eyes. Callaway turned back to look at the Mustang, and then looked again at Manny, who, to Callaway's horror, had removed his two-way radio from his belt holster, and was about to key the microphone.

"No!" Callaway roared, grabbing the man's wrist, and twisting it violently, flipping the device out of his hand and onto the concrete floor. Manny jumped back, pulling the nightstick from his belt ring, and cocked it over his shoulder, ready to strike at Callaway.

"Manny! Relax! If you pushed the button on your radio, it could set off the bomb!" Callaway said. "Please! Go to your office and call Fort Lauderdale PD on the telephone!"

Manny stared at Callaway for a moment, then he nodded his head, and ran into the building.

It took less than five minutes before he heard the wail of multiple emergency vehicles approaching across the Sunrise Boulevard Bridge. Some of them were easily distinguishable as Fire Department vehicles from the sound of their old-style, wind-up sirens. The first police car to arrive turned into the entrance of the garage, and stopped, blocking anyone from coming in. The officer exited his vehicle and motioned Callaway toward him. He obeyed, giving a broad birth to his vehicle, and never taking his eyes off it. When he reached the police car, he recognized Officer Steve Klauser.

"I didn't expect to see you again so soon, Mr. Callaway," Klauser said. "Head out, and around the corner, and you'll see the Mobile Command Post. Go on inside. The Bomb and Arson guys are suiting up to take a look at your car, just as soon as we get the building evacuated," Klauser said calmly as he eyeballed the mustang.

Callaway was breathing hard as he answered, "I didn't expect to see you, either, Officer Klauser," he said, trying hard to get the words out between breaths. "Tell the bomb guys that I saw a suspicious wire hanging over the left exhaust header," he stammered, then turned to follow the sidewalk that ran along the driveway.

"That dumbass spic security guard you got here was babbling like a baby when he called this in, from what the dispatcher told me," Klauser said with a laugh.

Callaway stopped, angry about the slur on Manny, but then kept walking towards the Mobile Command Post given the seriousness of the situation. The Command Post had been built from a one-million-dollar motor home that the Fort Lauderdale police had confiscated after finding two hundred kilos of cocaine tucked away in the vehicle's waste storage tank and ceiling.

It took two hours for the bomb and arson cops to go over the car. Then Officer Klauser poked his head into the motor home. "Okay, Mr. Callaway, they found and removed a device," he said.

The two men walked back into the garage and over to Callaway's car. "It was hooked-up to the transmission linkage, right above where you saw that wire," Klauser said, pointing at the shifter. "It would have gone off as soon as you shifted into reverse. Pretty damn good call on your part, Callaway. How'd you figure it out?"

Callaway looked over his car, and then back at Klauser. "Like I told you, I looked under the car, and saw a wire hanging down over the driver's-side header collector. That wire wasn't supposed to be there," he answered.

Klauser looked puzzled, "You must know cars pretty dammed well to have spotted that," he said. "I mean this

111

guy who's after you, that was a pretty unusual way he set up the detonator on the device. The explosives were sitting *on top* of the transmission, way the hell out of sight."

Callaway ran his right hand down the top of the driver's side rear fender. "I built this car, Officer Klauser," he said, smiling. "I mean, not the car itself. Ford did that. I put in all the high-performance equipment myself. I was the one who installed those exhaust headers, so I knew exactly what was and wasn't supposed to be there."

"Lucky thing for you that you did," Klauser said. "Uh, there's one other thing though, Callaway. When Bomb and Arson searched the trunk, they found a bag with some guns and ammunition in it. What's up with that?"

Callaway looked the man in the eyes. "I will not stay here and be a victim for this asshole that's gunning for me!" he said, becoming a little agitated. Detective Harkins has got this all wrong. This guy's a professional. Like you said that bomb wasn't some high school project. This killer's got skills. I need to get out of here and keep moving fast to avoid a bullet, or bomb, whatever. I was going to go out to the Markham Park Range to get some shooting practice. It's too late to go now, so I'll do it tomorrow after I have another sleepless night."

"Is that why you're carrying a piece under your shirt?" Klauser asked, pointing at the very slight bulge in Callaway's t-shirt.

Callaway was committing a crime, right in front of a police officer. He was no longer a federal law enforcement officer, a position that would allow him to carry a firearm concealed, nor did he have any permit from the state, county, or city to do so. He didn't know his accuser and wondered if he would be spending the night in the Broward County Jail for carrying a concealed firearm. He took a deep breath before he answered. "Look, Klauser, I'm fucking scared, okay?" he said, trying to keep from screaming at the officer. "You're a cop. You of all people should understand how I feel."

Klauser folded his arms before he responded, "Relax, my friend," he said in a calm voice. I didn't see a thing. I suggest you do a better job of hiding it, though. By the way, it's my day off tomorrow, and I was planning on going over to Markham to shoot, too. Maybe I'll see you there." He extended his hand. Callaway shook it.

"Thanks, man," Callaway responded, feeling relieved. "Maybe I will see you there."

He headed for the elevator, groaning over the thought of another night of intense fear, with no alcohol to run interference for him.

Chapter 12

"Been awhile, Callaway." Ron Fenton was the Range Master of the Broward County shooting-range at Markham Park. His auspicious career with the Broward Sheriff's Office, where he retired at the rank of lieutenant, came after working in their Marine Unit and running their Training Division. He and Callaway had crossed paths many times on the inland waterway and off the coast of Fort Lauderdale when Callaway was with U.S. Customs. "I was at your fiancée's funeral. I'm sorry for your loss, man," Fenton said. "I also heard about what happened at your place, with that DEA guy getting killed. I kind of figured you'd be showing up here after I read about that," Fenton said. Having trained most of the SWAT sharpshooters at the Sheriff's Office, Fenton had an appreciation for the killer's shooting skills. "Any idea how far the shot was?" he asked.

Callaway didn't look up from the range registration card he was filling out. "Over five," was all he answered.

Fenton's eyes got big before he spoke, "Five hundred plus yards, and the story in the paper said it came from the *water*? Crap!" he said. "Now I definitely understand why you're here. Too many people with guns here to try anything on you up close. You've got the target hill on one end, with the Everglades behind it, and now

114

they put that hill on the other side of the parking lot for the mountain bikers, so we're in a little, well-armed valley. Safe as can be."

Callaway didn't look up. "Yeah, safe," he said as he completed the card, and looked at his range bag. "Damn, I left my shooting glasses in the car. Watch my bag, I'll be right back," he said. Callaway walked out the front door and opened the driver's door of the Mustang. Reaching inside, he grabbed his yellow-tinted shooting glasses, closed the door, and touched the button on the key fob to lock it. He was about to re-enter the range building, when he heard laughter behind him coming slightly from above. He looked up to the top of a thirty-foot tall dirt berm, behind the perimeter fence of the range, and saw a man and a woman decked out in bright-colored shirts and helmets, riding mountain bikes along the top of the hill. *So, this must be the back end of the new mountain bike trail the County just built,* he thought as he walked back into the range office. *Where else but Florida would you have to pile up dirt to make fake mountains for the bikers to enjoy their sport.*

Fenton was still behind the counter. "Hey, there's a Fort Lauderdale cop, Klauser's his name, out on the range," he said. "He's been here a while today, but he said he knows you. He's holding the spot next to him for you."

Callaway gave Fenton a strange look as he handed him the five-dollar fee to use the range. "Yeah, I know him," he answered. "He came to my place after the shooting, and then yesterday, after I found a friggin' bomb planted in my car. Between you and me, the guy kind of gives me the creeps. A bit too 'Nazi, *mein herr,* if you get my drift."

Fenton laughed. "He's not a bad guy," he said. "He used to train the Fort Lauderdale SWAT guys at the

Sheriff's Office range at Port Everglades. Knows his way around a gun very well. I figured you two would get along fine. Anyway, the range is packed today, so if he's holding you a spot, be thankful."

Callaway put on his hearing protection and walked through the door to the outdoor range. Guns of every shape, kind and caliber were being fired up and down the line of fifty shooting stands as he walked behind the shooters to the only stand still available. It was right next to Officer Klauser, who greeted him with, "Callaway! Looks like it's a good thing I saved you a place, my friend. All the crazies are out here today."

Callaway saw what Klauser meant. There were several obviously first-time gun owners who hadn't read the signs at the range entrance explaining the art of safe gun handling. The range safety officers, most of them retired police firearms instructors, were running around trying to prevent a negligent shooting from happening. Callaway set his range bag down on the empty concrete range table and unzipped it. He pulled his trusty Smith & Wesson Model 686, .357 Magnum revolver, and a box of Federal hollow-point ammunition out of the bag.

He noticed Klauser eyeballing the revolver and the bullets.

"Well, Callaway. A bit old school, but very reliable," he said. "Slow rate of fire, but lots of power with those rounds. Back in the day, that set up was known as the King of the Street for its stopping power."

Callaway looked at Klauser's table, seeing a strange-looking pistol resting on a rubber mat. It appeared to have a break-open action, like an old- style single-shot shotgun with an exposed hammer, and a very expensive looking telescopic sight mounted on top.

"That's a Thompson Contender pistol. A 30-30 Winchester, my friend," Klauser said with a smile. "The other one in the bag is a .223 Remington."

Callaway had heard of the pistols. They both had twelve-inch barrels, and screw-on muzzle breaks on the end of the barrels.

"What in God's name do you use a pistol that fires high-powered rifle bullets for?" Callaway asked as he looked at the box of bullets next to the gun.

Klauser picked up the pistol from the mat and handed it to Callaway, who checked the chamber to make sure the weapon was unloaded. He marveled at the workmanship of the weapon, and in particular, the telescopic sight. Looking through it, he noticed that he had an extremely clear view of the target that was one hundred yards away, through the very crisp crosshairs of the scope sight. "That's a Leopold scope, set to eight-power," Klauser said as Callaway held the weapon at arm's length while looking through it.

Callaway was no stranger to telescopic sights like this, and he knew how expensive they were.

Klauser continued, "I shoot competitive silhouette with both of these pistols, my friend," he said, smiling at the pistol. "And sometimes I'll go out to the glades and pop a deer or a wild hog with them when I want some fresh meat."

Callaway was getting perturbed at Klauser for referring to him as his "friend."

The big pistol put a strain on Callaway's arms as he held it out in front of him. "Silhouette, huh?" he said. "That where you shoot at those plate steel animals, and try to knock them over?" Callaway said, as he held the pistol out in front of him.

117

"Yep," Klauser answered. "I shoot at those little steel critters out to two hundred yards. It's actually a lot of fun. If you hit them right, you hear a clang and down they go. You gotta practice a lot to do as well as I do at it. You should give it a try. I'm guessing you can afford the equipment, and you have plenty of time to practice. Since you don't work, and all."

Callaway smiled at the man, hearing the cockiness in his voice. It was almost like a taunt. He opened the cylinder on the revolver as he knew the range safety officers would stop the shooting soon, as they did so every fifteen minutes, to allow the shooters to set up new targets. When the whistle blew, he stepped back and watched as the Range guys walked the line, making sure everyone's weapon was unloaded with the cylinder or bolt open. Callaway grabbed a target stand and four bulls-eye targets and proceeded to walk to the fifty- yard line. *Well, Officer Klauser. I was going to shoot from twenty-five yards, but I think I'll put on a little show for you, cocky jerk,* he thought. Callaway got his target stand mounted, and the four small twenty-five-yard pistol competition targets stapled to it, while Klauser replaced his targets at the one-hundred-yard line. As Klauser returned, he held the targets in front of him for all to clearly see. Callaway noticed that the holes in the target were in a nice, little one-inch cluster, right in the X-ring at the center of the target.

Back at their shooting stands, both men donned their hearing protection and shooting glasses and waited for the range safety officers to advise them that the line was hot. It took about five seconds before they heard the call, "Ready on the right! Ready on the left! Ready on the firing line!" followed by the sound of a whistle. Instantly, gunfire erupted up and down the line.

Callaway couldn't help noticing that Klauser was watching him as he loaded six 125-grain magnum cartridges into the cylinder of the revolver. He closed the cylinder and held the weapon in front of him in a Weaver stance, feet at a forty-five-degree angle, with his shoulders slightly turned. He cocked back the hammer, sighted the target, and fired. The blast of the magnum round shocked the man shooting on Callaway's other side, but it didn't seem to faze Klauser at all. Callaway repeated the motions until the revolver was empty and noticed Klauser staring down range at the target.

"Nice, Callaway, six inside of the nine-ring of the target at fifty yards, off-hand," Klauser said. "Very nice!"

Callaway was a little doubtful about the report. "You can see all those little thirty-six caliber bullet holes in a black target, from fifty yards?" he asked.

Klauser gave Callaway a wink. "I have 20-10 vision, my friend. I think I'll fire one more, and then it will be time to head for home." He picked up the Contender pistol from the mat and loaded a 30-30-caliber rifle round into the chamber. Closing the action, he held the pistol up in front of him and pulled back the hammer. It locked into place with a loud click that Callaway could hear, even through ear protection. Klauser sighted in on the target, which looked pitifully small at that distance, took a short breath, let it slowly out, and squeezed the trigger. The blast and the flame that exited the barrel caused several shooters to stop and take notice. He opened the action of the weapon, removed the empty shell casing, and laid the pistol back on the mat, smiling. "Ten-ring, again!" he said, clearly looking for Callaway's reaction.

Callaway smiled and pulled his little Model 60 Chiefs Special revolver out of the bag and laid it on the concrete table. Klauser was packing items into his range bag when he saw the little gun. "Seriously," he said, giving Callaway a hard look. "You're going to shoot a revolver with a less than two-inch barrel at fifty yards? I've got to see this," he said in a very pessimistic tone.

Callaway was about to load when he saw an open bullet box on Klauser's table containing some strange-looking rounds. "What kind of bullets are those?" he asked as he pointed at what looked like a tiny bullet mounted in a much larger shell casing.

Klauser removed one of the rounds and handed it to him before he answered, "These are called Accelerators, my friend," he answered, sounding just a little condescending. "They load a little .22 caliber bullet into a sabot, a thirty-caliber plastic shoe. Then they load the shoe with the bullet into the 30-30- shell casing, and you end up with a very fast little bullet. When the bullet is fired, it leaves the barrel at about 4000 feet per second. Way faster than most rifles. The shoe falls off, and the bullet goes on its merry way to the target. "

Callaway reached into his bag, pulled out a box of .38 Special Plus Pressure rounds, and opened it. "All that stuff you have is a little too high tech for me," he said. Without looking at the man, Callaway loaded five rounds of the 158-grain slugs into the cylinder and closed it into the gun. "Watch and learn, *my friend,*" he said, without taking his eyes off the target. Raising the little revolver up in front of him, he assumed the Weaver stance again, only this time, he raised the barrel up about a half of an inch. Thumbing back the hammer, he let the air out of his lungs, relaxed, and imagining Derrick Drake's face as the target, he squeezed the trigger. The little gun barked, and he pulled the hammer back again. He repeated this action slowly, concentrating on the target until all five rounds were fired. Callaway placed the revolver on the table, again keeping his eyes on the target, and with a slight smile on his face, pulled the binoculars from his range bag, and gazed down-range. His smile got bigger when he saw five holes in the second target in a group that he could cover with his hand. With his right hand, he held the binoculars out to Klauser. "I know your eyes are good, but take a lo…" he said, stopping in mid-sentence when he saw the man was gone. In the time it took him to fire five shots, Officer Klauser had disappeared. He and all his equipment were nowhere to be found. Callaway turned around and looked for the man, but he was just gone. *I guess he can't take being shown up*, he thought, as he loaded the big revolver to shoot again.

Callaway went through two boxes of ammunition, feeling a bit more confident in his survival skills. Looking up at the dark, rain threatening sky, he decided to call it quits for the day. He packed everything up, grabbed his range bag, and walked back into the range office. Range Master Fenton was on the telephone, so Callaway waved and headed out the door to the parking lot, still wondering what happened to Klauser.

Seventy yards away, Officer Steve Klauser was watching Callaway through the 8-power Leopold telescopic sight mounted on his Thompson Contender pistol. The same pistol he had shown to Callaway on the range. It was also the same pistol he had used to shoot DEA District Director Alberto Cruz three days earlier. Klauser had removed the muzzle break from the threaded barrel of the weapon and replaced it with a can-style sound suppressor. He rolled down the heavily tinted driver's window of his white panel van and rested the

121

pistol on a custom-made mount attached to a steel plate bolted into the door frame. The mount held the pistol perfectly still but allowed Klauser a small range of motion from side to side. He waited patiently for Callaway to step off the porch of the range building and walk toward his Mustang and the bullet that was waiting for him. *"C'mon, Callaway. Step off that porch, so I can end all of your pain, and move on to the next guy on my list. Just you, Hidalgo and the Navy guy, and it's Miller time."*

Callaway took one step from the porch and heard a scream in front and above him. He saw something hurtling down the side of the brush-covered hill behind the chain-link fence separating the range from the mountain bike trail. He kept hearing the screams as a person slid through the brush and came to a stop wedged between the base of the dirt hill and the fence. As he sprinted to see what had happened, the hit man tried to swing his pistol to the left to catch him in his sights.

"Shit!" Klauser whispered as the weapon stopped against the left side of the mount before he could break the shot. He pulled the *Contender* out of the mount and tried to aim at Callaway free-handed. Callaway was crouched down, trying to give aid to what he could now see was a badly injured young female who had ridden her mountain bike off the path on top of the hill, and slid thirty feet down through the brush and rocks on the steep incline. The woman was trapped up against the fence. She was bleeding from cuts on her arms and legs, and he could see a bump in her twisted right leg that meant a fracture. "I need some help out here!" he yelled, as loud as he could, as he tried to pull the bottom of the fence up to get to the young woman.

Range Master Ron Fenton heard him yelling and

came out the front door. "Fenton! Call 911 and get a first aid kit," Callaway yelled. "And get some guys to help me pull up this fence!"

Fenton yelled into the office to some shooters who had just come off the firing line. "You men get out here and help him!" he yelled as he ran in the door. He told his assistant to call fire rescue and ran behind the counter. Grabbing a first aid kit, he sprinted back out and saw Callaway and the three shooters trying to pull up the bottom of the fence.

They couldn't lift it as it was clamped to a steel rod that ran along its base.

"Step back!" Fenton yelled, as he pulled his Colt Model 1911 pistol from the holster on his hip. He placed the muzzle against one of the clamps and pulled the trigger. The .45 ACP round shattered the clamp, allowing the men to pull the fence up, but not enough to pull the woman out from under it. He quickly moved around the men and blasted the second clamp off the steel rod. The three shooters lifted the fence, and Callaway gently put his forearms under the woman's arms and dragged her out.

Klauser had failed to kill Callaway. There were just too many people around, and they would certainly notice if Callaway was suddenly shot, with too many witnesses to see the van leaving the parking lot on the one road that meanders through the park to the exit, about a mile and a half away. *If I shoot him, the whole damned Broward Sheriff's Office will be waiting for me before I can get out of the park, that is if Fenton doesn't blow me away first,* he thought, as he put the Contender in his range bag, and removed the mount from the door. He moved from the passenger seat to the driver's seat and rolled up the window, watching the men work as he heard sirens approaching. It didn't take long for a Broward County rescue rig and fire truck to arrive. He could see Callaway holding a compress on one of the woman's wounds with his left hand, and gently rubbing her forehead with his right. "Nice, Callaway. That will keep her from going into shock," he said while he backed the van out of the space as he saw the rescue people taking over and Callaway standing up. Klauser pointed his right index finger at him. "Bang!" he said. "Only soon it will be for real." He shifted into drive and drove away.

Chapter 13

Callaway felt better after his trip to the range. Any time available to sharpen his skills always brought up his confidence a notch or two. Waking up the next morning, having consumed *no* alcohol the night before, he felt refreshed, but the fact that he was still a shut-in in his own condo reminded him that he was at the mercy of an unknown killer. Workmen had removed the section of bloodstained carpet from his living room where Al Cruz had died four days before, but the sight of him lying there dead still haunted him. *If he just hadn't opened those drapes, that damned hit man wouldn't have mistaken him for me, and he'd be alive right now,* he thought. His official sworn statement about the incident made at the Fort Lauderdale Police Department was relatively short, given what he had witnessed. Much of it centered on the connection between Carrie's death and what happened to Cruz in Callaway's living room.

Two other people were present while Callaway gave his recorded statement. Detective John Hessler had driven up from Miami Beach accompanied by his boss, Lieutenant Jeep Little. They were trying to find any links, other than the obvious ones, between the two murders. Given that the method of killing was so drastically different, there wasn't much of a connection. There were no new leads, either.

Callaway gave a second statement to the FBI, as agents from the Bureau were also investigating Cruz's death. The three law enforcement agencies were stymied in their investigations, having very little in the way of physical evidence, other than the bullet that was removed from Cruz. The one thing they did have was a person of interest based on motive, and that was Derrick Drake.

Detective Hessler was quiet on the trip back to the Beach, and Little couldn't help but notice.

"What's on your mind, John?"

Hessler twisted his mouth up then spoke, "What if it wasn't a case of mistaken identity? I mean, what if it was the hit man's intention that day to take out Cruz, instead of Callaway?

Jeep shook his head, "Why? If Drake is running this killing game, why would he go after Cruz? I mean it's obvious that he killed Carrie Marvin to hurt Callaway in the worst way possible. But what would be the point of killing a District Director of the DEA? From what I read about what happened last year, Cruz wasn't involved in killing Drake's father, other than supervising Marvin when she was running her undercover work on the island."

Hessler expanded on his theory. "What if Derrick's killing game places Callaway at the end of the murder list, so he will feel responsible for all of his friends' deaths? Talk about the ultimate way to burn someone, right?"

Jeep wasn't convinced. "I don't know. Seems like a lot of killing just to piss somebody off. The more murders, the more chance for a slip up on the killer's part that could directly implicate Drake. I just don't buy it. Stick with the investigation as it is. We need to close this case as soon as possible. Get with the feds again and see what they've got going on," he said, ending that conversation.

*****

Callaway drank a big glass of water and went downstairs for a workout. Even though only residents of the condo had access to the gym, he still had his little Chief's Special revolver in his gym bag, just in case. When he had finished hitting the weights and doing some time on the treadmill, he packed up his stuff and headed upstairs. The telephone was ringing when he arrived. It was Manny at the front desk.

"Hey, Mr. Callaway, your friend Jorge is down here to see you. I would have sent him up without calling, since I know him, but after what happened the other day, I figured I better call you," he said.

Callaway let out a breath and smiled as he spoke. "Manny, you are a good man and a good friend. Send my *other* good friend on up, please."

Two minutes later there was a knock at the door. Callaway looked through the peephole and made sure it was his old partner before he opened it. "Hor-hay!" he said, purposely exaggerating the Spanish pronunciation of his friend's name as he always did.

Jorge smiled as he walked in. "What are you doing, you rich piece of white-trash?" Jorge asked, grabbing his old partner in a hug. "Damn, Callaway! You're all covered with sweat. Did you tie one on again last night? Jesus! I'm gonna have to have my clothes laundered after hugging you!"

Callaway laughed at his friend's constant concern about the appearance of his clothes. "You know if you didn't always dress like you were going clubbing, you wouldn't have to worry about such things," he said.

Now Jorge gave him a sarcastic laugh. "So what? You want me to dress in a t-shirt and shorts like some friggin' fishing guide, like you?"

This is just what Callaway needed to break the tension that was constantly beating him up. He kept seeing Carrie's face in his mind, and every time he did, the rage grew stronger. He looked at Jorge, realizing he was here to try to cheer him up and get his mind on other things.

"Thanks, Bro," he said, smiling at his friend. "Hey, I just got through hitting the gym. Let me get a shower, and I'll take you out to lunch at Eddie's. I could use one of those big-ass corned beef sandwiches after my workout."

Jorge gave him a skeptical look. "Are we stopping at a bar before or after Eddie's?"

Callaway could see the concern in Jorge's eyes. He realized his friend wasn't there just to see how he was doing after the murders of Carrie and Cruz. "You think I'm hitting the sauce too much, don't you?" he asked.

Jorge sat down on the same chair where Cruz had been seated three days before. "Well, as a matter of fact, that subject did come up in a conversation I had with David Eldridge this morning. We both saw how you were when you came over to his house the night of Carrie's funeral. Cruz, God rest his soul, couldn't see it because he was pretty drunk himself. Hell, he ended up sleeping on the recliner that Eldridge offered to you that night. Poor guy. I miss him. I guess his family up north is burying him today."

Callaway felt the same loss, but he was able to make Jorge feel a little better. "Stop worrying, partner. The one and only good thing that came from Al's death is that it snapped me out of the hole I was falling into. I mean, I think if one more person told me I was heading to the bottom of a bottle of whiskey… I don't know, maybe I would have figured it out, but what happened here scared me big time. I think I'm good to go now, Jorge."

His old partner smiled at him. "Okay, so get your gringo ass cleaned up, and let's head for Eddie's. I needs me some corned beef, and if the hit man wants to try to get you, he has to go through me first!"

Callaway showered and dressed, and he and Jorge were about to walk out the door when the telephone rang. Callaway answered it and was surprised to hear it was Officer Klauser. "Mr. Callaway. Great news! We think we caught the hit man!"

Callaway let out a huge sigh. "So, tell me! Who is he? How did you get him?"

Klauser chuckled before he spoke. *Yeah, Callaway, get nice and comfortable, so you'll come out of your condo, and I can kill you*, he thought. "He was sitting in a panel van, right down the street from your condo. I thought he looked weird, sitting there like that, so I yanked him out of the vehicle, and ran him through NCIC and FCIC. He came back wanted in five states for basically doing what he's been doing here. Killing people. We found weapons in the van and a list of people he was supposed to kill. You're on it, a man named Eldridge is on it, and a guy named Hidalgo, too."

Callaway looked at Jorge, realizing at that instant that whoever this guy is, he was hired by Derrick Drake to kill him, and everyone else closely connected to him, to avenge the death of Drake's father, Anton. Looking at the floor where Cruz had died, he also realized that the bullet fired through the glass might have been meant for Cruz after all, and not him.

"What's up, partner?" Jorge asked.

129

"They got him, Jorge!" Callaway yelled. Fort Lauderdale bagged the hit man. My new friend, Officer Klauser grabbed the son-of-a-bitch right down the block from here," he said, starting to think that maybe Ron Fenton was right about Klauser being a stand-up guy. He spoke into the phone. "Hey, Klauser. Can I see him? I want to talk to this jerk-off."

Klauser laughed." Well, no, not now, anyway. We need to interrogate him and then the FBI and DEA get their turn. It will be a couple of days, but I think I can persuade Detective Harkins to let you meet with him. Oh, and keep this to yourself and whoever's with you. We don't want word getting out until the DEA can run this guy through the Wringer to see what he knows."

Callaway gave a laugh, looking at Jorge. "Are you off tomorrow, man?"

Jorge nodded.

"Okay then. Tomorrow, we're going fishing! Callaway said. Hey, Klauser. You want to go fishing with my old partner and me, tomorrow?"

Klauser smiled. *I'm fishing right now, asshole, and I've got you hooked. Now I just need to know where you're going tomorrow, and I'll have a little surprise waiting for both of you.* "Sure, Callaway. I love to fish. Where and when?"

Callaway grabbed his morning paper and looked at the tide chart for Miami Harbor. "There should be plenty of tarpon in the channel at Miami Harbor," he said to Klauser. "Meet us at the Miami Beach Marina at 4:30 pm. You'll find a seventeen-foot flats boat tied up behind an old shrimp boat named the *Orinoco Flow.* We'll get some dinner at the restaurant there, and then head out at dark to fish. Can you make it?"

Klauser was beside himself, as he leaned back in the seat of his old van. *This is great!* he thought. *I kill you two, then I just have to kill the old guy from the Navy, then this contract is done, and I disappear. Big money time!* "Yeah, I can find it. I will be there at 4:30 sharp. Now you two don't leave without me, okay?"

Callaway acknowledged and hung up the phone and looked at Jorge. "Let's eat, partner."

*****

The following afternoon, Callaway picked Jorge up at his apartment, and the two of them were at the dock at the Miami Beach Marina at 4:30 pm, on the dot. Callaway looked around for Klauser but couldn't find him. He and Jorge were standing by the bait shop talking to Mack, the old fishing guide who ran the marina at night to pick up extra cash. The man had gone drinking with Callaway and his close circle of friends occasionally, and he knew the men well. Jorge could see only the polling platform sticking up above the dock on Callaway's rejuvenated, low-slung flats boat, about fifty feet away. Mack told Callaway that he read about Cruz's murder in the newspaper, and then began telling them a story of how he strayed too close to Cuba on a fishing charter. He told Callaway and Hidalgo how he had to pour oil into the boat's fuel supply to make the motor smoke to dodge a Cuban gunboat chasing him and his clients. Callaway's cell phone rang, interrupting the tale. When Callaway answered it, he heard the soft-spoken voice of Detective Harkins from the Fort Lauderdale Police Department.

"Mr. Callaway, I said I'd keep you advised of our investigation of Director Cruz's murder, and that's why I'm calling."

Jorge, who had been bugging Callaway during the drive to the marina about letting him try the new remote starting switch for the flats boat, grabbed the device, pulling it off his friend's belt, and began walking towards the boat.

"So, what kind of great news do you have for me, Detective?" Callaway asked, watching Jorge walk towards the edge of the dock.

Harkins answered, "Well, this is a strange one. The bullet that the Medical Examiner removed from Director Cruz had no rifling grooves cut into it at all. Other than a slight deformation at the tip from the impact, it was practically undamaged. I mean, it doesn't seem to me that a shot as difficult as what killed Cruz could have been fired from a smooth-bore weapon and be that accurate."

Callaway thought about what the detective was saying. *Why is he bothering me with this stuff when he's got the guy in custody already?* he wondered. He was about to ask the detective if Fort Lauderdale P.D. didn't have any ballistics experts when it hit him. *The bullets that Klauser showed me at the range, he* remembered. *The ones with the plastic sabots. They wouldn't leave any rifling marks on the bullet itself because the bullet would never touch the barrel!*

"I'm sorry, Mr. Callaway, are you there?" Harkins asked.

Callaway realized in that second who the hit man was, and that he had been duped. Klauser could be anywhere in the area, sighting in on him and Jorge at the dock. He looked at his old partner who was standing on the edge of the dock, looking down at the flats boat. In what appeared to be slow motion, he watched Jorge hold the key fob with the auto-start up and push the button.

"Jorge!" Callaway yelled, as he began running toward his friend.

A white flash enveloped Hidalgo and the dock where the boat was tied up. Callaway heard nothing but felt the searing heat of the blast flinging him backwards. He hit the ground hard, flat on his back, while the concussion from a block of C-4 plastic explosive disassembled his flats boat into little pieces, throwing Jorge into the air and back towards the bait shop. Callaway felt something heavy hitting the concrete next to him as the pressure wave of the explosion compressed the blood vessels in his heart and brain, causing him to pass out.

He awoke to old Mack, the fishing guide, shaking him and yelling his name. He could barely hear him. He rolled over, and got on his hands and knees, trying to shake the pain out of his head and get his hearing back, when he saw Jorge a few feet away. Hidalgo's chest had been pushed in and distorted by the blast. He could see pink fluid pooling up on the concrete under both of his friend's ears, and he knew immediately his old partner was dead from a brain hemorrhage.

Mack, whose face had been cut by broken glass, was still yelling at him, and Callaway could hear somewhat more of what the man was saying. "Jesus Christ, Callaway! Somebody's killing all your friends!"

At that moment, Callaway realized who would be the last person on the list of names that Klauser, the hit man, was hired to kill.

Chapter 14

Callaway struggled to his feet, picked up his cell phone, and staggered through the marina building, and out the rear door into the parking lot. Pushing the button on the fob of his Mustang's key ring, he barely heard the chirp of the driver's door unlocking as his fingers curved under the door latch. He threw the door open and was in the driver's seat and starting the car before the door bounced back and closed. The 5.0 motor came to life at the first touch of the key, and Callaway was shoving the shifter into first gear as he stomped on the gas. The back tires clawed for traction as the rear of the car slid right and then left. Callaway felt the posi-traction rear-end finally grab the asphalt, rocketing the Mustang forward.

He had to dodge people running toward the dock to see what had happened, and he could already hear the sirens of police and fire units heading that way. Callaway grabbed his cell phone between shifting gears and was shocked when he could barely hear the beeps from the bashed-up *Nokia.* He tried to call Commander Eldridge, but the phone rang once, and then switched to the answering machine.

Next, he dialed 911. "Metro-Dade Police emergency," the 911 Operator answered. Callaway took a deep breath. "My name is Michael Callaway; I am a former Customs Service Special Agent. There is a hit man going to a house in Miami Beach to kill the resident that lives there. The man that lives there is named David Eldridge, and he's a Navy Commander. You need to send Miami Beach police units there now!" He gave the operator Eldridge's address as he slid the car through the Beach traffic. "The shooter's a hit man named Klauser. He's a Fort Lauderdale police officer, and he's going to kill Eldridge. Call Lieutenant Little or Detective Hessler at the Beach P.D. if you need confirmation."

"Where are you calling from, sir?" The operator asked.

"I'm on my way there, I'm about a mile out." Callaway yelled, squeezing the cell phone between his head and shoulder as he slid the Mustang around a corner.

The operator cautioned him. "Sir, I have dispatched units from Miami Beach, and they are running Code-3 to the location. You said you are a *former* federal agent. You don't have any police powers, so you need to stay away from the area until the police clear it.

Do you understand?"

Callaway hung up on the operator and called Eldridge's house. Again, it went to the answering machine. He cursed and threw the phone on the passenger seat. He approached an intersection, seeing nothing but brake lights ahead of him. The Miami Beach Public Works Department was digging up the swale of the corner house, bringing traffic to a halt. He slammed the shifter down into second gear and let go of the clutch as he steered the car up over the swale, getting about a foot of air under the vehicle. The Public Works' flagman began yelling obscenities at the red car as it flew across the nicely manicured front lawn of the residence.

Callaway crossed the swale at the other side of the house, snapping the steering wheel to the right, and turning down the side street towards Eldridge's house.

*****

The alert tone whining loudly over the radio got the attention of every on-duty officer in Miami Beach. The dispatcher gave out the address of Eldridge's house, reciting in a calm voice, "Any unit in the area, possible Signal 32 in progress at that address. Subject, male, with unknown description, possibly a Fort Lauderdale police officer named Klauser, may attempt to kill the resident Commander David Eldridge, United States Navy. Complainant, is Michael Callaway, and he is in route to the residence now."

Detective John Hessler was stunned by the broadcast. He sat in his unmarked car, just four houses south of Eldridge's house, realizing that his hunch may have just paid off. He stepped out, scanning the front of the commander's house. "Nothing," he said. He approached the house closest to his position and walked through the alley to the back yard. He looked at the low, sand-dune hill that stretched the length of the street behind the houses. As he slowly moved his gaze toward the rear of Eldridge's house, he thought he saw a slight movement. Running up the hill, Hessler drew his Glock 19 from under his coat. When he reached the top of the tree-covered dune, he turned and cautiously moved through the overgrowth on the dune. He stayed as much as he could on the sugar-sand areas where nothing grew to try to muffle his footsteps. Slowly getting closer to the spot where he thought he saw movement, he rounded one

136

of the Australian pine trees that grew there, and saw the figure of a tall, gray-haired man, standing and leaning against the side of another Aussie pine. The man moved slightly to his left, and Hessler saw the blue-steeled barrel of a firearm. He glanced down the hill and could see into the rear window of the Florida room at the back of Eldridge's house. He made out the figure of the commander lying in a reclining chair.

"Freeze, asshole!" the detective screamed as loudly as he could, while pointing the Glock at the man's back. "Miami Beach Police! Open your hands and let the weapon fall. Do it now!

The gunman lifted his head slightly, not turning to look at the person challenging him. He slowly opened his hands, letting the Thompson- Contender pistol slip through his fingers and fall to the ground. Hessler could see that his coat was open as the man slowly turned toward him. "Don't fucking move!" Hessler yelled. "Let me see your hands over your head…" Hessler was interrupted by a sharp, burning pain in his upper chest and right shoulder. He saw two puffs of what looked like smoke come through the right side of the gunman's coat but heard nothing but a pair of barely audible *clicks*. He spun backwards, his body reacting to the burning pain, slamming the back of his right shoulder into another Australian pine. The impact jolted the Glock out of his right hand, and he watched it fall to rest in the sugar sand about five feet from where he fell to the ground.

"I've practiced that shot a hundred times, but this is the first time I ever actually used it," the gunman said as he turned to face his victim on the ground. As he turned, Hessler could see his left hand clutching a small caliber pistol with what appeared to be a sound suppressor on the end of the barrel. "This little Beretta .22 is nice and quiet with this silencer on it," he said as he glanced down the hill at the window to Eldridge's house. Hessler looked down at the window, too, hoping that his yelling had awakened the Navy man.

"Shit," Hessler whispered. He could see that the television was on, and that Eldridge appeared to be sound asleep. He could hear the noisy, old window-shaker air conditioner rattling away, thinking, *He couldn't hear me yelling over that friggin bucket of bolts.*

"So, you're the Jew-boy detective that's been tracking me. I'm impressed, Hessler. You figured it all out, you found me, and you almost took me down. Nobody has ever got that close to me before. Either I'm getting old and slowing down, or you're *damn* good, my friend!"

Hessler looked at the blood soaking his shirt and sleeve. "How, how do you know my name?" he asked between painful breaths.

Klauser looked down at Eldridge through a range-finding monocular hanging from a strap around his neck and observed that the man still appeared to be sleeping in the chair. He stooped down and picked up the Contender with his right hand. He looked back at Hessler as he blew the sand off the rear lens of the Leopold telescopic sight. "Oh, I've got all kinds of information about everyone involved in this case," Klauser said calmly. "Callaway, all his friends, you, your old nigger boss, everyone. See, I've got a friend on the inside who has been giving me all kinds of good information about the Marvin homicide. I wasn't paid to take you out, but I'll call killing you a freebie." He turned the Beretta sideways, keeping it trained on Hessler, as he glanced at his watch.

Hessler couldn't believe how casual and cool this crazy man was. He had just shot a fellow cop, and he was speaking like he was discussing a golf match.

"Old Callaway and his spic ex-partner should be dead in the water by now," Klauser said. "The person who hired me was specific about how that was to be done. He said either shoot him or blow him up. Now, I kill the old Navy guy who ends my business here, and then I go on a permanent vacation with all the money I'm making off this contract. But, unfortunately for you, I've got one thing to do first."

He raised his left hand, pointed the little twenty-two at Hessler's head, and gave him a very warm smile. "*Mazel tov*!" he said, his finger tightening on the trigger.

You psychotic bastard! was all Hessler could think. But then he heard a strange noise, much like the sound that a baseball makes when it hits the catcher's glove. *Thump*! It was followed by a loud *crack,* off in the distance, well behind the gunman. Hessler saw the smile leave Klauser's face in an instant. His left arm dropped to his side, and the Beretta slipped from his fingers. He dropped the Contender from his right. He slowly turned to his left, falling against the pine tree, using it to hold himself up. Hessler's eyes opened wide as he saw a growing blood stain making its way down the man's coat, emanating from a hole in the garment up high on his back, to the right of his spine.

The gunman stared hard down the sandy hill. To his left, he saw a man leaning against another Aussie pine at ground level. Klauser reached down and pulled up the range finder with his right hand. He used the device, the one that was supposed to measure the distance for the shot he was going to take to kill Commander Eldridge, to get a view of the man who had apparently shot him. Shaking badly, he stared through the single, slightly magnified tube, looking many yards away. He was shocked. Michael Callaway was leaning against the tree, his tiny Smith & Wesson .38 snub- nose revolver pointed at the gunman, as a little trace of smoke curled from the barrel. He could see Callaway thumbing back the hammer on the Chief's Special, preparing to fire again. "Hell of a shot," Klauser wheezed as he slid painfully down the trunk of the tree, ending up in a sitting position, almost facing Hessler. The detective was in a lot of pain, frantically trying to slide his foot to his gun with the intent of retrieving it. His adversary had already retrieved his Beretta with his right hand and was raising it toward him.

"Drop it, asshole!" Commander David Eldridge, awakened by Callaway's gunshot, had sprinted up the hill, and was now holding a cocked-and-locked M1 carbine aimed at Klauser's face.

"God Almighty! I can't catch a break today," the gunman moaned. He dropped the gun, and Eldridge kicked it away.

Callaway made his way up the hill. He picked up the Contender, which was lying on the ground near the wounded hit man as he talked to the 911 dispatcher on his phone. "Yes, there's been a shooting, I've got a Miami Beach Police Officer down, along with the subject, both with gunshot wounds. Send two rescue units, Code-3."

Eldridge put a hand over the wounds in Hessler's upper chest and applied pressure to slow the bleeding.

Klauser just stared at Callaway. "How come you're alive? You're supposed to be floating in the waterway with your Cuban friend Hidalgo," he said. Looking around, as if to see if Jorge was anywhere to be found.

"Tell me, I at least got one of you, so my day isn't a complete waste of time."

It was all Callaway could do not to shoot the hit man between the eyes. But he needed answers. He gritted his teeth. "Who hired you, Klauser?" he asked, trying to overcome his anger and remember his interrogation training.

Commander Eldridge spun his head around and looked at Callaway. "You know this jerk?" he asked with an angry voice.

Callaway frowned as he answered, "Yeah. He's a Fort Lauderdale cop. He's been at my condo twice, the first time after Cruz was killed." Then he turned abruptly toward Klauser, "How *did* you shoot him and show up at my place in less than two hours?"

"That was simple," Klauser boasted. He began to cough and speak haltingly, puffed up with his own pride. "I was on a WaveRunner, right off the beach. One shot with the Contender, and good-bye Cruz. The little spic didn't know what hit him."

Callaway looked at Klauser, remembering that he used the same ethnic slur back at his condo regarding Manny. "You're a real tolerant son-of-a-bitch, aren't you, Klauser?" Callaway asked. "What are you, like some kind of white supremacist?"

The man gave a slight laugh as sirens sounded in the distance. He coughed up some blood before he continued speaking slowly, "Man, I am the king of white supremacists. Look at you, Callaway. Hanging out with all these spics, niggers and Jews! I choose to live a different way. If you don't like it, you can go to hell!"

"And our meeting at the gun range? What was that all about?" Callaway asked.

Klauser gave him a sinister look, now, his tone

141

sounding harder, "I've been doing this, killing people for money, so long that it's become like a sport to me," he said. I used to hunt animals, but for the last three years, I've been hunting the most dangerous creatures on earth. People! I was bored and decided to make it interesting. That's why I didn't arrest you for carrying that little gun. I figured you wouldn't be a match for me with it." He winced in pain, groaning as he continued, "In hindsight, that was a bit overconfident... On my part. I met you at the range because I wanted to see just how good you are. When I saw that you could shoot, I decided to take you out, there, in the parking lot. I would have done it, too, if that bitch hadn't fallen off her bicycle."

Callaway asked him again, "Who hired you, Klauser? I'm getting impatient."

The man shook his head, and asked, "You are amazing, Callaway, you know that? You made this incredible shot. Oh, by the way, my range finder said it was about 115 yards, with that little tinker-toy gun of yours, and all you're worried about is who sent me? Ha! Well, I'm not gonna tell you."

Callaway stared at the man, trying to control his anger. The cadence began its slow march in his head. *Revenge... Vengeance...*" Tell me or you'll die," he said, just louder than a whisper.

The gunman looked at him, and again shook his head. "What are you gonna do, Callaway, shoot me? I don't see that happening," he said, breathing heavily. "See, I know all about you. You're a by-the-book guy. You don't break the rules. You won't kill me in front of the good commander and the Jew cop over here. Hell, Mount Sinai Hospital is only five miles from here. They'll load him into one rescue truck and me in the other, and we'll both be on the operating table in twenty minutes. So, I'm not saying a thing. Call it professional ethics."

Callaway kept his revolver aimed at the man, totally amazed at his bragging. "I'm sure the police will find enough evidence to put you on Death Row for killing Cruz and Hidalgo even if you don't say a word," Callaway said as he picked up the sand- covered Beretta from the ground, looking it over carefully. "Spring loaded suppressor?" he said, holding the little .22 in his left hand.

The gunman said nothing, and Callaway thrust the muzzle of the silencer hard against the center of the man's forehead. Klauser snapped his head backward from the new pain caused by the impact.

"That was the old me," Callaway continued.

"Forget it, Callaway! I know you won't kill me. You want a shot at Drake…"

Callaway knew he had gotten the most obvious information out of the man. He wanted more. He needed something to make the man talk. "I'm not going to kill you, Klauser," he said. "See you don't understand how things work in Miami Beach. It's a lot different from Fort Lauderdale down here. This is an old city. The cops, the fire and rescue guys are all tight with each other. They don't like it when one of their own gets hurt or killed. So yeah, that first rescue rig will load Hessler up and haul him to Mount Sinai super quick, and you're right, they will have him on the operating table in minutes. Different story perhaps, for you, though. The second rig will load you up, for sure, but I think they might take you on a guided tour of the Art Deco District before they get you to the hospital. You know, just enough extra time for you to bleed out. Isn't that right, Lieutenant Little?" he yelled, having seen Jeep walking up the hill.

Jeep Little reached the top and stopped in his tracks when he saw Hessler on the ground bleeding. He frowned, looking over at the gunman with his eyes narrowed to little slits. "Yeah. . . Stuff like that *has* happened before," Little said, with unmistakable anger on his face from seeing one of his detectives shot. He pulled the handcuffs from his belt and secured Klauser's hands in front of him.

Now the gunman understood that Callaway's words were not an exaggeration at all, but what would become his fate if he didn't cooperate. He looked at Little, and then at Callaway, as the first rescue unit came screeching to a halt in front of Eldridge's house. The paramedics were carrying a backboard and med-box out of the rig and swiftly heading up the hill.

"Swear to me that you'll have the medics take me to the hospital! No tricks, Callaway! Swear to me, and I'll tell you what I know," Klauser pleaded.

Callaway looked at the man, then at Little, who nodded his head.

"Wait a minute," Little said, right before giving Klauser his Miranda rights.

"I don't know who hired me, Callaway, honest I don't," Klauser continued.

For the first time, Callaway saw fear in the man's eyes.

"It was all done by mail. I don't know who it is."

Callaway couldn't hold back any longer.

"Did you kill Carrie Marvin?" he asked, his finger tightening on the trigger of the Beretta.

The gunman looked him square in the eyes as he said, "No! I didn't have anything to do with killing your girlfriend. Matter of fact, from what I read about her death

144

in the paper, I wasn't hired until after she was killed. But whoever hired me wrote like he or she was involved. Whoever it was wrote something about wanting all of your houses to fall, or some crap like that. The person also asked me where they could get a hold of some explosives." The gunman coughed up some more blood before he continued, as the paramedics made it up the hill and began working on Hessler. Klauser watched them for a second, and as if on cue, one of the medics looked at him and gave him an evil look, putting a fine point on what Callaway said earlier.

"I was hired to kill you, Cruz, your buddy Hidalgo, and the commander, and that was it," he said. "I almost got you at the shooting-range, yesterday. Like I said, you got lucky. I got Cruz, and by the look on your face earlier, I got Hidalgo, and if it wasn't for Hessler and you, I would have got this old man, too," he said, glaring at Eldridge. "But give me time, I'll finish the contract eventually," he said, showing his arrogance.

"How you gonna do that from prison? That is, if you live?" asked Lieutenant Little.

The gunman gave a laugh through his pain. He could hear the second rescue truck pulling up. He got cocky, again looking straight at Little. "You stupid assholes don't know who you're dealing with!" he said as the paramedics from the second rescue reached him. "I'm a former CIA agent, Callaway. I've been trained to kill people in ways you've never dreamed of. I'm also pretty good at forging all kinds of documents. I created my own background to get hired in Fort Lauderdale. I came down here after I got booted out of the agency and got on with the police department as a cover, because there are all kinds of work in my profession available around here.

145

Every drug dealer in town has it out for someone else, or some bitch wants her rich husband to disappear. Business has been very good."

Callaway was a little confused. "So, you shot Cruz, thinking he was me…"

Klauser cut him off. "No, no, no! Cruz was on the list. From the way the person that hired me sounded in the letters, he or she really hated the little spic. Said something about revenge."

"So, killing people is all just a game for you?" Callaway asked. "A game you get paid for."

Again, Klauser frowned at Callaway. "And paid damn well!" he said as the medics began cutting off his jacket and shirt. "You are so small-minded, aren't you, my friend? You could do the same thing if you wanted to, except you could work for free, since you're already rich. I've killed so many people in my life that the work has become monotonous. I was bored until I tried to get you. My respect for you grew when you found my explosive device under your car. Not a whole lot of people would have picked up on that one. I wanted to see just what you brought to the game." He groaned as some more blood leaked from the corner of his mouth.

"I'm done talking now, assholes!" Klauser screamed. The medics put a pressure bandage over the wound on his back and slid him on to a wooden backboard. They stuck a large, #4 intravenous needle into his left forearm, and plugged in a bag of Ringer Lactate solution to provide volume to his depleted blood supply.

"Remember, Callaway, you swore that they'd take me right to the hospital," Klauser repeated.

The first rescue crew was carrying Hessler down the hill to their rig, as the second group lifted the gunman off the ground. The lead medic from the second rescue rig cautioned his people. "Gentle, guys, he's got a gunshot wound to the back with no exit wound. The bullet's still rattling around in there, and I think it may have nicked something important, the way he's bleeding and coughing it up. We need to go easy with him and keep him calm or it might tear whatever's leaking some more, and he'll bleed out. We'll get you to the hospital alive, sir."

The gunman noted the concern displayed by the lead medic, and instantly realized the mind game that Callaway and Little had played on him, fooling him into thinking the paramedics would kill him. Both men followed the medics down to their truck as Klauser began yelling, "You son-of-a-bitch, Callaway! You lied to me!"

The lead medic tried to caution the man. "Sir!" he said, in a commanding voice. "You need to calm down. If your blood pressure goes up, you will rip whatever's bleeding in your chest wide open and you'll die!"

The gunman was breathing hard, not heeding the warning at all, letting his anger get the best of him. The medics loaded him into the rear of the rescue rig where he began to struggle with them as if he wanted to jump out of the rig and attack Callaway, even though he was handcuffed to the gurney. Callaway could still hear him bellowing from inside the rescue rig, even over the noise of the big diesel engine that powered the truck. "I'll break out of prison as soon as I heal," Klauser yelled. "I swear I will! I broke out of jails all around the world when I worked for the agency. I WILL do this. Then I'm coming for all of you bastards!"

Callaway walked between the two rescue vehicles and just stared at Klauser through the open door as the medics taking care of Hessler were preparing to transport him to the hospital. He heard the medics try to calm Klauser as they watched the numbers from the blood pressure cuff keep climbing. They put him in a MAST suit, just as the Fort Lauderdale medics did with Cruz, in case they had to force blood from his legs to his heart and brain.

"I'll kill you, Callaway! You and all your pals, and you won't be able to do a goddamned thing to stop me!" Klauser continued to yell, as the medics tried to stabilize him.

Callaway's mind was twisting into a knot, just as it did after he found out that Carrie was dead. He felt the same pain in his head. That same relentless cadence and throbbing he had felt when he saw Cruz on his apartment floor and Jorge's mangled body on the dock. He walked to the front of the rescue rig that contained the hit man and put his arms on the front edge of the fender, laying his forehead on top of them. The pain in his head grew worse as he heard the gunman's continued rant. He could hear one of the medics talking to a surgeon at Mount Sinai over the radio speaker in the cab of the rescue rig. The doctor was advising the medics not to administer Valium, or anything else to calm Klauser down, since it could disguise signs and symptoms of his wounds. He heard the lead medic respond that they would transport as soon as they could restrain their "combative" patient.

"I will kill all of you, and your families, too!" Klauser screamed, beginning to slur.

Callaway desperately wanted to walk to the back of the rig and put a bullet in the man's brain. But the gunman was right. If he killed him, he would be arrested, and he wouldn't be able to find Carrie's killer. The throbbing in his head became worse. He turned his head to the right, taking a deep breath, still resting his head on his upper arms, and opened his eyes slightly, sweat pouring out of every part of his body. He could see the pile of scrap lumber from Eldridge's remodeling job sitting on the grass in the swale. One ratty, termite-eaten two-by-four beam, with two large nails sticking through the end of it, stuck out of the pile, mere inches from the truck's left front tire. He stared at the two-by-four intently as he listened to the man still yelling obscenities. The pounding in his head continued to get worse. He moved his right leg around the bumper of the truck, placing the side of his sneaker underneath the two-by-four. Slowly, he pulled the beam further out of the pile, until the nails contacted the sidewall of the tire. He waited until the air conditioner compressor kicked in, adding more noise to the already loud diesel idle. Using the noise as cover, he gave the board a hard kick. The sharp nails dug into the sidewall of the heavy-duty tire but didn't penetrate. He kicked it again, just before the compressor cycled off. He waited, tensing up even more, hoping to get another kick in before the driver finished assisting the lead medic in restraining Klauser to drive them to the hospital. The compressor finally cycled on, and as soon as the idle on the engine came up, Callaway kicked the two-by-four as hard as he could. He exhaled as he heard the telltale sound of air hissing from around the nail now thoroughly embedded in the sidewall.

The gunman stared at Detective Hessler through the open door of the other rescue rig, parked back-to-back with the one he was in. The driver of that rig hopped out and began closing the doors.

"I'll be coming to see you soon, Jew-boy! Remember that!" Klauser yelled at the detective.

The driver climbed into the cab, and the truck carrying Hessler disappeared down the street, siren blasting, with a police car running ahead to block intersections for a brother officer.

Callaway walked around to the rear of the unit and just stood there, looking at the gunman. He folded his arms over his chest, staring at the raging man. Klauser pulled his right arm free from the medic's grasp and began flailing. He tore the oxygen mask from his face and tore the hose off the IV needle. Blood spurted all over the lead medic. "He's as stable as we can get him, let's roll," the lead medic yelled, trying to reattach the hose. The driver hopped out and ran around to the cab of the vehicle.

Klauser stared at Callaway. Fuming with anger, he asked, "What the hell are you looking at, Callaway?" You should have killed me when you had the chance! I swear I will come back and get your ass!"

The lead medic responded to the flow of blood from the man's mouth, "Sir! You need to calm down, or we won't be able to help you."

The other medic grabbed one of the rear doors to close it.

The gunman laughed at Callaway, who had a strangely calm look on his face. "It's just a matter of time, my friend, before I come for you, like the angel of death in the night!" Klauser said.

The lead medic heard cursing from the cab and the words, "Shit, we've got a flat tire!"

Callaway watched the look on the gunman's face change from cocky to horrified, as the lead medic felt the fight go out of the man. The other medic saw his blood pressure spike at the sound of the driver's words, and then plummet to zero. Klauser's breathing quickened, the stress of knowing that he would not see an emergency room causing the small tear in his aorta from the bullet wound to open even more. His look of astonishment showed that he realized the flat tire was no accident when Callaway looked at him. Callaway slowly raised the middle finger of his right hand, as he held it tight to his chest, and told Klauser, "Go to hell, *my friend.*"

The gunman's eyes rolled back, and he was gone. The lead medic began chest compression, as the other medic increased the pressure in the MAST suit, trying to save the man. It was a waste of time and effort.

Jeep Little walked up and stood next to Callaway, observing the situation in the rescue rig. He stared at the flat line on the heart monitor and shook his head.

"Dead, huh? What a shame," he said sarcastically. "You'll need to come down to the station to give us some information, Mr. Callaway. My detectives are sweeping the crime scene and doing an area canvas for evidence and to find Mr. Klauser's vehicle. They have Commander Eldridge's written statement, but we want to get yours on tape. Oh… and I'll need the gun that you shot this man with," he continued, pointing at Klauser.

Callaway reached under his shirt and pulled out the little revolver, handing it grip first to the lieutenant. "My cars around the block," Callaway said, pointing to the corner. I'll walk down the street to it, so I won't mess up your crime scene."

Little nodded and turned to walk back to the scene. Callaway walked down the street, his previous massive adrenalin rush subsiding quickly, causing him to feel slightly lightheaded. When he rounded the corner, he could see his Mustang parked diagonally across the swale of a lone house at the end of the block, with the front tires of the vehicle on the sidewalk. As he got closer, he saw the deep thirty- or so-foot long gouges his tires left in the grass as he was stopping the car when he arrived.

Oh, these people are gonna be pissed off at me when they see what I did to their swale. I had better go give them some cash to fix it, he thought, as he walked up the driveway past a beat-up old white van. He rang the doorbell while looking through the glass panel next to the door. *Vacant. Totally empty,* he thought. He turned around, looking at the van, when he saw a sign lying in the yard next to the vehicle. He walked over to it and flipped it over. "For sale?" he whispered to himself. He looked at the van again when it hit him. "Klauser said the bad guy that he faked arresting yesterday when he called me was driving a white van," he said. "Could it be?" He walked to the passenger door and looked through the window. He could see a notepad on the dashboard, and he could barely make out Eldridge's address written on it from the glow of a streetlight two doors away. He looked down at the floor on the passenger's side and saw a black nylon bag, with the zipper partially open. He went to his car and grabbed a flashlight from the interior.

Shining the light down through the windshield illuminated the inside of the bag enough for Callaway to see the grip of Klauser's another Thompson Contender pistol. He could see that the passenger door was locked from the position of the lock button on the top of the door. He shined the light across the front seat and was amazed to see that the lock button was up on the driver's door. He walked around to the door, looking to see if any of the Beach detectives were nearby. When he saw that he was alone, he wrapped his right hand in the bottom of his shirt, and pulled the door handle up. The door opened. *He must have left it unlocked in case he had to make a fast getaway,* he thought. Callaway carefully reached across to the passenger seat and grabbed the bag, knowing that the coarse woven material on the handle would not hold a fingerprint. Placing the bag on the driver's side floor, he again wrapped his fingers in his shirt, and pulled the zipper open. He looked at the pistol for a moment, thinking of what he intended to do soon. *I sure could use something accurate at long range for my upcoming hunting trip in the Bahamas,* he thought. He removed the pistol and two boxes of ammunition from the bag. He placed the bag back where he had found it and quietly closed the door. Looking around again, he saw he was alone, and he walked over to the Mustang. He opened the trunk with the key instead of using the key fob, which would have emitted a loud *chirp*, and placed the pistol and ammunition on the floor. He then pulled his cell phone from his belt and called Miami-Dade 911 to advise he may have found the hit man's vehicle.

Within minutes, the Beach cops swarmed the house where he was, tearing through the van looking for evidence. They found the notepad with all the notes Klauser had taken about his victims and intended victims. They also found a box of 30-30 *Accelerator* bullets, just like the one in the chamber of the Contender pistol that Klauser had been pointing down the hill at Commander Eldridge.

Callaway advised the officers that he was going to their station to give a statement. Climbing into the Mustang, he exhaled a big breath. As he drove to the police station, he thought about how he had just broken several laws. He looked at himself in the rear-view mirror and gave himself a slight smile, while at the same time feeling no sense of regret. "I guess the Boy Scout is dead," he whispered.

*****

Later that evening, another session of questioning and statements regarding the shooting took place at the Criminal Investigations Unit of the Miami Beach Police Department. The Beach detectives investigating the incident that had occurred in Commander Eldridge's back yard handled the process quickly as they were happy about the news that Detective Hessler would make a full recovery.

Detective Harkins from Fort Lauderdale arrived at the Miami Beach police station, accompanied by a forensic firearms technician. The technician used an Exacto Knife to scrape tiny shards of plastic from the rifling inside the barrel of the Contender pistol with which Klauser had intended to shoot Commander Eldridge. This would link the weapon to the murder of Alberto Cruz. Harkins had also brought a detective from his department's Internal Affairs unit who wrote a report about Officer Klauser's previous illegal activities while in the employ of the Fort Lauderdale Police Department.

Callaway was not charged with any crime since he had shot Klauser in defense of another person's life. And that person happened to be a Miami Beach police detective. In the eyes of his comrades, Callaway was a hero for saving Detective Hessler's life. Sergeant Rodriguez even went so far as buying Callaway a late dinner from Wolfie's Restaurant, to show his respect.

At 9:00 am, Callaway drove home, this time to his boat in the Miami Marina, burping all the way from the massive amount of corned beef he had consumed. When he pulled into the parking lot, he noticed that somebody had parked a shiny new dirt- bike style motorcycle in his assigned parking space. Looking around, he could see that the nearest empty space was at the other end of the long lot. Shaking his head, he shifted the Mustang into reverse, and backed up half a block to park. When he walked back to where the *Orinoco Flow* was tied up, he couldn't help but pause. He looked at the wreckage of his flats boat that had been hoisted out of the water and on to the concrete dock by a crane barge by order of the Coast Guard.

Sadness overwhelmed him as he sat down where Jorge had been standing when Klauser's bomb exploded. He could see some damage on the back of the *Orinoco Flow* along with some cracked windows. His anger came back, with that same knot of pain in the back of his skull. "I'm sorry, *hermano*," he whispered. I shouldn't have fallen for such a stupid trick. I will find whoever paid Klauser to do this to you, and Cruz, and whoever killed Carrie, and I will mess them up, even if it's the last thing I do." He went aboard the *Orinoco Flow* and sat down at his desk. He could see the icon indicating there was a message waiting for him on his shiny new computer. Opening up his email, he saw the message was from Avengeher. He opened it and read slowly, through tired eyes.

"I think we've hit the jackpot. I researched the poetic writing that was found on both Carrie Marvin and Melinda Eagle when they were found murdered. It occurred to me that whoever our mole is, he or she might have background in poetic study. I researched the college transcripts of every-one, agents, administration, and civilians in the Miami office, and I only found one person who had an apparent love of poetry." Callaway finished reading with his mouth hanging open. "Son of a bitch," was all he could say.

Chapter 15

It took only about three minutes to pick the lock. He removed the heavyweight chain that looked strong enough to have stopped the British Navy from passing West Point during the Revolutionary War and drove through the gate. He stopped to reattach the chain to the concrete-filled ten-inch steel pipes so that no one would notice his forced entry. He drove his vehicle down the dirt road with the headlights turned off and the taillights carefully covered with duct tape so no one traveling on U.S. 27 would see his brake lights. When he reached the end of the road, DEA Special Agent in Charge David Howe exited his agency vehicle. His hefty Chevy Suburban's black paint made it almost impossible to see from the roadway that was three miles distant. The truck was perfect for carrying the items he was looking for in this remote area off U.S.27 and the Florida Everglades in the City of Miramar. The only other people in the immediate area were the workers and customers at a 24-hour fishing campground and truck stop on a spur road about three and a half miles north of where he stood. He couldn't see the lights of the truck stop as they were blocked by a stand of pine trees just north of the bunker area.

The next step in Howe's quest would be more difficult. He stood looking at a bunker built into the ground on a small, man-made island. The bunker contained five hundred thousand pounds of explosives jointly owned by seven engineering and construction companies operating rock-mining pits in the area. Those companies dug holes in the nearby ground fifty to one hundred feet deep, mining limestone and silica sand used in everything from making concrete to building roads. The pits would fill with water as soon as the hole in the ground passed ten or so feet deep, because the drag lines would penetrate the Florida Aquifer, releasing millions of gallons of fresh water from the underground river that ran the length of the state. Explosives were used to soften up the underwater rock, which saved the companies millions in broken drag line cranes and steel scoops that the mining companies used to pull the rock out of the ground.

The poured concrete and steel bunker was only a few years old and way more secure than the one that the companies had used before it. The old bunker was merely a corrugated metal building with a big padlock securing the front door. This much more sophisticated version was built after some teenage boys, out shooting snakes in the area, decided to find out if a .22 long rifle bullet would penetrate the walls of the structure. One of the bullets did, and the subsequent explosion left only bits and pieces of flesh as their remains.

Howe surveyed the situation, using all his Navy SEAL training. As a precaution, the owners of the bunker had built an old-style rotating swivel bridge leading to the island from the entrance road. The problem he now faced was that when the bunker was closed, the bridge was left sideways in the lake, restricting access to swimming in the cold, sometimes alligator-infested water to the island and the bunker. The bridge control switch, one hundred feet off the island, could be utilized only with a control panel that was removed whenever the bunker was not manned. Howe's original plan was to break into the box and jump the wiring to make the bridge turn.

"Crap!" Howe mumbled when he saw the control panel was missing from the box. The box itself was made of welded half-inch steel plate, with three recessed holes to insert the plugs into the control panel. Since he had not brought a cutting torch with him, he would have to resort to a less glamorous method of getting the bridge to turn. He smirked at the sign next to the box that stated:

ANY   EMPLOYEE   CAUGHT   FEEDING ALLIGATORS WILL BE TERMINATED ON SIGHT.

He would need the bridge to remove the number of explosives required to accomplish his mission. He walked back to his truck, scanning the highway three miles away for headlights, and opened the lift-gate in the rear of the vehicle. The dim glow of the rear interior light allowed him to see the items he had brought with him.

Plan B, he thought. He opened a bag and removed a silencer suppressor for his weapon. Removing his jacket, he reached back along his right hip and unsnapped his holster. Instead of drawing his agency-issued SIG Sauer pistol, he withdrew a beat-up Glock 18, 9 mm that he had removed from the DEA property room late one evening nine months ago. The functional pistol was a beater with much of the finish trashed by salt water from the previous owner's many nights of smuggling drugs across the ocean waters surrounding the state before he ended up in the federal prison in Tallahassee. Howe knew that with the flick of a lever on the left side of the slide, the pistol would instantly transform from a semi- automatic weapon to a fully automatic machine pistol. The only part of the gun in good shape was a shiny new Bar-Sto replacement barrel that protruded a half-inch out of the front of the slide, threaded at the muzzle. This would allow him to use the pistol without forensic specialists linking any recovered bullets to the original barrel that had already been tested and documented by a "ballistic fingerprint."

He had also equipped the weapon with a brass-catching device that resembled a small net mounted on the right side of the pistol's ejection port. Howe would not have to worry about law enforcement recovering any shell casings from the pistol. He screwed the suppressor onto the barrel, as he looked around the area. *Well, I put you together for when I kidnaped that Seminole chick for Herrera,* he thought, *but you'll come in handy in case anyone wanders up on me out here, and I'll use you on any gators that might be in the lake.*

He pulled a neoprene wet suit from the cargo area, and in the process, knocked over a satchel, the contents of which spilled on the floor of the cargo area. He immediately grabbed three large pieces of paper from the contents and stared at them. The papers were copies of blueprints of the DEA and Customs Service headquarters in Miami, along with the Federal Courthouse in that same city. He looked at the figures he had written in pencil on each piece of paper, indicating just how much dynamite it would take to bring all three of those buildings down. This was the mission his new boss, Derrick Drake, had given him. Derrick had taken control of his late father's drug smuggling operation, and his mole in the Drug Enforcement Administration in Miami, as well.

Based on his computations, and the demolition training he had received as a SEAL, Howe had

159

determined he would need four cases of Alfred Nobel's 1866 creation to get the job done. He put the blueprints, along with some homemade timers for the explosives, back into the briefcase, and put on the wet suit. He buckled on a nylon duty belt, with a holster for the silenced Glock and a Velcro pouch for his lock-picking tools.

He walked to the lake's edge, and again, looked out toward US 27. "No cars. Time to do a little hunting." Howe said, as he pulled an aluminum four-cell Kel-Light flashlight from a holder on the belt. Holding the flashlight in his left hand, he drew the Glock from the holster with his right, making sure it was in semi-auto mode, and pointed it at the lake shoreline. He then placed the back of his left hand, with the flashlight, against the back of his gun hand, in a firm bond, bracing one against the other. He was now able to sweep back and forth across the lake, using the push-button switch on the light to flash it at suspected large, toothy reptiles in the water. "Bingo! Red eyes," he said. "One round in the *sweet spot* should do the trick," seeing the telltale sign of an alligator. Again, he glanced at the road, looking for headlights. Again, the road was clear. From the distance between the creature's eyes, he estimated its size at around seven feet long. At a range of twenty yards, he leveled the pistol and the flashlight at the scaly looking reptile and squeezed the trigger on the Glock a split-second after he blinked the light on and off. The pistol bucked, emitting only what sounded like a puff of air along with the click-click sound of the slide moving backward and forward. The alligator thrashed in the water for a couple of seconds, and then sank to the bottom with a 9 mm full metal jacket bullet lodged in its poker-chip sized brain.

Howe searched the rest of the lake area for more gators while constantly looking at the highway for headlights before he waded into the cold water. He held the Glock out of the water out of habit, although he knew the pistol would fire under water if needed. He was counting on that in case another alligator came nosing around. He reached the island and holstered the pistol and climbed out of the water, walking to the main control system for the bridge. It was now a simple matter to jump the wires on the island control box. The electric motor on the swing assembly came to life and the bridge creaked around until the ends lined up with the roadway on the land side and the fifty- foot road leading to the bunker on the island. "Now let's see what you've got for me," he said aloud as he looked over the lock on the steel door of the bunker. The lock was large and complex, but Howe's skills were up to the task. After about five minutes, he heard the *click* of the final tumbler as the lock opened. He put his lock-pick tools into a pouch on his belt and pulled the heavy steel door open. He found a light panel by the door and threw just one switch to dimly light the interior of the windowless building. Immediately, he began searching the stacks of boxes. He found some boxes of an explosive known as ANFO, a combination chemical explosive made up of ammonia nitrate and fuel oil, along with many crates of a slurry explosive made of extracts of different explosives suspended in a water-resistant gel. These high-tech rock-breakers were very effective but hardly portable. He kept following the stacks of crates toward the back of the building until he found what he was looking for. "There you are. Good old-fashioned dynamite!" he said, smiling.

Dynamite was the go-to explosive that the miners

used until the new chemical stuff came out, and since high explosives are not something you throw in a dumpster to get rid of, he knew there would probably be some left over in the bunker. There were two old-style plunger box detonators sitting on top of the cases. There were eight cases of the explosive, all of which were probably manufactured in the 1960s. He needed four cases for his task of blowing up three federal buildings.

Howe carried the cases, one by one, to an area just inside the front door. He also grabbed two boxes of blasting caps, and, just to be safe, a hand- held detonator. Howe brought along both antique plunger detonators, too, thinking one would look great as a decoration in his house. The other one he would give to Derrick Drake as a gift, to go along with the destruction of the federal buildings that he ordered.

Reopening the front door of the bunker, he drew the Glock from the holster and quickly stepped out, pointing the pistol in a sweep, from left to right. Seeing nobody, he carried the first two cases out to the bridge, which had an electric cargo carrier built onto the right railing. He loaded the cases and one of the old plunger detonators onto the carrier, and merely pressed the switch on the control panel to ferry the explosives across the water. Howe walked on the bridge alongside his precious cargo until it reached the end. He carried all the items to his truck and loaded them into the rear of the vehicle. Back across the bridge he went to get the other two cases of dynamite and the other things he needed. He walked into the dimly lit interior of the bunker, bent down to pick up the third case, and froze. Howe heard the distinctive two clicks of a revolver being cocked. He only knew one person, in this day and age, who still carried such a wheel-gun.

162

"Well… Mr. Callaway, what are you doing out on a beautiful night like this?" he asked without turning around.

Callaway eased in through the door, keeping his distance from Howe.

"I was just taking a stroll up the Everglades levy, and I saw the light on in here, so I figured I'd take a look see, and find out what was goin' on," Callaway said, mimicking Howe's Tennessee drawl. "Don't turn around Howe!" he said sharply, knowing that this man could move as fast as a coiled rattlesnake.

Howe kept his back turned, instinctively holding his hands over his head. "I guess it wouldn't make much difference if I told you that I was investigating a hot lead on some terrorists that were out to steal dynamite, huh?" Howe asked, hoping that Callaway would get closer.

"Nope! I bagged your hit man yesterday," Callaway answered. "He didn't tell me who you are, but he gave me enough clues to let me figure it out. He said you were looking for explosives, and I remember reading about this place when it blew up years ago. So I figured I might find you here, and… Here you are." Callaway didn't tell Howe about the source inside the agency that was feeding him info, should something go wrong.

"Damn, boy!" Howe answered. "I'm shocked. You're sharper than I thought you were. That crazy son-of-a-bitch hit man even scared the crap out of me just dealing with him by mail. How'd you get him?"

Callaway kept moving a few feet right and left every time Howe was speaking, not wanting him to get an audible fix on where he was standing. "Shut up and walk forward to the wall, Howe," Callaway ordered. He had to immobilize the man, quickly.

Howe stepped up to the wall, staring at the structure closely for the first time. He noticed that it was covered with a thick, grainy rubberized coating. "Pretty smart, these demolition people," he mumbled. "Covering the walls with rubber to stop anything from sparking and…" Howe was interrupted by the touch of Callaway's revolver pressing against the base of his skull.

"Listen to me real close, asshole," Callaway hissed. "I'm holding the hammer back with my thumb, and I've got the trigger pulled, so the trigger safety is disabled. You make a move on me, my thumb comes off the hammer, and your brains will be all over that nice rubber wall. You understand?"

Howe swallowed hard while Callaway reached his left hand behind Howe's lower back, and quickly pulled the Glock from his captive's holster. Callaway reached around his own back and slid the suppressor and front of the pistol into his belt in the small of his back. He knew that Howe was still very dangerous, even without a gun.

"Left hand behind your back, now."

Howe complied, and Callaway clamped a handcuff on his left wrist. He pushed the muzzle of his six-inch barrel harder into the back of Howe's head. "Now the right one, slowly," he growled.

Howe knew he had no chance. If he put a move on Callaway, his brain would be dripping like oatmeal thrown against the wall, courtesy of a .357 Magnum contact wound. He felt the cold steel of the *Peerless* cuff locking down on his right wrist making three audible *clicks*.

Callaway held on to the chain between the handcuffs. He wasn't done with Howe yet. "Take a step back, and put your feet together," Callaway ordered.

Howe did so, nonchalantly, not expecting what would happen next. Callaway yanked hard on a rope noose that Howe had stepped into. The force pulled his feet backward and out from under him, dragging his face down the rough, rubberized wall as he fell.

"You fucking asshole!" he yelled, instantly rolling over on his back and kicking at Callaway with his hobbled feet. Callaway had taken the precaution of using a long piece of rope to make the noose. The kick did not come close to touching him. Howe lay there spitting dirt, blood, and a front tooth that the trip down the rubber wall had broken off.

"What are ya gonna' do now, Callaway, shoot me?" he asked, trying to spit out all the blood pooling in his mouth.

Callaway lowered the hammer on the revolver, while keeping it pointed at Howe, as he spoke. "No, I'm going to call the local police, and the FBI, and have them come out here and arrest your ugly ass," he said.

Howe gave Callaway a weird smile. "Yeah, you do that, just don't do it from here," he yelled as Callaway pulled a zip-lock bag containing his cell phone from his pants pocket. "You make a call in here, and your cell signal will make all the blasting caps in this building go boom! And there are enough of them in here to set off everything else in the building. Look, Callaway, let's make a deal. You leave, and I'll find a way out of here. You go play with Drake, and I'll leave y'all alone. I'll consider it a fair trade for not killin' me, okay?"

Callaway gave the man a look that told Howe he didn't believe a word he was saying. Howe tried to convince Callaway that he was right. "Look, dumb ass, who do you think anyone's gonna believe came out here to steal explosives, me, or the guy who wants to avenge a bunch of people by blowing up Drake's island?" he said, still spitting out blood. "Hell, all I have to do is tell the FBI that I had a feelin' you'd came out here, so I came to check it out, and you got the drop on me. They'll lock you up in a heartbeat. So, you just walk out that door, and we'll be square, okay?"

Callaway thought about what Howe said and realized he was probably right, at least about whose story would be more believable. He sat down on the two cases that Howe intended to take before he replied, "You know what, Howe, you may be right." He pointed his revolver at the man's face. "But if I kill you, and make it look like self-defense, you won't be able to say a thing."

Howe lay there shaking his head. "They still won't believe you, boy! Basic criminology, right? You've got a motive. What motive would the best DEA agent in Florida have for stealing dynamite?" he asked, with a bloody grin.

"You mean like blowing up three federal buildings? All of your houses will come falling down around you?" Callaway answered.

Howe's grin quickly disappeared, as he asked, "How'd you know about that, Callaway?"

"Let's just say I have great intuition. Whoever wrote that on Carrie is a very deep thinker," Callaway answered, trying to get an answer to his ultimate question.

"You liked that, huh…" He stopped short, knowing he had just admitted his guilt.

Callaway stood up quickly. He cocked the hammer on the revolver and pointed it at Howe again. "*You* killed her, you piece of shit!" He ran to Howe and kicked him hard in the side. Howe let out a yell from the pain that Callaway knew was coming from a couple of broken ribs.

"Callaway, no, I didn't kill her! Honest to God I didn't!" he pleaded.

Callaway dropped his right knee into the man's groin, causing another satisfying yell. Shoving the muzzle of the revolver under Howe's chin, he pushed up hard, cutting off the man's air supply. "Tell me everything that went on in the safe-house that night, or I swear I will cut your balls off and force-feed them to you!" he said, grinding his knee hard into the man's testicles.

Howe was in a lot of pain, and for the first time since he saw combat while in the Navy, he was scared out of his mind.

"All right! All right! I didn't kill her," he gasped. "It was Herrera! He said he would kill her! I just handed her over to him! I gave him the idea for the writing on her belly, but I didn't write it. I don't speak Spanish."

Callaway smacked him across the face with the barrel of the revolver. "Why?" he yelled. "How could you do that? How much did Drake pay you to hand her up to be killed, you low-life scumbag?" He pushed the muzzle of the revolver hard into Howe's throat, hard enough to make him gag. He could barely hear his next words.

"Th... Three million!" he said, gasping out the words.

Callaway was breathing hard. He pulled the revolver away from Howe's throat, yelling at Howe. "She had two agents guarding her. How did you get past them?"

Howe stared up at Callaway, "They worked for me," Howe said. "I was their supervisor. When I arrived, I took them to one of the bedrooms, like I wanted to talk to them, and then I shot them with the Glock you took from me."

Callaway continued to glare at him. "And?" he asked. Howe thought his next statement would be his last. "She was asleep in the master bedroom," Howe said, taking a deep breath. "I spiked her wine that afternoon with some sleeping pills. And after I killed the two agents, I snuck into her room with a hypodermic full of some kind of sedative that Herrera sent me. That stuff knocked her out cold almost instantly. She didn't get to struggle much at all. I disabled the surveillance cameras and wound them back to erase my arrival. Herrera and his men showed up a half-hour later."

Callaway listened intently, still seething with anger. "What happened next?" he asked.

Howe took a deep breath before he answered.

"DEA took that house from a guy who was laundering a lot of money. It was right on the inland waterway, near Boca Raton inlet. Herrera and his men pulled up in one of Drake's speedboats, and they carried her away. That's it. I swear I did not kill Marvin!"

Callaway sat down on one of the cases of dynamite again. He looked at the old plunger detonator. Reaching over with his left hand, he lifted up the T- shaped handle, extending the rod that went from the handle through a hole in the top of the wooden box. He pushed it down hard, hearing the whining "ZZZ" sound that he remembered from many old movies. He stared inquisitively at the box. "So how does this thing make the dynamite go boom, Howe?" Callaway asked. "I've always been curious about that. You just plug the wire into a stick of dynamite and push the lever down?"

Howe rolled on his back groaning, staring at the ceiling of the bunker, trying to find a way to get loose and kill Callaway as he answered. "No, you've got to put a blasting cap into the stick, and then connect the wire between that detonator and the cap," Howe said. "Only the cap will set it off. The stick won't explode even if you set it on fire. You have to hold the safety on the side of the box to make it throw current to the cap. It's nothing but an electrical generator, like a magneto on an old car."

Howe kept feeling around on the floor under his back, hoping to find a piece of wire, or anything else that he could use to unlock the handcuffs. The small talk would give him time.

Callaway pulled the plunger up, and rammed it down again, the detonator emitting the same menacing "ZZZZZZ" noise, as the gears and magnets inside spun at high speed. "You know I've been thinking about what you said earlier, about which one of us could explain his way out of being out here," he said.

Howe rolled on his side to face his captor as Callaway continued.

"I think I'll be able to convince the police, and the DEA, about what you were doing out here, all right. I have enough evidence for you to get the death penalty, or at least get you locked up for the rest of your life."

Howe looked at Callaway and nodded. "Yeah, Callaway, you're probably right," he said. "Cruz told me that you were a by-the-book Boy Scout. I'm glad he was right." His voice sounded almost thankful. His mind, though, was racing, thankful that Callaway didn't kill him, while at the same time thinking of what he would do as soon as Callaway left. *Sure asshole, leave me here on the floor,* he thought. *The minute you leave, I'll get out of these cuffs within thirty seconds, and then I'll be on your tail. And when I catch you, I will kill you very slowly, and you will just disappear.*

Callaway got up and walked over to Howe. He kicked the man in the stomach. Howe rolled into a fetal position to try to protect his middle from any more blows, when

Callaway hit him hard on the right side of the head with the heavy barrel of the big L-frame Smith & Wesson, knocking him unconscious. Callaway walked out of the bunker, closing the door behind him. After crossing the bridge, he walked to Howe's truck, and looked over all the items in the rear compartment. He emptied the contents of the bag on the floor of the cargo area, amazed to see the homemade timer-detonators Howe had rigged to hook up to the blasting caps and dynamite.

"The SEAL's taught you well boy," he said, smiling.

The simple devices appeared to be nothing more than a couple of D-cell batteries hooked up to a plastic-cased dive watch. The wires went through holes drilled through one side of the watch case and ended up soldered to the bottom of the hour hand, which was set at twelve o'clock. There were two corresponding wires connected to the minute hand, which could be set for as many as fifty-nine minutes before the wires would touch, sending the electricity of the batteries out of the other side of the watch, and then to blasting caps stuffed into sticks of dynamite. The three targeted federal buildings were close enough to each other for a highly trained and motivated individual like Howe to set the explosives in all three buildings to blow up at the same time.

All your houses will come falling down around you, the ultimate screw-you from Derrick Drake, he thought, looking at the two cases of dynamite and the old plunger detonator. "You know what, Derrick, I'm gonna make your house, and your drug lab fall down, on *you,* you little shit ball," he whispered. Callaway grabbed eight of the timer detonators and two handfuls of blasting caps and stuffed them into his pants pockets. Lifting one case of dynamite, he carried his prizes over to some bushes where he had hidden the Yamaha dirt bike he'd found parked in his private space at the marina. *Thanks for buying a bike with an ignition system just like the ones on the outboard motors I used to work on, stupid,* he thought. *I hope you don't notice the extra miles I'm putting on this thing!* He secured the items on the rear package rack before reaching for his cell phone. He could immediately tell that there was no service this far away from civilization. He thought again about what Howe had said about proving his real intent on being out here in the first place. He also knew that it wouldn't take but a quick inventory by the mining companies to figure out that the one case of dynamite that he would need for his mission of revenge was missing. Then he would be in trouble as his story would instantly fall apart.

He looked at the bunker thinking, *only one last thing to do then.*

Chapter 16

About fifteen minutes went by before Howe regained consciousness. Searing pain came from the right side of his head. Taking a hit from the underside of the barrel on Callaway's revolver was like being struck with a piece of half-inch rebar. His head throbbed as he cursed his tormentor. "I am gonna make you hurt so bad, Callaway! I am gonna mess you up real bad!" he said.

He rolled over twice to the stacks of wire bundles used for detonating the explosives that came from the bunker. Howe rolled up on his side, searching until he found what he needed: a piece of bare solid copper wire that one of the mining company demolition people probably dropped when cutting wire from a roll. The piece was about three inches long and perfect for his needs. Pushing against the floor with his knees, he was able to get his back into a position where his fingers could reach the discarded piece of wire. He deftly held the wire between the thumb and index finger of his right hand, about an inch from the end. Howe inserted the short end of the wire between the thin, smaller, bottom part of the cuff, and the upper part that contained the locking mechanism. He pushed the wire in and began tripping the ratcheting pin in the upper part, that locked into the serrated notches on the bottom part. He pushed until he heard an audible click, and the cuff would open about a quarter of an inch each time. He continued this painstaking task until the cuff was open enough for him to slip his hand through.

Howe left the cuff attached to his right hand and worked on removing the noose that had been binding his feet together. Standing up he felt dizzy, and instinctively brought his hand to the injured part of his head. "Son-of-a-bitch," he hissed. The pain increased from his touch. His anger got the best of him as he headed for the door of the bunker, intent on finding Michael Callaway and killing him with his bare hands, even though he was swaying like a drunk. He reached the door under a full head of steam, when all the training the SEALs had beaten into him kicked in. He looked around for anything he could use as a weapon and spotted a four-foot long, polished stainless-steel rod leaning against the wall, the kind that explosives engineers used to clear out holes that were to be filled with the volatile stuff that would crack a boulder like an egg. Howe grabbed it with the tremendously strong grip of his right hand, as he put his left hand out to touch the door. *What if Callaway was screwing with me about calling the FBI?* he thought. *What if he's hiding in the bushes out there, waiting to drop me with his gun? Or maybe, he's waiting for me right outside the door!* Howe paused for a few seconds, his anger getting the best of him, and kicked the heavy steel door as hard as he could. It flew around on the hinges, but it made an odd noise as it struck something. A noise that Howe had heard twice while Callaway held him captive: the unmistakable "ZZZ" of an old-style plunger detonator that Callaway had positioned so the door would strike the handle, sending a bolt of electric current through wires that were right under Howe's feet. The current traveled through those wires to the rear of the bunker. In a split-second, the current reached the blasting cap. A blasting cap that Callaway plugged into the end of one stick of dynamite, in a case with many others just like it.

"God damn…" was the last thing DEA Special Agent in Charge David Howe would ever say.

*****

"You want a small one or a big one, Jack?" Officer Fred Benini stretched his back as he poured sugar into the steaming cup of coffee before him on the counter. His partner, Officer Jack Flowers, was standing about fifteen feet behind him at a magazine rack reading a newspaper article about the Miami Hurricanes. He stood with his back to his partner, so absorbed in the story about his favorite college football team that he didn't even hear Fred's question.

Benini laughed to himself, knowing his partner's absolute obsession for and dedication to "The Canes," as the locals referred to the team. He turned back to the counter, smiling at Rae, the one- toothed owner of the lonely truck stop, fish camp, and campground that sat at the edge of the Florida Everglades off US-27 in Pembroke Pines. The Miramar Police officers were about two miles north of the northern boundary of their jurisdiction, but no supervisor would ever bother them about putting in at the store, as there was no other place to get coffee on the graveyard shift for ten miles. Neither of the officers had worked Seven Zone since that cool night a little over one year prior, when they responded to the mysterious crash of a Beechcraft King Air airplane at the unmanned airstrip known as Opa Locka West, at the extreme south end of their jurisdiction. They had responded to the call of an explosion and a large fireball at that location, only to find the burning wreckage of the aircraft belonging to the late drug kingpin, Anton Drake.

The officers had no way of knowing that Anton's son, Derrick Drake, had been the only passenger on that flight, and that he had exited the aircraft prior to the explosion. The vengeance Derrick had sworn that evening succeeded in murdering three of Callaway's friends. Now, in the opening of the door to an explosives bunker a little over three miles from where the two Miramar officers stopped to get coffee, he was about to finish the life of the traitorous dog that had handed his fiancée up to die.

Flowers was immersed in the news story about the Canes, but still noticed the truck driver who walked in after parking his tractor-trailer rig on the north side of the truck -stop, between the building and the officers' patrol car. Flowers followed the movements of the newcomer as the trucker walked by him, and gave the officer a frosty look, and then stood next to him at the magazine rack. The officer took note that he was a very large man, with tattoos all over his arms. *Somebody's trying to look like a bad a*ss, he thought.

The driver looked over the fare on the rack, smiled, and selected a copy of *Penthouse*.

What's the matter, pal? The hookers at the truck stop up the road too expensive for you? Flowers thought. Flowers had his teeth clamped on his ever-present plastic cigar holder, containing an unlit cigar, which dangled from his mouth until a movement ahead through the window caught his eye. He could see a bright whitish-orange light behind the stand of trees south of the store. The light grew in a millisecond to a gigantic fireball above the trees. The officer's mouth opened slightly, and the cigar and holder fell from his mouth, hitting the hard old terrazzo floor below where the holder broke in two with a loud crack.

Benini spun around to check on his partner and saw the hell that was rising from the swamp off in the distance. He also saw the stand of trees disappear, revealing the height and mass of the explosion.

"Down!" he yelled, spinning around, and hitting Rae in the chest with an open hand. She yelled as she bounced off the table behind her and fell to the floor behind the counter that separated her from the officer. Flowers dropped the newspaper and waist-tackled the truck driver. Benini dove to the floor and covered his head with his arms as the shock wave from the explosion struck the building, blowing all the windows on the south side out, and showering the occupants with broken glass. The sound of the blast was deafening, but what came next was even more terrifying. Several of the tall pine trees from the stand that was rooted between the store and the explosion were snapped off like twigs, and hurled through the air at tremendous speed, flying through the broken windows, passing through the building and the windows on the north side, and penetrating the side of the tractor-trailer parked next to the patrol car.

Flowers rolled onto his left side, looking at the trucker. The man was lying there shaking and crying, and the officer detected a strong odor, indicating that *Mr. Bad Ass* had soiled his pants. "

Fred, you okay?" Flowers asked.

Benini was carefully trying to push himself up from the floor, avoiding the broken glass and shards of wood that now littered the place.

"Yeah, I'm all right. What the hell was that?" Benini asked as he stood up, and checked on Rae, who was still on the floor in a fetal position, crying, but unharmed.

Both officers looked in the direction of the explosion. "Don't tell me we have another plane crash?" Benini continued.

Flowers, breathing heavily from the shock of the blast, got on the radio. "Twenty-Three Alpha Twenty-Seven, 10-33 traffic!" he shouted.

The dispatcher at the Broward Sheriff's Office Central Dispatch immediately keyed an alert tone, clearing the air for the Miramar officer and advising him to go ahead with his 10-33 emergency radio traffic.

"We just had a big explosion south of Pembroke Road and west of US 27. I think it may have been a big airliner, or maybe something military that went down. Check with the FAA, and Homestead Air Force Base. Maybe they lost a B-52 or something. We're heading south to see what happened. Start the fire department out here, Code-3. We got a big brush fire going."

The BSO dispatcher acknowledged, repeating what Flowers had said, and advised his supervisor of the situation. The officers jumped into their patrol car and slowly weaved between the broken glass and shattered tree limbs that littered the driveway of the building. They drove out on the spur road, and turned right on US 27, heading south with their emergency lights on. As they arrived at a point parallel with the blast site, they saw a massive fire burning in the swamp, and trees, palmetto palms, and even a dead alligator littering the roadway where they had stopped.

"Twenty-Three Alpha Twenty-Seven," Flowers called over the radio, as Benini brought the vehicle to a halt by the entrance to the dirt road that traveled west from the highway. The dispatcher acknowledged and Flowers continued. "Be advised the explosion appears to have come from the commercial explosives bunker three miles south of Pembroke Road and three miles west of US 27, This is not a plane crash. It appears that the explosives bunker blew up again. We can't get any closer because the chain-gate at the entrance is still up, and there appears to be a large object blocking the road behind it. Send somebody from one of the mining companies out here with a key or have the fire department bring out a cutting torch. Also, have Florida Highway Patrol block and re-route traffic at the Dade County line and on Pines Boulevard."

The dispatcher acknowledged, and the two officers peered through the smoke and darkness, trying to determine the extent of damage. A large object rested against the inside of the chain-gate. They exited the patrol car and walked toward it, shining their flashlights into the smoke. As soon as they got within ten feet of the object, they could see it clearly.

"Oh shit! It's a vehicle. Or what's left of one," Benini said. They ducked under the heavy chain and slid around the vehicle. The hulk was twisted like a dishrag, with all of its windows blown out.

"Looks like a Tahoe, or maybe a Suburban," Flowers said. He made his way to what he thought was the rear of the vehicle. He crouched down and was astonished to find the license tag dangling by just a sliver of metal from its mount. "Fred, we got a tag, I'll run it," Flowers said.

Benini lit up the interior, which looked as if it had been crushed by the hand of a giant. *Nobody home. Where is your owner and where the hell did you come from?* he wondered as he looked through the passenger compartment of the vehicle.

Flowers called in the tag number. "Twenty-Three Alpha Twenty-Seven," Flowers said. "I need a 10-28 on Florida tag 107 T-Tango W-Whiskey B- Bravo."

The Sheriff's Office Dispatcher responded immediately, with "Alpha 27 that tag does not show up in the system, can you repeat the number?"

Flowers read the tag again, and they received the same response. He and Benini stared at each other for a long couple of seconds, realizing why the tag did not show up in the Florida system.

"Feds?" Flowers said, as Benini nodded his head. Both men had distinguished themselves for many years as detectives before they were rotated back to road patrol. They knew the practice of the state issuing untraceable Florida tags to federal law enforcement agencies that worked undercover in Florida. They also knew that it would take some time and work to figure out who the vehicle belonged to.

The on-duty Miramar PD desk officer called out to Central Dispatch, "X-Ray 23, have Alpha 27 go over to two-channel."

Both officers switched their radios to an auxiliary channel that could be used for private chatter with Miramar P.D. Desk Officer Jeff Parker at the communications center in their police station. "Jack, give me a couple of minutes and I'll get you the information on your tag," Parker said.

Flowers acknowledged, smiling. If anyone could cut through the red tape to determine who owned what was left of this vehicle, it would be Jeff. The man had contacts everywhere with local, state and federal law enforcement agencies. After only one telephone call, he had the answer, and he called the two officers back over to the auxiliary channel to give them the news. "Alpha 27, your vehicle is registered to the Drug Enforcement Administration, and assigned to a David Howe, Special Agent in Charge of the Miami office," Parker advised.

The officers looked at each other again.

"Son of a bitch," Benini said, as he walked to the rear of the vehicle, shining his light on the tag. He raised his light a little higher, illuminating a big gap that the explosion had made between the rear hatch and the floor. Benini stared into the cargo area and saw a large, broken wooden box with writing on it. He bent over and could see the words *DANGER - EXPLOSIVES* stenciled on the side in red paint and several red-colored sticks of dynamite hanging out of it, with more scattered about the rear compartment. He quickly stood up straight. "Jack, we gotta go!" He grabbed his partner by the shoulder and pulled him up to a standing position. "There's dynamite all over the back of the truck!"

They heard the fire department approaching with their sirens blasting through the night. Both men broke into a run, jumping into their patrol car and driving toward the fire department units as fast as the vehicle could go. Flowers got on the air to tell the firefighters to back off. "Twenty-three- Alpha-27!" Flowers shouted into his portable radio. The Sheriff's Office dispatcher acknowledged. "Advise the fire department to stay away! We have explosives inside the vehicle we found. Have the Sheriff's Office Bomb and Arson Unit respond Code-3, and have our supervisor give us his ETA. We are clearing the scene, right now.

Chapter 17

As Michael Callaway rode his "borrowed" dirt bike southbound on the Palmetto Expressway, he could feel the motorcycle vibrate beneath him. He looked at his rear-view mirror and saw a bright flash of light to the northwest behind him. *Enjoy your stay in hell, Mr. Howe*, he thought. He struggled to keep the bike at the posted speed limit. As much as he wanted to get back to the *Orinoco Flow* quickly, the last thing he needed was to get pulled over by a state trooper while carrying a case of dynamite and a bunch of detonators. The Glock machine-pistol wouldn't help matters either if he were stopped. He had already decided to flee if any police vehicles lit him up while trying to stop him. *Don't think I can bullshit my way out of this one!* he thought. Callaway had taken the precaution of wrapping the wooden box that had the words *EXPLOSIVES* and *DANGER* stenciled all over it in bright red lettering with his jacket. The bone-numbing chill of the cool night air of January, even in Miami, was a little tough to stand while riding at sixty miles-per-hour on a motorcycle wearing a damp tee-shirt. Still, he surmised, it was better than having the uncovered box of dynamite observed by a passing police car. *Don't want to just hand them the probable cause to take me away and throw me in jail, either* he thought.

He continued south until he reached the Dolphin Expressway and turned east, past Miami International Airport, heading for the safety of his boat in Miami Beach. *Hope I didn't hurt anyone, or cause much damage with that little explosion,* he thought as he traveled through the night.

*****

Back at the entrance gate of the dirt road to the explosives bunker, deputies from the Broward Sheriff's Office Bomb and Arson Squad were gingerly prying open the remains of the rear hatch on the DEA vehicle assigned to Special Agent-in-Charge David Howe. After determining that the dynamite in the rear compartment was not wired to any kind of booby-trap or detonating device, they crow-barred open what was left of the latch holding the door closed and slowly lifted the hatch open.

The midnight shift supervisor from Miramar PD, Sergeant Pete Tambor rolled up and parked near Benini and Flowers's police car. The smoke from the explosion was starting to clear courtesy of a cold wind blowing from the northwest out of the nearby Everglades. He shown the door-mounted spotlight on his vehicle out towards the spot where the bunker should have been, three miles away and saw nothing. No trees, no building, nothing.

"I don't think this was some kids shooting .22 rifles this time," he said as the two officers walked up to him.

"Did you hear what Parker found when he searched for the tag, Sarge?" Benini asked as he lit a cigarette.

"Yeah, I put a call in to DEA in Miami," Tambor replied. "They can't locate the guy Howe who the vehicle's assigned to. I asked them to send someone out here, but that's a problem since Howe is the Agent-in-Charge, and their District Director Cruz was killed last week in Fort Lauderdale. They said the people in DC would find someone with authority to send them out. Obviously, something is beginning to stink with all the DEA people who've died around here lately."

The three men looked up into the clear sky at the sound of an approaching helicopter. The BSO Aviation Unit came roaring over the scene after a quick run from their base at Fort Lauderdale Executive Airport.

"Poppa-One arrival over the scene in Miramar," the officers heard over their radios. Benini and Flowers looked at Tambor, who was staring at the green and white Bell Jet Ranger helicopter. The pilot switched on the Midnight Sun spotlight under the belly of the chopper and began flying a search pattern around the scene.

Tambor got on the radio with the intent of hitching a ride with the deputy in the sky. "Twenty-Three-Delta-3," he said. "Have the Poppa-Unit advise if he can pick me up, so I can observe the extent of the scene from the air."

The pilot responded instantly that he would, and the three officers on the ground turned on their vehicle headlights to create a landing zone on the roadway. When the sergeant became airborne, he was shocked at the devastation below him. The pilot of the Sheriff's helicopter widened the powerful beam of light projecting from the Midnight Sun, illuminating a large area where the explosives bunker used to be. He called the two officers on the ground, advising them to go to the private chat channel on their radios. "You're not gonna believe this!" Tambor yelled over the radio. "There's nothing left of the bunker but a big smoking water hole in the ground! All the trees and vegetation are blown down flat for about a mile around. There are pieces of corrugated metal and junk all over the place. As soon as Bomb and Arson clear the entrance, have the fire department move in and put out the small fires that are burning along the entrance road. I'll be back down in a few minutes."

The Jet Ranger helicopter circled, making larger and larger turns, and then returned to where Benini and Flowers were waiting. Playing with the spotlight control lever, Tambor spotted a long and shiny item about fifty feet away from where Benini was standing. He asked the pilot to hover and keyed the shoulder microphone of his portable radio, trying to talk over the noise of the rotor four feet over his head. "Twenty-Three-Delta-Three!" he said. "Freddy, there's a shiny object on the ground, about fifty feet to your right. It's away from the SUV, so go check it out."

Benini acknowledged, walking to the area where Sergeant Tambor shined the light. When he looked down, his mouth dropped open. He keyed his radio to advise Tambor of what he found. "Sarge, you're not going to believe this, but I've got a shiny steel bar with a human hand and forearm attached to it! And it's got handcuffs on its wrist," he said.

There was silence on the radio for about ten seconds before Tambor responded, "After what I've seen out here tonight, nothing surprises me. Mark the location, and we'll let our crime scene people deal with it."

The pilot landed and Tambor joined Benini to see the grizzly sight. The hand and forearm appeared to have been ripped from the body by the blast, never relinquishing its grip on the steel rod.

The Bomb and Arson deputies completed their investigation and signaled that the demolished SUV could now be examined for clues, since they had removed anything from the interior that could explode. Now the sun was beginning to rise, casting a bluish light over the smoky woods out towards the location of the former explosives bunker.

Tambor's radio crackled with a message from one of the Miramar officers blocking the road on the perimeter of the scene. "Sarge, I just let a supervisor from the DEA through, and he's heading your way," the officer said.

A black Ford Crown Victoria pulled up to Tambor's parked patrol car. The driver, wearing what looked like a windbreaker from a country club, exited the car and walked toward him while looking at the mess west of the roadway. The damage was more apparent as the sun started to rise in the eastern sky. The sergeant walked to meet the man. "Sergeant Pete Tambor, Miramar PD," he said, extending his right hand.

The DEA representative's head snapped around, eyes wide open. "Richard Todd, sergeant. Acting Special Agent in Charge, DEA," he said, shaking the sergeant's hand, again looking at the carnage in the woods.

"I don't know you, sir. How long have you been the Acting Agent in Charge, Mr. Todd?" Tambor asked, noting the man's somewhat jerky movements.

Todd looked at him with an exasperated expression. "About an hour and twenty minutes, Sergeant," he answered.

"I know you," Officer Flowers said as he walked up to the men. "I was on the Federal Money Laundering Task-Force a couple of years ago when I was working narc. I worked with some of your Customs guys when you were Agent in Charge in Miami. You moved from Customs to DEA?"

Todd stiffened. He ground his teeth, as he thought of the man responsible for the loss of his supervisory position with the Customs Service and the auditing job he was shoved into as a result: Michael Callaway.

"That's not really important now, is it, Officer?" Todd asked, glaring at Flowers. "I'm here to find out why a vehicle belonging to the Agent in Charge of the Miami DEA office is at the scene of an explosion. The FBI is on its way with their crime scene and lab people, and we will be taking over this investigation.

Sergeant Tambor squinted his eyes and smiled at the acting Agent-In-Charge from the DEA. "Look, Todd, I just met you, and already I don't like you," he said. "This crime scene, and yes, the Miramar Police Department considers it a crime scene, is in our city. The only connection with the federal government here is the fact that one of *your* agency vehicles is at the scene with the crap blown out of it, and that a box of dynamite from a bunker in *my* city was inside of that vehicle. We *will* be part of this investigation, sir!" Tambor said with authority.

Todd's mouth twisted up like he just bit into a lemon. "All right, Sergeant," Todd said. "Call out your investigators and have them join in the fun."

Tambor pointed at Benini and Flowers. "These officers did their time as investigators," he said. "They're two of the best we have. They can do the initial findings. Have you located the agent this vehicle was assigned to? David Howe, right?"

Todd's eyes narrowed upon hearing that the local police were able to learn the identity of the Miami Agent in Charge, obviously from his vehicle, so quickly. "How did you find that out, Sergeant?" he asked in a low tone.

Tambor didn't mention that his desk officer had so

many good connections. "Let's just say we're a little more sophisticated than the federal agencies think we are," he responded. "And I know people who know people. So where is David Howe, Mr. Todd?"

Todd rolled his eyes, again looking out towards the woods. "We haven't been able to locate him," he said, knowing that an attempted trace had been made on the tag of Howe's vehicle by the Sheriff's office dispatcher.

Tambor also looked out at the site of the explosion. "So, we must assume that he may be out there," he said. "In many places by the looks of the blast. And the fact that we just found a human arm and hand about one hundred feet from here. Any bets on whether they used to belong to David Howe?"

Todd wiped the sweat from his forehead, looking very nervous, as Tambor continued with, "I mean, can you think of anyone who may have been out here with him or involved in this mess?"

A smirk came to Todd's face as he answered, "Yes. I can think of one other person."

*****

Callaway was cuddled up in his bed aboard the *Orinoco Flow* when he was yanked from a deep sleep by a stern knock on the cabin door. He rolled over and stared at the clock as the knocking continued. He grabbed a pair of shorts from the chair near the bed. About halfway to the door, he stopped.

"Who is it?" he yelled in a gruff voice.

"Miami Beach Police, Mr. Callaway. We have someone here that wants to talk to you."

"Give me a minute so I can put on some clothes,"

Callaway yelled back. He opened a drawer to get a shirt when he noticed the boots and fatigue pants on the floor covered with mud from the previous night's activities. He needed to act fast. He pulled open the access hatch to the boat's wiring and plumbing pipes and pushed the muddy items down into the space, brushed off his hands, and then walked to where his guests were waiting.

Two uniformed Miami Beach police officers stood on the deck, one who he knew from his Customs Service days, and behind them, a familiar face greeted him. "Hiya, Mike," Commander David Eldridge said.

Callaway was bewildered at seeing his good friend with the Beach cops. "Hey, David. What's going on?" he said, as he backed away from the door to let the men in. Callaway sat in a chair and invited the three men to sit. Only Eldridge did, taking a spot on the couch with the officers standing behind him.

Eldridge twisted his mouth into a strange smile. "Sleep well last night, Mike?" he asked, raising and lowering his eyebrows.

Callaway immediately got the message. "Yeah, David," he answered. "I slept real well last night. Why?"

Eldridge leaned back on the couch and exhaled. "There's a meeting at the Miami DEA office up in Doral in an hour," he said. "I was sent here to make sure that you attend that meeting."

Callaway tried to act surprised. "Why would I be invited to a meeting with the DEA?" he asked. "Did they come up with anything new about Carrie's murder?"

Eldridge shifted on the couch, clearly uncomfortable. "Nooo, this has to do with a big explosion up in Miramar last night, he answered.

Callaway looked at the two Miami Beach officers,

who both appeared to be there only because they had to. He quickly sized up the situation. *If they were here to arrest me for what happened last night, it would be Miramar cops or someone from the feds. So why do they want me at this meeting?* he thought. "So, what does an explosion in Miramar have to do with me, David? Who's holding the meeting?" he asked, trying his best to sound sincere.

Eldridge looked at his watch. "I don't know who is running the meeting, other then it's some big dog from the State Department, along with the new acting agent-in-charge for the Miami DEA office, whoever that is," he answered. "It appears that your old *friend* David Howe is missing in action. They can't find him, and they brought in an acting to take his place until they find out what's going on."

"David, I had a rough night last night, thinking about Carrie. I'm really not in the mood to go to some government dog-and-pony show," Callaway said, looking away from his friend.

Sounding exasperated, Eldridge answered, "Look, they said it was important. My boss, Admiral Slingo, will be there. DEA came to her and told her that we're friends, so that's why I was sent here to bring you to the meeting."

Callaway thought hard about that last statement about their friendship. *Huh! Obviously, no evidence for the cops or the feds to question me, or they'd be here doing the talking, and I'd be in handcuffs. So, they sent my buddy to drag me to this meeting. This new DEA boss and the admiral are either pretty sharp… or desperate.* "Your Admiral a stand-up lady, David?" he asked.

Eldridge's eyes got squinty, "No! She is a bitch on

wheels," he answered. "And she doesn't care much for people who are late. Look, Callaway, we're wasting time, so get some presentable clothes on and let's get going, okay?"

Callaway stood up and began walking to the stateroom. "Relax, David," he said. "We'll get there. I wouldn't want to be late for the new DEA guy or Admiral *Bitch*, either."

Eldridge stared at him, suddenly recalling John Paul Jones. *You are definitely heading into harm's way, my friend.*

Chapter 18

Callaway felt kind of odd riding in a government vehicle again. The beat-up U.S. Navy Chevy Caprice bumped and squeaked along on worn-out bushings. Callaway smiled as they were driving through the parking lot of the marina, seeing that the two Miami Beach officers who'd escorted Eldridge to Callaway's boat had obviously been waylaid by the owner of a certain mud-covered dirt bike. The mood inside the vehicle was about as wretched as the condition of the car. Callaway kept trying to start a conversation, but Eldridge just wouldn't say much of anything.

"You pissed at me, David?" Callaway asked.

The big man turned his head toward Callaway with a scowl on his face. He looked over the top of his mirrored Ray Ban fighter pilot sunglasses for just a moment before turning back to the road. "Mike, I don't want to talk to you right now," he said. "Obviously someone thinks you're connected somehow to whatever happened in Miramar last night. You are my friend, and I don't want you to get in any more trouble, so I'm not going to ask you the obvious. My boss thinks that I will get it out of you, and hand you up. And I just won't do that, no matter what she does."

Callaway looked at his friend, and then stared out the passenger door window for a few minutes before he answered. "Everyone has a price, David. Remember that." He thought about how Eldridge, Cruz and Hidalgo helped cover up the fact that Callaway blew up and sank a cocaine-hauling submarine that belonged to the late Anton Drake, in violation of several international laws. "But thank you for being my friend," he said. "And for covering my ass down in the Bahamas about me sinking the sub. I'll shut up till we get there."

Forty minutes later, Eldridge turned the Caprice into the parking lot of the Miami district headquarters of the U.S. Drug Enforcement Administration and parked, giving Callaway a stern look. "Just don't get your ass out there too far for me to cover it, okay." he said.

They entered the building and were directed to a conference room, with several people waiting for them. The most prominent was Eldridge's boss, Vice Admiral D. May Slingo. Callaway had once asked Eldridge what her real first name was when the Commander was assigned to her office. He had had a good laugh when he heard that the D stood for Dorcas. Eldridge, who was a big reader of the Bible, told him that she was probably named for a person described in the good book as being very charitable.

The Admiral stood up upon seeing Eldridge entering the room with another man. She walked around the table towards Callaway. Seeing this tall, scrawny person, about the same age as Eldridge, brought a grin to his lips. She walked up to him, and very officially thrust out her right hand to greet him.

"Admiral May Slingo," she said tersely.

Callaway grasped her hand, noticing how she grasped his high up above his fingers, as though she was trying to push his thumb back to his wrist and applying a considerable amount of pressure at the same time. He looked her in the eye, and muttered "Ma'am?" *Trying to establish your dominance, Dorcas? That didn't seem very charitable,* he thought, and wanted to shout her first name, but she already looked pissed off. *Why make things worse?*

"Have a seat, Mr. Callaway," she said, as she let go of his hand and pointed at a chair in the center of the room. "Oh, and you may sit, too, Commander Eldridge," she added.

Eldridge moved to one of two empty chairs at the end of the table and sat down.

Callaway knew one of the men at the table as Jerry Donavan, Agent-in-Charge of the Miami office of the FBI, but he couldn't figure out the identity of the other suits. There were several other people seated behind Callaway, watching the proceedings. Callaway noted with a grin, that Slingo remained on her feet and wondered if this was another show of dominance.

"Mr. Callaway," Admiral Slingo said. "I believe you know Mr. Donavan from the Federal Bureau of Investigation? This is Mr. Theodore Robinson, from our State Department, and Mr. Enrique Garcia, the new District Director of the Customs Service."

Callaway had heard of Garcia but had never met him during his time with Customs.

"At the other end of the table is Detective Denise Carpenter, from the Miramar Police Department. Slingo continued. "We're still waiting for the new Interim Agent-in-Charge of the DEA… ah, here he is now."

Callaway turned to see the door opening behind him. His teeth clinched as his former boss, Richard Todd, the man who tried his very best to fire Callaway from the United States Customs Service, walked into the conference room. Instantly, Todd locked his eyes on the man who had forever stuck him with the nickname *Major Dick*.

"Mr. Michael Callaway," Todd said, in a very low voice.

Callaway now believed that this *meeting* was about to turn into an *execution.* "Nice to see you again, Todd," Callaway said smiling. "I see your job writing interagency audits didn't last too long. When did you get the new gig as Interim with the DEA?"

Todd looked at Callaway with even more disdain as he answered, "Last night. All because of the mess that occurred in Miramar." For the second time that week, Callaway was read his Miranda rights, by Todd this time.

"Do you know anything about the rather large explosion that happened up there?" Todd asked.

Callaway just shook his head and smiled. "No sir don't know a thing about any explosion," he answered politely.

"And I suppose you can account for your where-abouts last night?" Todd continued.

"Well let's see. I was involved in a shooting incident a couple of days ago." Callaway responded.

Admiral Slingo interrupted him. "Yes, I understand you saved Commander Eldridge's life." Slingo said with a weak smile.

Callaway continued with, "I went to the Miami Beach police station to give a statement after that, and then I went to my boat at the Miami Beach Marina," he answered. "I did a little fishing off the back of my boat and just hung out yesterday, and then I went to bed about eleven, eleven-thirty. That's about it."

Todd was persistent, "Can you prove that?" he asked. "Did anyone see you, talk to you, whatever?"

Callaway smiled, "No sir. Didn't talk to or see anyone that I can recall. I'm still in a bad way over the murder of my fiancée, so I just hung around on my boat," he said, not lying one bit about his feelings. "Would someone please explain what I am suspected of being involved in? Am I under arrest? What and where was this *explosion*?"

Showing no concern about Callaway's loss, Admiral Slingo asked Commander Eldridge, "Did he say anything during the ride over here?"

Eldridge sat up straight in his chair and answered, "No ma'am. Not a thing."

She looked at him and slightly shook her head, "Why do I get the impression that you didn't press him too hard on the subject, Commander?" she asked.

Eldridge hesitated, seemingly at a loss for words.

"You still haven't answered my question, Admiral," Callaway broke in. "What the hell happened last night, and how does it concern me?"

Slingo gave Callaway an icy stare. "All right, Mr. Callaway," she answered. "Early this morning, a few hours before daybreak, a dynamite storage bunker near the Everglades, in Miramar, blew up. It caused massive damage to the area around it. Mr. Todd seems to think you may have had something to do with the explosion. That is part of the reason we are here."

Callaway was tired of the attitude of the lady in the white uniform. "Why would I be involved in something like that, Admiral?" he asked. "I mean, how do you know the bunker didn't just blow up? Accidents do happen, right?"

There was an uneasy silence for a few seconds until Miramar Police Detective Denise Carpenter spoke up.

"Why don't you tell him about your DEA guy who died out at the scene, Admiral?" she asked. Again, silence, until Carpenter continued, "Mr. Callaway, the DEA Special Agent in Charge, David Howe's agency vehicle, what was left of it, that is, was found at the scene," she said. "There were a couple of cases of dynamite in it, along with building plans for three federal buildings ..."

Admiral Slingo interrupted her, saying, "Detective, with all due respect to your city, this has become a federal matter. We can take over the conversation from here."

"With all due respect to you and the federal government, Admiral, this incident occurred in my jurisdiction," Carpenter shot back. "And from the pieces and parts we found, the explosion probably took the life of what is looking more and more like a bad federal agent. My department will investigate this no matter what you say."

The admiral seemed stunned by the response. Robinson, the man from the U.S. State Department, began to speak, "Detective," he said in a calm voice. "You don't seem to understand that there may result in international problems resulting from this incident . . ."

Now Carpenter cut him off with, "And you don't seem to understand, sir, that a death that occurred during the apparent commission of a crime, resulting in a large amount of property damage, and the loss of about a million-and-a-half dollars' worth of explosives is not just going to go away," she said, shifting her gaze to the admiral and then back to Robinson. "If you have a problem with what I'm saying, sir, I suggest you call my chief, or the mayor, because until I'm told to back off by one of them, I will investigate this case."

Nicely played, Detective Callaway thought. He was pleased to see that Carpenter could handle the situation.

He decided to squeeze Slingo and the weenie from the State Department, just a little, "Again, exactly why am I here, Admiral?" Callaway asked. I mean, it's obvious that if Mr. Howe was trying to steal explosives, then he had to be the mole that'd been handing agency information out to someone offshore. And that someone is Derrick Drake, and he was probably doing the same thing for Anton Drake before that. It's also obvious that you bozos couldn't figure that out." He noticed a quick grin from Detective Carpenter as he continued: "If Howe was stealing dynamite, it wasn't to sell to Derrick Drake. Drake can get all the explosives he wants from Fidel Castro through his Security Chief, Martino Herrera. Detective Carpenter said that there were building plans for three Federal office buildings in Howe's vehicle. We all know that Drake either killed, or ordered the death of my fiancée, and he hired a hit man to kill Alberto Cruz, and Jorge Hidalgo. And that Commander Eldridge and I were also on the kill list. Remember what was written all over Carrie when they found her? 'All of your houses will fall?' Looks to me like Howe was going to blow up some of your buildings on behalf of Derrick Drake, like some kind of crazy vengeance thing." Callaway could see that the Admiral was getting visibly angry.

"Now look, Mr. Callaway!" she said. "You don't seem to understand the gravity of the situation!" Her voice rose to a bit of a shriek. "Everyone in this room knows that you are bent on going out to Derrick Drake's Island and killing him. We have been in contact with the Bahamian Government about the investigation of the murders you talked about. We are very close to obtaining an arrest warrant for Mr. Drake and the Bahamians say they will work with us, if this is handled by the letter of the law, their law, and by their people. We just need to let them know when we have the warrant, and they have assured us that *they* will secure Mr. Drake for us. They don't want any violence out there."

Callaway stared at Slingo for a good five seconds in disbelief. "Are you out of you out of your fucking mind?" he roared. "Are you that dumb that you think the Bahamians will really help you? Most of you know damn well that Drake's daddy owned about half of the members of the Bahamian Parliament. The minute you tell them you have a warrant, they will call Derrick, and he will rabbit out of there and head for Cuba, or Venezuela, and you won't be able to get him!"

Slingo yelled back, "You know, for a guy who was a cop, and from what I've heard, came from a Navy family, you sure don't know much about duty, mister!" Her face started to turn red. "I'm sure your father would be real damn proud. Do you think we're going to let you just go crazy and shoot up the Caribbean because you think Drake killed your girlfriend? We do things by the book, and that's all there is to it. Do you understand?"

Callaway looked at each of the people behind the table. When he got to Eldridge, the big man looked him in the eyes and shook his head slightly from side to side, trying to tell him to shut up. It didn't work. Callaway looked at the admiral, narrowing his eyes to little slits. With a nasty grin, he answered, "Tell me something, Admiral. Did you come up to your rank by way of sea command, or have you been ashore throughout your career?" he asked.

" It's none of your god dammed business how I made rank!" she yelled. "I worked my ass off to get where I am. Don't try to change the subject. I'm warning you that if you even get near Drake's island, I will have you locked up instantly."

Callaway shot right back, "Really? You have no authority in Bahamian waters," he yelled. "What are you going to do, call their defense force out to arrest me? Good luck with that. I know their islands better than they do."

Slingo stood up fast. "I don't need to call the Bahamians, Callaway! she roared. "I'll find a way to nail your ass. It's a big ocean out there. Strange things can happen," she said, her face bright red, as she lost all control of her temper.

Callaway thought to himself, *it's time to go.*

"How would you know that, Admiral? He spoke. "Obviously, the most water you've ever been in was in your frigging bathtub. My Dad had a name for people who made Flag Rank without ever having a command at sea. He called them Land Tortoise*s*. Big and slow."

"Callaway!" Major Dick screamed as he jumped to his feet. "Admiral, I have a way to make sure that Mr. Callaway stays away from Drake's Island. I've taken the liberty of requesting assistance from the United States Marshals Service. They've sent me two marshals, one of whom I know very well. He's very good at what he does, and he will keep a close eye on Mr. Callaway. I'd like to introduce Marshals Tucker and Rodriguez. They will be assisting us in making sure that Mr. Callaway doesn't do anything stupid."

Callaway heard a chair rattling behind him and turned to see a female, wearing a dark pantsuit, and a tall, very overweight man, stand up and walk to the front of the room. Todd pointed at the female. "This is Marshal Elaine Rodriguez, and this is Marshal Clarence Tucker," he said.

Callaway looked at the two United States Marshals.

Rodriguez appeared to be kind of quiet, as well as being extremely good-looking. Tucker, on the other hand, was a gigantic beast of a human being, wearing a suit that came from the tall and big man section of a cheap department store. Callaway also couldn't help but notice his strong body odor as he walked past him to the front of the room. He couldn't help but chuckle.

"*Marshal Tucker*?" he whispered.

The large man glared at him as he spoke. "Yeah Callaway, what about it?" Tucker replied.

"Nothing, man. I just really enjoy your music," Callaway said.

"Gee, I've never heard that before, Callaway," Tucker said. "Let me tell you something, pal, I am going to be on you like stink on shit. You got that?"

"Yeah… I kind of got that when you walked past me," Callaway said, wrinkling his nose. "You all do whatever you feel is necessary," Callaway continued. "I'm telling you right now that I have no intention of going after young Mr. Drake. I'm going to the marina and getting on my boat, and I am heading to the island of *Eluthera,* where I will try to get through the grief of losing my fiancéee, and my friends."

Eldridge tilted his head back and stared at the ceiling in relief, as Callaway, having not been charged with any crime, stood up and walked to the door. He turned and looked at Admiral Slingo with a big grin on his face.

"Have a nice day, Admiral!"

*****

When he arrived back at the *Orinoco Flow,* Callaway fired up the diesel engine and untied the boat from the dock. As he idled the shrimper out of the marina and into Government Cut, he thought about the horrible things that Derrick Drake's thugs did to his lover. *I won't let Drake get arrested, Carrie,* he thought. He rubbed the half-world pendent on the chain around his neck. *Drake's not going to prison as long as I'm alive. He's going to hell on a bullet train!* His thoughts were interrupted by the sound of loud engines as a DEA chase boat idled out from a nearby slip. He smiled at how bored the *chase* boat operators would be, following a very slow, converted shrimp boat in a chase-boat that could hit seventy miles-per-hour. When he reached the deep water a few miles offshore, he turned and looked at the Miami skyline, thinking this would be the last time he would ever see it. He would have time during the transit to figure out how he would get to Drake's island, and to get close enough to get to Derrick and Herrera to kill them.

*****

He reached the island of Eleuthera in the Bahamas two days later. His escorts left him and roared off in the direction of Miami. He figured that Mr. Robinson from the State Department would get permission from the Bahamian government to allow the Marshals to act as watchdogs on him, to report to the Bahamian Defense Force, and Admiral Slingo if his boat even left the dock. If it did, Callaway thought, the Bahamians would probably receive a request from State asking them to apprehend him for whatever nebulous reason they could think of. Tucker and Rodriguez arrived by air before Callaway did and picked up a car from the DEA office on the island. They began working twelve-hour shifts watching Callaway. Tucker, as senior agent, opted to take the night shift. Callaway would have to wait two days more for conditions to be just right for his assault on Drake's island. He would have to find a way to make his move without being discovered by the two U.S. Marshals that were assigned to watch him day and night.

Sitting out on the deck at the stern of his boat, he waved at Marshal Tucker, wondering how he could slip away under the man's watchful gaze. He looked north, up the channel when he heard a loud noise.

"I think I just found my ticket to ride."

Chapter 19

"No moon, and glass calm seas," Callaway said as he watched the sun setting into the Caribbean Sea to the west. He looked out the opposite window of *Orinoco Flow* as she sat at the dock on the island of Eluthera. He could see U.S. Marshal Clarence Tucker sitting in the DEA Chevrolet Impala, watching his every move. Callaway had watched the U.S. Marshal cram his three hundred pounds into the car that evening, along with some water and a bag full of junk food of suspicious quality from one of the local food stands.

Callaway chuckled, thinking of what kind of awful scents Marshall Rodriguez would have to endure in that vehicle after relieving Marshal Tucker. *He doesn't bathe much, and he eats all kinds of crappy food. It's gonna smell like a lion cage in that car tomorrow. Hopefully, I'll be alive, and back aboard my boat to witness the changing of the guard,* he thought.

He tried to relax, waiting for night to come, thinking about the strings that the U.S. State Department had to pull to get the Bahamians to allow two armed U.S. Marshals to watchdog him. The last thing he would do before leaving his boat was to contact Avengeher online, advising them of his plan to attack Golgotha, and thanking them for all the information they gave him.

Callaway also told his mystery friend that he didn't expect to return, since he would probably be killed on the island, and how even if he survived, the WaveRunner could only carry enough fuel to get him halfway back to Eluthera. He was shocked to receive a response stating that Avengeher would attempt to rescue him at daybreak, at a point halfway between Drake's island and Eluthera.

When the sun dipped low behind the horizon, Callaway donned his black wetsuit, strapped on a scuba tank and buoyancy vest, and grabbed his dive mask and fins. He tied a strong knot in a thick piece of rope to the boat railing facing the channel. He lowered the other end of the rope, with a large bag secured to it, down into the water. Quietly, he climbed down the rope into the water, and pulled the fins onto his feet. The January water was cold, even with the wetsuit on, as he untied the bag and went under. Submerging about ten feet, he swam up the channel until he reached Mary's engine shop, where he would prepare his transportation for a visit to the island of Golgotha.

Mary trusted Callaway enough to leave him a key to the shop while she was off visiting her family in England, courtesy of the airline ticket he had bought for her. He had told her he would be moving the WaveRunner to Fort Lauderdale, and if all went well, she would never know his new use for the watercraft. Instead of being his new go-fast toy, it would become the means of speedy transport to get at Derrick Drake. He kept picturing Carrie on the slab in the Medical Examiner's Office, Cruz, dead on his living room floor; and Jorge, as his partner lay dead in his arms. He felt the hard, fevered knot of anger throbbing in his temples again, as he reached the workshop. "I'm gonna kill that little bastard Drake for you, partner, and for Cruz, and especially for you, Carrie," he said to himself.

Climbing up the ladder on the dock behind Mary's shop, he unlocked the door, and hauled all his equipment inside. He immediately set to work that early evening, timing his departure to Golgotha for the 10:00 pm take-off time of the last Chaulk's seaplane flight of the day. Out of his bag he pulled three large spray cans of flat-black paint. He began coating every inch of the watercraft above the waterline, covering the garish Yamaha factory paint job. The flat paint seemed to absorb all of the light in the room, which he surmised should render the vehicle almost invisible at sea on this moonless night.

Working on a swing-down trolling motor bracket, he drilled six holes through the rear deck of the craft. He ran the mounting screws through to a backing plate that he was just able to squeeze through the access port on the rear deck. He knew Drake's men would hear the screaming wail of the supercharged engine before he could get close to the island, so he mounted the silent fifty-five pound/thrust Minn-Kota electric trolling motor powerhead to the bracket and rigged the wiring for the throttle control and battery connection. *If I'm not spotted by one of his patrol boats, and if the guards on shore do not see me, I should be able to sneak right up on them. Sure! Easy, right?* he thought.

Thinking of the absurdity of what he was about to do, he took a deep breath, and paused from his work, seeing Carrie's face in his mind. *I'm going to the island, and I'll kill every son-of-a-bitch there that gets between me and Derrick. And then I will kill him and Herrera, too. Or die trying. I don't care,* he thought as he began loading equipment into the Yamaha's watertight forward compartment. He thought about how most of his friends were cops, and those who were closest to him were dead.

"If I win, the world will be less two killers and their henchmen. If I lose, nobody will care very much," he said to himself.

He placed the first items inside a waterproof cushioned bag. Ten large "explosive devices," as his former associates at the Bureau of Alcohol, Tobacco and Firearms would call them. These included three sticks each of dynamite he'd removed from Howe's DEA truck. He'd use these to take out Drake's new drug lab. He also made three smaller devices using only one stick of dynamite with seven-second timers, for use against Drake's thugs. Callaway inserted a blasting cap into each stick of each device, which in turn was connected to one of the ingenious timers that Howe had built. "I must say, Mr. Howe, you may have been a colossal asshole, but you did some fine work. Amazing craftsmanship!" he said. I hope you're still enjoying your permanent vacation, *all over* the Everglades," he said with a smile.

Next, he added the pistol and ammunition that he'd liberated from Klauser's van, after his failed attempt on Commander Eldridge's life. Callaway had examined the Thompson-Center Contender on his boat. He read the inscription *Custom Shop* engraved on the barrel and, with further research, learned that the single-shot pistol was a match grade gun that should be able to hit a small target at a very long distance. Callaway wondered why Klauser felt he needed so many types of ammunition for the Contender, including hollow points and tracer rounds. He wondered why, since each tracer bullet contained a chemical compound that would ignite upon firing, causing the round to glow red in the darkness as it flew through the air.

You never know, he thought. *They might come in*

handy for something. Lastly, he stuffed a flare pistol into one side of the storage compartment. *If my ride home does show up, I guess I'll need some way of flagging him or her down. Big If. He* checked the flare pistol to make sure it was loaded. He wondered if the mystery person who gave him all the information on Drake and the status of his little army was on his side or not.

What if this person was working for the nasty admiral? he thought. *I may go flying towards the island and find half of the Atlantic Fleet waiting to pick me up. Or worse, what if the information came from one of Drake's people? They could be waiting for me. I could be dead meat as soon as I hit the beach, or I could be in for some pretty evil torture before I die. I'm guessing Derrick will opt for the torture. But I've got to try. I'll probably get killed in the process, anyway, but I've got to try.*

Callaway zipped up his thin black wetsuit, which would conceal him on the island and keep him somewhat warm if he ended up in the cold January Sea, but instead of wearing dive boots, he laced up a pair of black combat boots to give him better traction on the sandy island. Last of all, he strapped on a gun belt and holstered the Glock 18 and the silencer that he had *confiscated* from Agent in Charge Howe. In addition, he placed four extra magazines for the pistol in Velcro-secured pouches on his left side, opposite the pistol. Two of the magazines were the standard seventeen-round type, loaded with Federal 147grain Hydra Shok rounds. These sub-sonic rounds would travel less than one thousand feet per second and be very quiet when fired through the silencer. The other two magazines carried thirty-two rounds each, in case he needed to toggle the selector on the left side of the slide from semi to fully automatic. They were loaded with

Winchester 127 grain Black Talon rounds. He remembered learning that these rounds were the deadliest that the company made. As efficient as they were, the bullets would be useless for secrecy through the silencer, as they traveled at a very high velocity and would still make a lot of noise. He also attached a net bag normally used to collect lobsters to the left side of the belt. He would use this to throw the magazines in when they were empty, since they all came from his private collection of toys that go bang.

True to his somewhat anal-retentive nature, all the magazines had his initials stamped on them. He would collect them, in case he did survive, so there wouldn't be any evidence of the hellfire he planned on raining down on Derrick Drake.

Callaway rolled the davit that held the WaveRunner through the door and onto the dock. He hooked the davit up to the cables on the crane boom and hit the Up switch, lifting it into the air. He pushed the crane boom around until the craft was above the water next to the dock. He then lowered it into the water until the hoist lines went slack. Unhooking the lines, he jumped onto the back of the *Little Beast,* switched on the ignition, and pushed the starter button with his gloved index finger. The turbocharged engine came to life with a high-pitched roar that bumped up his adrenaline, bringing him to a quick realization. *I'm really going to do this,* he thought. *I'm going to Golgotha to put a bullet right between Derrick Drake's beady little eyes or die in the process, even if I have to kill fifty people to do it.*

He was beginning to realize how much he'd changed. The Boy Scout that his friends, associates, and enemies knew before had died. He was no longer Saint

Michael as the drug lords referred to him when he always went by the book.

"I burned that fucking book," he mumbled to himself, as he coasted the WaveRunner into the channel. He cruised south, almost invisible in the darkness, idling toward a place near where the *Orinoco Flow* was docked. He stopped in a small cutout in the mangroves growing near a seawall, waiting for his *cover* to arrive. The machine that would shield him and his craft, from the watchful eyes of Marshal Tucker, came idling by in the channel preparing for a water take-off about ten minutes later. Callaway watched from the cover of the mangroves, waiting for the Chalk's Airlines Grumman Albatross to power up.

As he waited, he pictured Marshal Tucker snoozing in his vehicle. He was sure the noise made by the Albatross on her take-off run would awaken the man. The question in Callaway's mind was would the aircraft provide enough cover to conceal him from Tucker's eyes?

Callaway waited until the plane passed him. He pulled the face shield down on his helmet and idled out and around to the left side of the aircraft, cruising just behind the wing. He had to stay next to the left side of the airplane, opposite from where Tucker was parked, to be shielded from view, since this was the only way out of the channel. He could see up into the cockpit, which was dimly lit by the instrument panel. Both the pilot and the copilot of the Grumman placed a hand on the ceiling mounted throttles of the aircraft and pressed forward, releasing 1425 horsepower from each of the Wright Cyclone engines. Callaway mirrored the speed of the aircraft as it roared down the channel. The Albatross passed by the *Orinoco Flow* just prior to reaching her takeoff speed.

*****

Agent Tucker watched the aircraft go by as he did every night since he'd taken the assignment watching Callaway. As the aircraft gained speed, the pilot glanced out of the left side cockpit window, and in the reflection of the flying boat's running lights saw what looked like a man running alongside of his aircraft, on the water. The blacked-out hull of the watercraft was almost invisible in the darkness. He stared at the man, who appeared to be wearing a motorcycle helmet flying alongside and below his left wing. As the hull of the flying boat left the water, he saw the man give a slight nod to him, and then accelerate away from the aircraft. His copilot was curious as to what his captain was looking at.

"What do you have out there, boss?"

The pilot turned his head and looked at the copilot, with his mouth slightly open. "Nothing! Not a god-damned thing!" He turned to look, in vain, for the *person* that he saw pulling away from him.

*****

Once he reached the cool water of the Bahamian Sea, Callaway pushed the button on the GPS built into the dashboard of the watercraft. Instantly a course directly to the island of Golgotha appeared. Callaway slowly squeezed the throttle lever on the handlebars of the WaveRunner, feeling the little craft continue to pick up speed as he watched the digital speedometer blinking numbers at him in bright green. "90, 97, 98."

210

There was a subtle pause in acceleration, when suddenly all hell broke loose. The little craft bolted forward as he watched the speedometer break one hundred miles per hour and continue to climb to a top speed of one hundred five.

Mary had told him that the race-prepped engine could probably run for at least a half an hour at top speed without any damage. That would be all he would need to get within a couple of miles of his target. Callaway leaned forward, resting his chest on the Yamaha's center console. He had nothing to do but keep the craft level on the water and think during the run to Drake's island.

At first all he thought about was what would happen if he hit even a coconut floating in the water. At the speed he was traveling, the floating object would rip his little craft to shreds and most assuredly kill him. Then he began thinking about Carrie, picturing her beautiful face. Her incredible smile burned into his brain as he traveled along. He thought of how they had met for the first time, at the Federal Law Enforcement Academy in Georgia. It was there that their love affair had begun, only to be cut short by her job as a deep-cover agent for the DEA. He hadn't seen her again until they met in Greasy Dick's Bar in Nassau, where he found her acting as a bodyguard for Anton Drake while working her undercover operation on the drug kingpin. He remembered how they had made love on a tiny island, where he gave her the gold half-world pendant and told her he loved her and how he wanted to explore the world with her. Then he thought of the last time he had seen her, lying on a cold stainless-steel table at the Miami-Dade County Medical Examiner's Office when he and Mrs. Marvin identified her. He kept seeing her slashed throat, and that knot of anger began twisting in the back of his skull again. His eyes filled with tears as he tried to squeeze even more speed out of the engine in his little watercraft. But the WaveRunner had no more to give him. The only relief he would get would come with the death of Derrick Drake by his own hands.

When he came within two miles of Golgotha, he slowed down and brought the watercraft to a halt. The ocean was still dead flat, even though he could feel a slight breeze on his face coming from the direction of the island. Callaway reached around behind him and pushed the lever that dropped the trolling motor assembly into the water behind his little vessel.

Grabbing the hand control for the trolling motor, he flipped the switch that was marked *forward*, and ran the unit up to top speed. He was now only moving at 10 mph, but he was doing so in total silence. He kept turning his head, listening for any of Drake's go-fast boats in the area. Callaway could hear one of the boats running far off in the distance on the other side of the island. He continued to ride the Yamaha parallel to the beach, passing Drake's house and the compound for the tourist submarine that the drug smuggler used as his *legitimate* business.

He reached a dark part of the beach, about an eighth of a mile from Drake's compound. Jumping off the watercraft, he waded out of the cold sea after flipping the trolling motor up on its mount and out of the water. Tying the watercraft's rope to one of the stern cleats, he walked ashore and tied the other end of the rope high on a large piece of driftwood washed up on the beach.

Callaway scanned the area and then moved up the beach towards the jungle that covered the area leading to the drug lab. As he approached the woods, he heard footsteps coming his way. He lay down on his back in some sea grape bushes as he drew the silenced Glock from his holster. He could see the figure of a man now, walking out of the jungle toward him. Callaway lay there with his weapon on his stomach pointed upward. The person walked to Callaway's position and stopped just short of stepping on him.

Callaway could see that the man was holding a shotgun, and he appeared to be staring in the direction of his watercraft floating just a few feet from the beach. The man had figured out what he was seeing, as he quickly grabbed for the portable radio on his belt. Callaway moved the barrel of his pistol slightly, aiming for the man's throat. He saw the gunman look down, obviously noticing the movement below him, as he squeezed the trigger. The only sound the weapon made was a *puff* and the *click-click* of the slide rocking back and forth. The heavy bullet struck the gunman just below his chin and then exited through the crown of his skull, taking a large part of his brain with it. Callaway rolled to his left as the man's body crumpled to the spot where he had been. He pried the shotgun from the dead man's hands and examined it.

A Remington 870 with an extended magazine tube. Thank you very much! he thought. He slung the weapon over his shoulder, scanned the area one more time, and started up the path toward the drug lab. After traveling about three hundred yards, he reached the edge of the clearing where the lab was being built. He could see a large double-wide trailer with some fifty-gallon metal drums lined up near a door. It appeared to him that the doublewide was being used as a temporary lab until the new, larger lab was finished.

The lab building was much further along in

construction then he thought it would be. The shell of the building, including the roof, was complete. He peered through the empty window openings, and with his flashlight could see that some of the equipment for handling the chemicals used in the production of powdered cocaine had already been installed. He could also see that barrels of highly flammable chemicals used to process cocaine were in a large rack on the rear exterior of that building, too. He removed his backpack and began walking around the building. He stopped about every ten feet to set one of his dynamite bombs in place, including one under the larger center barrel that contained one hundred gallons of explosive Ether, in the rear of the building. All of the timers that had been expertly constructed by the late David Howe were set to go off in one hour. Callaway expected that a total of twenty-one sticks of dynamite would level the new structure and the temporary lab in about three seconds.

Clearly, this Drake was not concerned about having the drug lab and all of its chemicals so close to his house, as his father had been. The previous drug lab was on the adjoining island that had been blown up one year ago.

As he was cinching up the top of his backpack, Callaway again heard footsteps coming his way. Dropping to a crouching position, he again removed the Glock from his holster, holding it to his chest in the ready position as he scanned the area. He saw a lone figure, tall and slightly bent at the waist, coming around the building and walking toward what appeared to be a vehicle maintenance building next to the drug lab. Callaway kept to the sandy ground as he quietly crept around the drug lab to sneak up on this new threat. He reached the corner of the vehicle maintenance building and peeked around the corner just in time to see the person light up a cigar, the smell of which wafted down to where he stood. Callaway instantly realized that he was twenty feet away from the man who had killed his lover. Martino Herrera, Drake's Chief of Security, was speaking in Spanish over his portable radio, telling somebody that they had forgotten to turn off the compressor in the repair building, and how they had better get to that building to shut it off quickly.

Callaway started to breathe hard as he could feel the anger building. There was no doubt in his mind that he would kill this man, but he needed answers to the questions that had haunted him from the minute he was told that Carrie was dead.

Callaway waited, hearing Herrera having a coughing fit, confirming rumors of lung cancer. The coughing got louder as the man walked along the building toward Callaway. Callaway took a step back and picked up a coral rock about the size of a softball. He stood up just as Herrera cleared the corner of the building. Herrera turned towards him, instinctively grabbing for the gun holstered on his right side, when Callaway smashed the rock into the side of the man's head, knocking him to the ground unconscious. Callaway took Herrera's pistol and threw it into the woods. Finding an open door to the maintenance building, he dragged Herrera inside. He lifted him up and rolled him onto one side of a drive-up ramp vehicle lift. Herrera lay on the ramp on his stomach as Callaway secured him to the ramp with some engine lift straps that he found on a nearby workbench. He then pulled the lever and elevated the ramp and Herrera to a level just above his own waist.

Callaway sat down on a stool at the mechanic's bench and watched as Herrera began to regain consciousness.

215

The groggy man winced in pain as he came to, rolling his head from side to side as if trying to figure out what had happened to him and where he was. He stared at Callaway for a good five seconds before he spoke.

"*Hijo de puta!*" he said, with an astonished look on his face. "You have some balls coming here, Mr. Callaway! You will never get off this island alive."

Callaway sat back on the stool, holding the Glock in his right hand and pointing it at Herrera's face.

"I really don't think I'll make it out of here, either, Martino," Callaway said. "And even if I do, I'll get arrested and probably thrown in prison for the rest of my life. But I really don't give a good goddamn about that since I've already got half of what I came here for. As long as I kill you and Derrek Drake, I really don't care what happens to me. I've got nothing to live for since you killed my fiancée. You did kill her, didn't you?"

Herrera began coughing hard again, trying to speak, "So you kill me, so what? I have lung cancer. I only have a year to live at the most, so you'll probably be doing me a favor," he said.

Callaway leaned forward, staring deep into the man's eyes as he replied, "A year is a long time. And besides that, I'm going to make your death as painful as I possibly can."

Herrera appeared visibly shaken by the look on Callaway's face, as if he knew that whatever the man had in store for him would not be pleasant. He coughed as he spoke, "Callaway, listen, I'll help you kill Drake and let you leave the island if you let me live. I'm going to die a painful death anyway, so what's the point of killing me now?" he asked, sounding desperate.

Callaway snapped up from the stool and walked to

his left, standing in front of his prey. The shotgun he had taken from his first victim dangled muzzle down from the sling over his left shoulder. He grasped the pistol grip, raised the muzzle, and pressed it against Herrera's forehead.

"So, tell me more, Martino, did you rape her? Were you the one that held her under the water? Are you the one that gave her the *Colombian necktie*? I got a pretty good idea of what you did from your mole, Mr. Howe. Tell me the truth and I'll consider your offer," he said as he lowered the shotgun.

Herrera let out a breath and suddenly seemed a little more relaxed. "You know Callaway, I've studied everything about you, trying my best to have you killed. The one thing I know about you that is certain is that you are an honest man," he said. "You go by the book. That's what everybody says about you. Swear to me that you won't kill me, and I'll tell you anything you want to know, but I warn you, you're not going to like what you hear."

Callaway looked at the man, knowing what he had learned from Special-Agent-in-Charge Howe, smiled slightly, and whispered, "I swear."

"It was all the hit man Howe hired," Herrera said. "He sent that guy to Boca Raton to kidnap your girlfriend and then kill her the way that Derrick Drake wanted it done."

Callaway grabbed the front strap that secured Herrera's neck to the cold steel ramp of the lift. He pulled the strap, tightening down on the back of the man's neck, causing terrific pain. Herrera began coughing from a combination of his lung cancer and the pressure on his throat.

"So, you had nothing to do with Carrie's death, right? I mean you never laid a hand on her?" Callaway asked in a soft voice.

Herrera strained to lift his face to stare into Callaway's eyes. "No, Callaway. I never left the island," he said. "It was all the hit man that Howe hired. I mean, look, I know Drake wanted her to die in a horrible way, but I respect that she was a professional, just like me. I would just shoot her in the head and end it quickly instead of drowning her. That is a horrible way to die, don't you agree?"

Callaway looked up above the area above the lift, seeing an air hose and a grease gun hanging from the ceiling. He spoke without taking his eyes off the devices.

"So, Drake came up with the stuff that was written on Carrie about all of my houses falling, right?" Callaway asked.

"No, that was Howe, he came up with those words," Herrera answered. "He told us how he wrote it in Spanish on her belly at the safe house, just to screw with you."

Callaway lowered his head and stared deeply into Herrera's eyes. It was a cold, deadly stare that caused Herrera to suck in a deep breath.

"You are a lying sack of shit!" Callaway yelled. "Howe doesn't even speak Spanish! He couldn't have written that stuff on her body. You did it, you son of a bitch! But I will agree with you about one thing. Drowning is a horrible way to die. And you're about to know exactly how horrible it is!"

Callaway reached up and grabbed the grease gun from its hose reel mounted three feet above his head. He pulled the device down and set its adjustment dial to its lowest pressure rating. Herrera looked at him as Callaway stuck his left index finger under the man's nose and pushed hard, upward. The pain inflicted by doing this caused Herrera to open his mouth in an attempt to scream. Callaway stopped the sound by shoving the two- foot long, flexible grease wand down the man's throat, causing him to gag and vomit. Again, Callaway stared into Herrera's eyes as he squeezed the trigger, slowly pumping thick lithium axle grease down the man's throat, into his lungs and stomach.

"This is for Carrie and Melinda Eagle," he said, glaring at his captive. "Oh yeah, Juan Jimenez said to tell you hello."

Herrera struggled against the straps, looking pleadingly into Callaway's eyes. Callaway turned the pressure dial up to its maximum power and squeezed the trigger again. Herrera's body began to shake drastically, as his eyes looked straight up. Callaway continued to squeeze the trigger on the grease gun until he heard a loud *pop* coming from the man's chest cavity. Herrera's body went limp. A stream of blood and axle grease poured from his mouth and nostrils, snaking down around the grease wand. Callaway let go of the wand, slowly backing away from Herrera's body. He wiped grease off his gloves with a shop rag from a nearby toolbox. He looked at the open lid on the toolbox. On the inside of the lid was a mirror in which he saw his reflection. He stared into his own eyes, as the knot of pain in the back of his head subsided. *My God, I've become what I set out to kill,* was all he could think. It was an instant realization that *Saint* Michael Callaway had become, in a period of weeks, no better than the man he had just killed, or the hit man, or David Howe. He became damaged goods, just as Carrie had after the murders of her father and her first fiancée.

He looked down and began to cry, but his attention was drawn to the mirror on the toolbox by a bright red glow. In the reflection he could see that the glow was coming from a cigarette being smoked by someone looking at him through a window. He saw the person in the window raise something up and put it to his shoulder. Callaway swiftly spun around, raising the barrel of the 12 gauge, getting off a shot just before the man in the window could pull his trigger. The nine 30 caliber lead balls from the shotgun shell burst through the window glass and tore through the man's face and upper chest. His body pitched back striking the man behind him and throwing him off-balance. Callaway ran out through the door with the shotgun leveled to his left. The second man regained his balance and attempted to fire, but Callaway let fly with two rounds of buckshot, catching the man in the abdomen and groin. The gunman fell backward, screaming in agony, while his finger squeezed the trigger of his AK-47, firing the gun wildly in the air, instantly alerting everyone on the island that there was an intruder. Callaway ran toward the path that he knew would take him to the area near Drake's house. Before crossing the clearing to the path, he heard gunshots and saw clumps of sand jumping into the air all around him. He turned in the direction of the gunfire and fired two more rounds, dropping another one of Drake's men.

Callaway ran down the pathway but stopped when he saw flashlights ahead of him. He crouched down, looking through the tritium night sights on the shotgun, and waited. Three men appeared, running down the path toward him. He leveled the shotgun, took careful aim, and fired, quickly working the slide action of the weapon. All three men dropped to the ground. He could now hear voices from the clearing behind him and footsteps coming in his direction. Reaching into his backpack, he pulled out one of the single sticks of dynamite with its timer set for seven seconds and put it on the ground. He laid the now empty shotgun on top of the stick of dynamite with the glowing night-sights upward, hoping they would be seen by the approaching men.

Callaway waited until the men were almost on top of him, then he touched the switch to start the timer, and ran down the path. Six men came down the path. One of them stopped when he saw something glowing on the pathway. They slowly approached with their rifles aimed at the glow on the pathway when the time expired on the explosive. The concussion of the blast killed all six men instantly.

Callaway continued down the path. He passed an intersection with another path and could hear more people approaching from his right. He pulled the Glock out of the holster and removed the seventeen-round magazine, carefully placing it in the magazine pouch on his gun belt. He inserted one of the 32 round magazines and flipped the selector switch to fully automatic. He was no longer worried about how loud the weapon would be.

"Time to make some noise," he said to himself. Continuing down the path towards the beach and Drake's house, Callaway heard shots coming from behind him. He could make out a slight hill in the white sand path ahead of him. He stepped up onto the hilltop and jumped in the air, spinning, and spraying the path behind him with the deadly Black Talon rounds. The extra power of the rounds upped the cyclic rate of the pistol, while overwhelming the suppression capabilities of the silencer, creating a sound that was more like a chainsaw than a firearm.

221

Hitting the ground on the other side of the hill, he dropped to a kneeling position, quickly removing a long magazine and instinctively placing it in the net bag at his side. He loaded the weapon with another thirty-two round magazine and waited to hear more incoming rounds. Instead, he heard moaning coming from the path behind him. He moved off the path into the woods, carefully walking towards the lights he could see glowing on the building next to Drake's house. When he reached the building, he could see the back of Drake's house, located next to the dock that ran out to the barn, housing the tourist submarine along with the pier where all of Drake's go-fast boats were tied up. A gas pump on the pier was fed by an above-ground pipe running along the dock, and up to a large fuel tank about ten feet away from him. He saw more of Drake's henchmen running down the beach to take up positions near the entrance to the path.

They think I'm going to come down the path and right into their arms. Not too bright, boys, Callaway thought.

He looked up at the back wall of Drake's house. From the plans *Avengher* had sent him, he could tell that the extension was Drake's safe room. He figured that Derrick would run in there if the fighting got close. He ducked down behind a large one-thousand-gallon fuel tank, trying to figure out what he would do next. He knew he could not fight all the remaining thugs Drake had running around looking for him.

Well, Callaway, he thought. *You can try to get back to your WaveRunner and make a run for it, but if you do that, Drake stays alive. You won't get a second chance, because if they don't kill you here, you'll either die on the way back home or be thrown in prison for the rest of your life. Think quick, boy.* He looked down and saw a hose reel with a gas nozzle hanging from a gasoline tank. The hose reel was very large, and it occurred to him that this was probably a backup hose for fueling the go-fast boats or some other vehicles on the island. Again, he looked up at the roof of Drake's house, remembering that the safe room had a ventilation pipe that ran out of the building's roof. *Maybe I could give Derrick a reason to leave his house*, he thought, as he grabbed the fuel nozzle and switched on the pump.

Callaway tied the gas hose around his waist and began climbing up the drainpipe to the roof of Drake's house. He believed he would not be easily visible to Drake's men since he was climbing in the alley between the two buildings. The hose got caught up on one of the drainpipe brackets. Callaway gave the hose a hard yank, freeing it from the bracket, but at the same time nicking a small hole through one side of the hose. Reaching the roof, he pulled the hose up and found the air vent he was hoping for, almost directly in the middle of the safe room roof. He stuck the nozzle of the hose into the vent and pulled the trigger, starting the gas flowing. Taking a piece of nylon strap from his backpack, he tied the lever in place to keep the fuel flowing, noticing the small amount of gasoline leaking on to the roof. He placed another single stick of dynamite next to the vent and set the timer for ten minutes, hoping he would have enough time to get off the island, while still allowing enough time for a large amount of gasoline to accumulate in the safe room. *Now, if you just haven't closed the vent from the inside,* he thought.

He clambered back down the roof, slid down the pipe, and jumped back down into the alley. He checked his watch to see how much time he had left before the explosive went off. Working his way around the back of the building adjacent to Drake's house, Callaway again cut through the woods, heading back to the WaveRunner.

*****

"Have you killed him yet?

"Derrick Drake had been pacing about in his house like some kind of agitated zoo animal since the first gunshots were heard ten minutes prior. His guards had been attempting to give him information on the intruder or intruders on his island.

"Is it Callaway or the cartel?" he screamed at his security men who were guarding the front and only entrance to his late father's house.

"I don't know, Mr. Drake," one of his security men answered. "By all accounts it's only one man, but by the number of our men that have been killed, it seems like we're fighting an army."

Drake shook his head, anger seething in him. "Callaway! It's got to be Callaway. Where the hell is Herrera?!" he asked.

"We don't know, sir. No one's been able to find him," the security man said, shaking his head. Drake kicked a chair over in his anger. "I want ten of your best men with you guarding my front door! I don't want that son of a bitch getting near me," he said in the clipped version of his British accent that he picked up from all the boarding schools that he had been thrown out of when he was young.

The security man gave Drake a very distraught look. "Sir, with the exception of a few men that are still out hunting for the intruder, I only have ten men left."

*****

Callaway made it to the edge of the woods near where he'd tied up the WaveRunner. He scanned up and down the beach looking for any more of Drake's thugs and broke into a run down the beach toward the water, scrambling to make it to the WaveRunner. He was greeted by the sound of automatic weapons fire and felt a burning pain in his side under his right armpit. Falling to the ground, he crawled behind a small dune. Callaway reached down and pressed against the wound that felt like a graze under his arm. He took his left hand up, and even in the darkness he could see that his glove was soaked in blood, even though the wound didn't seem too deep. Peeking over the top of the dune, he saw muzzle flashes coming from two areas in the woods about thirty feet apart. He looked at his watch, trying to determine when the dynamite stick on the roof of Drake's house would explode, hopefully blowing the building, and Derrick Drake, straight to hell.

He lay there applying pressure to the wound, as he counted the seconds down, figuring this was the end of the line.

The time ran out, but nothing happened.

"Well, shit, Howe, I guess you got in your last shot at me after all, since your damned detonator didn't work this time," he whispered in anger.

He pulled the Glock from his holster and set it down near the top of the dune. *Gotta keep going*, he thought. His mind jumped back to all his training at the Federal Law Enforcement Center. "Never give up in a fight. Roll and go!" he said.

Callaway pulled the remote starter from his pocket,

pushed the button, and heard the engine on the watercraft come to life. He then pulled the one remaining single stick of dynamite from his bag. Knowing the single stick had a detonator set for seven seconds, he pushed the switch on the timer, counted to three, and painfully heaved the explosive as hard as he could toward the gunfire coming at him from the right. His timing was accidentally perfect, as the explosives that he set around the drug lab building and trailer all went off, shaking the ground and distracting the men shooting at him.

He then grabbed the Glock and rolled to his left, to the side of the dune. He fired one long burst, emptying the weapon at the men to the left of his position. He popped loose the 32-round magazine and again stuck it in the bag hoping to leave no trace of his presence on the island known as Golgotha. He loaded one of his 17-round magazines into the weapon, jumped up and ran towards the water, firing the pistol at the woods while pulling the knife from the scabbard on his belt with his left hand.

He could see that the outgoing tide was pulling the WaveRunner tight against the rope securing it to the beach, with her bow facing the open sea. He continued to fire as he swiped down at the rope, cutting it clean, while trying to secure the pistol in his holster. The pain in his side made him lurch while doing this, causing him to inadvertently hit the magazine release on the side of the pistol. The magazine popped out of the grip of the pistol and landed in the water near the edge of the beach.

Bullets began striking the water all around him. Callaway made a desperate dive onto the watercraft. His left side and legs hung off the craft into the water as he grasped both of the handlebars and squeezed the throttle. The WaveRunner jumped forward, dragging Callaway along its left side. He pulled himself up onto the machine and gunned the motor to full throttle, flying across the water and into the darkness. Drake's men continued to fire at the sound of the craft, when the last stick of dynamite exploded in front of them, killing two of them instantly but only knocking the third one to the ground.

Callaway ran out about a half a mile from the shore and then circled around towards Drake's house. He shut down the gasoline engine and flipped the trolling motor off the rear of the WaveRunner, cruising silently towards the beach, shielded from view by the darkness. When he got within an eighth of a mile from the beach, he shut off the trolling motor and flipped the bracket out of the water. Reaching into the watertight compartment in front of him, he pulled out a towel and pressed it against his aching side. He pulled off his gloves, and feeling the area above his ribcage, he could tell that the bullet creased deeply into his flesh, and then kept on going. Reaching back into the compartment with his left hand, he unzipped the gun bag containing the Thompson Contender single shot pistol that he had taken from Klauser's van. He opened one of the plastic bullet boxes containing military armor piercing bullets, loaded a round into the chamber, and closed the breach. Laying the wooden front of the pistol on the windshield of the WaveRunner, he looked through the ten-power telescopic sight, zeroing in on the front of Drake's house. He could see a man walking up to the house, coming from the direction of his last battle on the beach.

Yeah, that's it, asshole. Tell him that you ran me off the island. Tell the little son-of-a -bitch that he's safe now, so he'll come out of his house, and I can kill him, he thought. The front door of the house was open, yet there was a second door that appeared to be made of steel bars, like the door of a jail cell, still closed. He recalled a report that there was an iron-barred inner door which braced the front door in the event of an attack.

Straining his eyes, Callaway could see the figure of a man standing behind the iron-barred door. Hard as he tried, he could not sight in on the figure he assumed to be Drake, with very little chance of hitting him. He let out a deep sigh, believing the game was over and that the man who ordered the death of his lover would continue to live.

"I'm sorry, Carrie, I tried my best, but I guess the man that had you killed will go free," he said. Callaway unloaded the pistol and began placing it back into the gun bag in the waterproof compartment. He felt the breeze on his face, just as he did when he arrived at the island, only this time it was tainted by a peculiar smell.

"Gasoline!" he whispered to himself. Pulling out the Contender, once again, he sighted in on the roof of Drake's house with the little scope turned up to the maximum power. He could see a dark, shiny stain seeping down the roof from the area where he had placed the gasoline nozzle into the roof vent of Drake's safe room. Lowering the site slightly, he could see liquid dripping from the eaves. He smiled, and reached back into the compartment, pulling out the other box of .223 rounds for the Contender. He removed a single tracer round and loaded it into the chamber of the weapon. Callaway again rested the pistol on top of the windshield of the WaveRunner and pulled back the hammer. Given the long distance to the house and the wind coming directly at him, he aimed about three feet above the stain on the roof. He knew that he would get just one shot, as the red glowing streak of the tracer flying would reveal his precise location to Drake's men. He took a breath and let it out slowly, trying to steady himself when he began to squeeze the trigger, and found himself praying as he did so.

The extremely loud boom produced by a rifle bullet coming out of a short pistol barrel rocked Callaway back in his seat. He quickly recovered and laid the pistol on the windshield while looking through the scope again. He could see that all eleven of Drake's men were standing directly in front of the door, like defensive lineman guarding their quarterback in a football game, and they were pointing their guns out toward his position on the water. He knew that if they all fired at once, the chances were better than good that he would be hit.

He lifted his head and saw the bright red streak made by the tracer round arc down and strike the roof of the house. Almost immediately the rooftop burst into flames which continued down the side of the building. The fire burned its way up to the roof vent. Following the fuel arcing over the top, it then traveled down the vent into the safe room below. A huge amount of aviation-grade gasoline instantly caught fire within that steel and concrete room. The pressure produced by the heat and expanding air within the room, began to buckle the steel door leading to the inside of Drake's house.

Derrick Drake heard the gunshot coming from out at sea. He immediately retreated from the steel barred door back toward the steel door of the safe room. The room quickly became hot. He ran to the steel barred door, trying to pull the keys from his pocket. He kept looking back at the door and saw it buckling as more and more heat poured out from its edges. He turned back to the steel barred door, but only managed to break the key off in the lock in his haste. His safe room was about to become his death chamber. He screamed at his security men in a high, shrill voice. "Get me out of here, now!"

All of his remaining men came to the door and began pulling at the iron bars. Drake was screaming, his body pressed against the door, his arms through the bars, flailing, as the safe-room door gave way. A giant gush of orange flame poured out through the open door, engulfing the room and Derrick Drake. With no place else to unleash the pressure that built up in the room, the fire vented through the bars of the front door and through Derrick's body, at such a velocity that it burned all the flesh from his bones. The fire continued outside like a blowtorch, burning, or suffocating every last one of Drake's men to death.

Callaway looked through the telescopic sight, watching the carnage. He could see the figure of the man at the door hanging lifeless from the bars. He placed the pistol back into the compartment, started the engine, and turned his little craft for the open sea.

Chapter 20

The sea was starting to get rough as Callaway made his way back toward the island of Eluthera. He was trying to travel fast enough to reach his supposed pickup point near where he estimated the WaveRunner would run out of fuel. The sun was peeking over the horizon to his east when he heard the engine on the watercraft begin to sputter. The little craft slowed down to a halt and began to drift. He was pleased that he had accomplished his mission, but now reality was setting in.

"Well, Carrie, this is just great. I'm either going to die out here from exposure or get arrested. One of the two," Callaway said as he scanned in all directions looking for the boat that was supposed to pick him up. The morning was beginning to warm up, so he removed his boots and wetsuit and buckled his gun belt around the waist of the black bathing suit he had been wearing underneath. "It doesn't look like my rescuer is trying to find me," he said. "I guess this Avengeher person isn't gonna show."

Callaway found out that he was quite wrong when he saw a low-flying seaplane that almost flew right over him. Not knowing if the pilot had seen him, he opened the center console of the watercraft and retrieved his flare pistol. Aiming the device straight up, he cocked the hammer and pulled the trigger, launching the 12-gauge flare high into the air. The red, glowing projectile rose in the sky, and then arced over and dropped into the sea.

He watched the seaplane as it made an almost perfect 180° turn, then the pilot started back toward his location. The engine throttled down as the pilot deftly lowered the nose of the aircraft while turning into the wind, showing Callaway some excellent flying skills. The plane slowed, and the pilot raised the nose while settling the rear hull of the aircraft into the water. After a slight bounce upward, the plane sat right down in the chop and turned toward Callaway.

He watched the plane approaching him, trying to determine who the pilot was. He couldn't tell if it was Todd's former secretary Donna Kendall, or Detective Jimenez from Miami-Dade PD, or whoever else Avengeher might be. The windshield of the cockpit was darkly tinted, allowing him to only see a figure in the pilot's seat. The pilot continued to steer the aircraft toward him, cutting the throttle completely as the seaplane came close. The now silent machine drifted up to Callaway's watercraft, softly bumping into the starboard side.

Not wanting to take any chances, Callaway un-snapped his holster and drew the Glock, pointing it at the cockpit. It was at this point that he realized the weapon did not have an ammunition magazine in it. He kept the gun aimed at the solitary figure inside the plane, knowing he only had one round in the chamber if things went wrong. Callaway heard the right-side cockpit door crack open, and when the door came fully open, his mouth dropped open in total surprise.

"Todd?" was all that he could say.

"Jesus, Callaway!" Todd yelled. "This is the way you treat people trying to help you?"

Callaway lowered the pistol. "You are Avengeher?" he asked, twisting his head to one side.

"Who were you expecting, Callaway?" Todd asked. "The First Sea Lord of the Royal Navy?"

Callaway continued to stare at Todd, confused by the mutual hatred between them. "Well, are you just going to sit there?" Todd asked. "We have very little time to get you back to your boat before everybody in the world knows what you've been up to. I suggest you get aboard so we can get going."

For the first time since he had met this man, Michael Callaway obeyed an order given to him by Richard Todd. Without saying a word, he climbed off the WaveRunner and into the cockpit of the little seaplane and sat down in the right seat. He couldn't help but stare at Todd, trying to figure out exactly why he had helped him track down the mole, David Howe, and provide him with up-to-date plans and photos of Drake's island. He was absolutely stunned by the fact that Todd was rescuing him now.

Todd pushed the starter button and brought the single pusher engine of the seaplane to life. The noise of the engine and the propeller directly behind the two men was almost deafening, with the cockpit door open, but he could still hear Todd speaking to him.

"Uhh... don't you think you should get rid of the large piece of evidence floating in front of us?" he asked, pointing at Callaway's watercraft.

Callaway couldn't help but notice that Todd was wearing a weapon in a shoulder holster under his left arm. He could see two magazine pouches hanging from the holster rig, under his right arm.

"Are those Glock 9 millimeters?" Callaway asked. Todd nodded, as Callaway reached over and pulled one of the mags from its pouch.

"I seem to have lost my last magazine somewhere between the island and here." Callaway said as he slipped the magazine into the grip of the Glock 18. He opened the right cockpit door, pointing the weapon at the WaveRunner and paused. He knew he had to sink the watercraft since the Navy and the Bahamian Defense Force would be swarming through the area soon. All they would have to do is find the watercraft and they would know that Callaway was involved in the mess on *Golgotha*.

"I'm sorry, my friend," he said to the watercraft, as if it was his warhorse, and then looked at Todd and said, "Ears!" as he stuck his arm outside the cockpit.

Todd stuck his fingertips in his ears, as Callaway raised the weapon back up and squeezed the trigger. Set to fully automatic, the eighteen bullets came out of the pistol like water from a garden hose and stitched the hull of the little craft from bow to stern. She immediately took on water and began to sink, which wasn't surprising given the weight of all the extra hardware that Callaway had brought along on his trip.

"Don't forget the pistol," Todd said, as he advanced the throttle of the seaplane, taxiing for takeoff. Callaway watched the bow of the WaveRunner slip beneath the waves as he dropped the pistol and his gunbelt into the water and slammed his cockpit door shut. He knew that all his equipment would be tough to find as they were over the Bahamas Trench in about 7000 feet of water.

Todd turned the seaplane into the wind and rammed the throttle forward. The Lycoming engine howled as the pusher prop bit into the air. Callaway buckled his seatbelt as the seaplane bounced over a couple of waves and rose out of the water. He winced from the pain of the wound under his arm and Todd asked, "Are you all right?"

Callaway looked under his arm and saw dried blood. "Yeah, I got nicked a little, but the bleeding stopped," he answered.

Todd reached under his seat and produced a first aid kit. Callaway was able to patch the wound with a couple of gauze four-by-fours and some adhesive tape.

Todd kept the throttle up, trying to gain altitude as quickly as possible, while turning toward Eleuthera. The two men sat silent as Todd climbed the plane to 6,500 feet and leveled off.

The silence became eerie.

"Well, aren't you going to ask me?" Todd asked as he backed the throttle off at a speed of 110 mph.

Callaway didn't say a word for about ten seconds before he looked straight at the man and spoke. "Why? Why would you of all people help *me*?"

Todd grinned slightly, "A long time ago, right after I retired from the Army, I was hired by the Drug Enforcement Agency and several other federal agencies as a recruiter. They sent me up to Northwestern University to check out an applicant that appeared to have a lot of potential to become an agent. That applicant was a young woman named Carrie Marvin. She appeared to be just what the agency was looking for in a deep cover operative. Smart, strong, and damaged, mentally. I didn't know what to expect before I met her. I read her profile, and I knew about the murders of her father and fiancée. Just talking to her, I knew she was all business, and that she had vengeance in her heart for anyone dealing drugs."

Callaway listened quietly, as Todd let out a long sigh, and continued. "I figured that she would fit the psychological profile of a deep cover agent," he said. "What I didn't figure on was falling for her, in a big way."

Callaway's eyes widened.

Todd continued with, "Oh, don't worry Callaway, nothing happened between us," he said. "She was way out of my league, and I knew it. But for some reason, she got to me. Since I recruited her, it was my job to keep tabs on her performance after she went into the field, just as I did with all my applicants. I was able to follow her exploits down in South America. She was quite impressive. I continued to check on her even after you caused me to lose my job with the Customs Service. If you thought I hated you for that, you can imagine how mad I was at you when I heard you two were together." Todd shifted in his seat and continued with, "The government moved me to a position auditing the DEA office in Miami to find the mole that they believed had been giving information to the Drakes. When I heard that Carrie had been murdered, I was so angry I wanted to fly out to Drake's island and kill everybody there myself. But I know my limitations. I was never a field man. But I had to do something. I wanted to find a way to help anyone who would bring a fierce vengeance upon Derrick Drake and all of his thugs. I only knew one person who would be angry, capable, and crazy enough to do the job, and that would be you."

Callaway sat there, stunned by this revelation. Something just didn't seem right. "But what about your former secretary?" he asked.

"I saw her standing by you at Carrie's funeral. I was surprised to see that. I thought she hated your guts. And then she came up to me after the ceremony and told me that a lot of people wanted to help destroy Derrick Drake. What's up with that?"

Todd sat up straight in his seat, grinning again. "Yes, she was in on the joke. So was a certain older narcotics detective from Miami-Dade PD. We all managed to dig up some information on Mr. Howe and Mr. Drake."

Todd's smile got a little bigger. "Oh, and by the way, Donna and I are a bit of an item now," he said. "Yes, I know she hated my guts when I was her boss, but they sent us both to work at the DEA, and somehow or other we became friends, and… much more. She helped me put aside my hatred for you and focus on figuring out who the mole was."

Callaway laughed. "You're not kidding, she hated you. She used to refer to you as a walking prostate exam for all the male agents," he said. Callaway looked at Todd for a long moment, and then painfully reached out his right hand. Todd glanced over at him, smiled, and shook his hand, just as the plane started to bounce around in the air.

"Dammit!" Todd shouted. "This is the same headwind that slowed me down when I was heading out here to find you."

"I can handle the bumps, the bandage seems to be holding," Callaway said.

Todd shook his head. "That's not the problem," he said as he looked at his watch, and then at Callaway. "In about ten minutes, the satellite that's been watching Drake will be over his island. I'm guessing you left enough wreckage there that will be noticeable for anyone watching the screen to notice?"

Callaway nodded. "You could probably see it from Mars."

Todd advanced the throttle a little more, trying to coax more speed out of a seaplane with the aerodynamic qualities of a cinder block as he replied, "As soon as the NSA person sees what you did, he or she is going to get on the phone to the DEA and they are going to call the

US Marshal watching your boat. If he goes aboard and you're not there, you're done," he said.

Callaway rubbed the stubble of his beard. "I guess old Marshal Tucker will have his day with me after all if we don't get in there pretty quick," he said.

Todd gave a little laugh. "You know I asked the Marshal's Service for him specifically to watch you," he said. He's such a dumbass I figured that he would never catch on to you."

Callaway stared at Todd, as Todd laughed again. "Oh, I did his background, too," he continued. "He was only hired because his uncle is a congressman. I followed his career, too, just for laughs. He's a total moron."

With Eleuthera coming into view, Todd began his descent. "If we see that the Marshal is on your boat," Todd said slowly. "I'm just going to keep going. I can drop you on some other island, which will give you time to make a run for it. You'll be a fugitive in both the US and the Bahamas, though."

Callaway clutched the wound in his side, trying to think this through. "If Tucker's in his car, do you think you can make a touch-and-go landing in the channel next to my boat?" he said. "It's early in the morning; there won't be anybody up except fisherman. If you can just get her down low enough, I'll push open the door and jump out."

Todd looked at Callaway, his mouth agape. "We'll still be moving at about sixty miles per hour," he said. "If you don't get splattered on the tail of the plane, you'll probably crack your skull on the water at that speed. You sure you want to do this?"

"I don't have much of a choice, now do I?" Callaway answered. "If I survive the jump, I'll swim to the boat and see what happens from there. If I don't, you just keep on flying. You were never here, and we never saw each other. I couldn't have killed Drake and Herrera without help from you and your friends, Todd. I am very grateful to you, Sir, and I don't want you getting into trouble for what I did."

Todd looked at Callaway and nodded. His expression softened at Callaway's calling him "sir" for the first time. He took the plane around to try and line up on the channel where the *Orinoco Flow* was berthed.

*****

"You are late again!"

Maggie Burke came running into the large room with her snow-soaked shoes sliding on the slick linoleum floor. She was twenty minutes late for her shift, and the analyst who had been on duty all night did not look pleased. "Yeah, Maggie, this is the third time this week," the analyst continued. I may not have the party lifestyle that you have, but I do still have things to do before I go to sleep. If you worked the graveyard shift once in a while, you might understand."

Maggie was suffering from a terrible hangover and had heard enough of this junior analyst's complaining all week. She was about to scream at him when alarms started going off all over the console.

"Which one of the birds is it?" she asked as she put on her headset.

"Thirty- one, Area 1260, Southeast Bahamas!" the analyst responded.

The satellite and ground computer worked in unison and would send out an alarm whenever the satellite in orbit observed something unusual.

239

"Pulling up the satellite video now," she said as she watched the picture materialize on the monitor in front of her. "Oooo… shit."

The heat sensor on the camera of satellite number 31, in low Earth orbit, showed an extremely hot area on the island of Golgotha.

"This is the one that we've been watching for any new activity, right?" she asked.

The other analyst nodded, staring dumbfounded at the screen. Maggie grabbed the telephone and called DEA headquarters on the other side of the district.

"Hey, this is Maggie Burke at NSA," she said, trying to hide her excitement. We've been watching Area 1260 for you guys, Golgotha Island, monitoring it for any activity. Something happened there. Either a volcano erupted, or somebody nuked the place, because it has a heat bloom over it the size of Arlington."

*****

Todd put the seaplane into a steep bank and lined up with the channel where Callaway's boat was docked. Callaway could see Tucker seated in his vehicle while the aircraft banked. Todd wrestled with the controls, as the ungainly little aircraft had some quirky handling characteristics at low speed. The channel itself was only about one hundred feet wide, which allowed plenty of room for taxiing a seaplane, but not a heck of a lot to land, or in this case, do a touch-and-go. The plane slowed as he lowered the flaps and was floating just above the water as Callaway unlatched his door and prepared to jump. He had to push hard against the resistance of the wind but managed to squeeze through the opening and drop into the water. The impact hurt him badly, as his body skipped and tumbled, and then sank into the cold water. Todd gunned the motor and flew low down the channel, narrowly missing a building as he climbed.

"Good luck Mr. Callaway," was all he said as he turned the seaplane on to a heading for Florida.

*****

"Tucker! Wake up. I'm here to take over," Marshal Rodriguez said, shaking her head while looking at her partner through the open car window. Tucker's eyes popped open at the sound of her voice. He wiped the drool from his cheek.

Rodriguez backed away from the door, her nose wrinkling." "Do you ever bathe, man? Jesus! The inside of the car smells like something died in there."

Tucker's cell phone rang, and he grabbed it off the seat, giving Rodriguez a dirty look.

"Tucker," he answered. His eyes got very large. "What! Holy crap!"

He threw the door open, screaming as he squeezed out of the vehicle, and ran past Rodriguez. "He hit the island; we need to secure the boat!"

Callaway surfaced brief seconds after the water impact. He coughed from swallowing seawater. He didn't feel as if anything was broken, although the wound on his side was killing him. He began to swim to the boat when he realized his bathing suit was gone, ripped off by the impact. When he reached the port side of the *Orinoco Flow*, he could hear Marshal Tucker screaming from the parking lot. He painfully pulled himself up the rope that he had used to escape from the boat the night before. He climbed over the rail standing next to the side door. He could feel the concussion of Tucker's huge body hitting the rear deck of his boat. He knew the man would be coming into the cabin through the rear door. He stepped inside just as Tucker slammed into the other door. Callaway saw the towel that he had left on his dining table after his previous day's shower. He grabbed it, pressing it painfully against the wound and held it under his arm.

Tucker forced the door open. He was apparently startled to see Callaway standing there and drew his pistol from his belt holster.

"Freeze, Callaway!" he screamed, pointing the pistol at Mike's face.

"Whoa, Marshal Tucker!" Callaway yelled. "What the hell are you doing, man? Get that gun out of my face!" Callaway put his hands in the air, but kept his elbows against his sides, keeping the towel in place over the wound.

Tucker still had the gun aimed at Callaway as Deputy Marshal Rodriguez reached the door. Callaway, standing there naked, looked at the woman and smiled. "Marshal Rodriguez. Of course, *you* are welcome here anytime, ma'am," he said.

She let her eyes roam down his body. She looked up with a slight smile, and then with a look of scorn, she turned to her partner. "Tucker! What the hell is wrong with you?" she yelled. "He's here on the boat so that means he couldn't have gone to Golgotha. The Bahamians only gave us permission to carry weapons to protect ourselves. Get that damned gun out of his face."

Tucker lowered his weapon and moved closer to Callaway, who looked at the man and shook his head. Tucker was looking furious. "I don't know how you did it, but I just got a call telling me that Golgotha Island had been trashed. I can't think of anyone else who would want to do that."

Callaway closed his eyes and again shook his head. "Oh, so I guess the three Colombian cartels that Derrick Drake deals with wouldn't be suspects, you dumb asshole?" he asked, sarcastically.

Tucker was fuming as he moved in even closer. Callaway was getting concerned that he might notice blood on the towel pressed between his arm and his side.

"Oh, yeah, Callaway? Then why are you soaking wet? Did you go out for a morning swim?" he asked, spitting as he spoke.

Callaway gave Tucker a very stern look. "No, actually I just got out of the shower," he said, sniffing the air. "Something that you might want to try, man, cause you stink really bad."

Marshal Rodriguez rolled her eyes. "Tucker, you've got nothing here, let's go," she said.

"Callaway, I'm sorry about my partner's actions, and what he did to your door." Callaway noticed that she kept losing eye contact with him while talking.

"Not a problem, Marshal Rodriguez. I kind of understand what you're dealing with. But again, for the record, you're welcome to come back here anytime you want."

Tucker opened the broken rear door to the cabin and walked out, cursing under his breath. Rodriguez followed him out the door and Callaway collapsed into a chair, physically and mentally drained from pain, stress and the physical exhaustion of the last twenty-four hours. He managed to apply a butterfly bandage to the wound and drank half a bottle of Crown Royal. He settled back to await any further repercussions.

Chapter 21

It was a true *déjà vu* moment for Commander David Eldridge. He was landing on the island of Golgotha, just as he had one year ago when he was part of a task force that invaded the island in force. The purpose of the first landing was to arrest Anton Drake, a former Royal Navy Commander, for smuggling drugs. This was after Michael Callaway unintentionally sank the man's tourist submarine turned drug smuggling submarine, resulting in a warrant from the Bahamian Government for Anton's arrest. Unfortunately, Anton had left the island, but when Eldridge and others searched the place, they found evidence of many horrors that the Drakes had committed during their reign as the drug kingpins of the Caribbean.

Eldridge slogged ashore with a detail of people, including agents from the DEA, FBI and U.S. Customs, along with members of the Bahamian Defense Force and police. Eldridge's boss, Admiral Dorcas Mae Slingo came ashore, too, leading the American contingent. She was resplendent in shiny new combat boots and a Navy jumpsuit a few sizes too big for her frame. Eldridge heard her barking orders as soon as they were feet dry on the island.

"I want everyone to break into groups of three! Fan out and search the island for anything that might identify whoever did all this. I want evidence, and I want answers!" the Admiral demanded.

She turned around and looked right at the Commander. "Eldridge! You're with me," she said. "You've been here before. I want you to show me around."

Eldridge sighed, dropping his right hand on top of his Beretta M9 pistol, in his holster. *Maybe they'd let me go home if I accidentally shot off one of my toes,* he thought. He motioned to Slingo and a sailor carrying an M-16 to follow him. They walked to the area of Drake's house from the opposite direction of where Callaway had landed and observed the carnage there. They found eleven burnt bodies, laid out like bowling pins outside of the door. The ground around them was scorched black from the flames that had shot out of the front door of the house the previous evening, like the fire from the engines of an F-18 fighter on afterburners.

Admiral Slingo, having never seen any blood and carnage during her career, immediately started retching, but managed to keep from vomiting, until she saw what was left of Derrick Drake. While the other bodies were burned black, there was nothing left of Derrick but his skeleton, with bits of flesh here and there, held together by cartilage. His bones hung from the bars of the steel door like some Halloween horror house decoration. What was left of his mouth hung wide open, as if ready to bite someone. "Oh God!" Slingo whispered, as she fell to her knees and began to vomit.

Eldridge turned away to avoid embarrassing his boss. "You aren't tough enough for this, are you, Admiral?" he whispered.

Slingo struggled to her feet and stumbled over to the fence that led to the dock.

"Both of you come here!" she yelled, gesturing at Eldridge and the sailor. "You two are the only ones who saw what just happened," she said. "If I find out that you've told *anyone* about this, I will bust you both down to nothing. Do you read me?" she hissed.

Eldridge and the sailor came to attention. "Aye-aye, Admiral!" Eldridge shouted, looking at the young sailor, who was white as a ghost.

The three moved down the beach while Slingo received reports of what the others searching the island had found. She was told about a building that had been thoroughly destroyed, apparently by some type of explosive, a few hundred yards away in the jungle. They also reported the grim discovery of a man strapped to an automobile ramp that they found in the wreckage of the building next door to the lab. The DEA agents identified him as Martino Herrera. Slingo stopped occasionally to write everything down on a pad as she followed Eldridge down to the beach.

The trio came upon the remains of the men that Callaway had fought down the beach from the house. Two of them had been blown apart by Callaway's last stick of dynamite, and the other was face down in some sea oats with the top of his head blown off. Slingo turned her head and walked away, avoiding the gruesome scene.

It was low tide, and the commander looked out to sea, thinking how much nicer his life was when he was commanding U.S.S. Pegasus, cruising the islands, and looking for trouble. He looked down and saw a rope in the water. He followed the rope out of the water until he found the other end tied in a neat knot to a large piece of driftwood. He grabbed the rope, pulling it out of the water. It was cut clean by something very sharp. He turned to his right to see what Slingo was doing and saw her by the edge of the jungle looking very pale. "Damn! I wish I had a camera right now," he muttered, as he took a step and bumped something with his right foot. Looking down, he saw dried blood in the sand. He crouched down and pulled the object out of the sand. He let out a sigh. He picked up a seventeen-round Glock magazine, knowing full well where it had come from. He turned it around, praying at the same time. "God, no. Please don't let it be…" he whispered.

Eldridge looked at the left side of the magazine, and there he found *M. Callaway* engraved, as he knew he would, confirming his expectations.

A year ago, Eldridge, Cruz, Hidalgo, and others had found Callaway's name engraved on a piece of the bomb that accidentally sank Anton Drake's submarine. He and the others had falsified information to cover Callaway that night, and here he was again in the same situation.

"Did you find something, Commander?" Admiral Slingo asked in her shrill, startling voice. He stood up with his back to his commanding officer, as she walked up behind him. *Do or die,* he thought. *Do I do my job and hand up my friend to this bitch?"* He slipped the magazine into the right slash pocket in the front of his jacket. "No ma'am," he said, turning around. "Not a thing." He shuffled his feet, covering the blood with sand.

All the searchers met up on the beach to discuss the mayhem and destruction they'd observed on the island of Golgotha. The one thing they didn't find, except for Commander David Eldridge, was anything that would link Michael Callaway to what Slingo was calling a crime. She was angry that she had nothing to use to charge the man she'd apparently grown to hate. As she was boarding the boat to return to their ship, she stared at the back of her recalcitrant subordinate, Commander David Eldridge, thinking of a way to use him to trap Callaway.

Chapter 22

"I want you to get it out of him, Commander. I mean, he is your friend, right?"

Commander Eldridge stared sternly at his boss, Admiral Slingo, standing in the conference room of her office suite, wanting seriously to tell her to go to hell. "You want me to betray a friend?" Eldridge asked, turning his eyes away from her.

"Yes, Commander, that's exactly what I want you to do. And I expect you to get the information I will need to have Mr. Callaway prosecuted to the fullest extent of the law," she replied.

Eldridge looked at her and smiled, "What if he clams up?" he asked. "What if he denies that he was there? I can't shoot him up with truth serum. We do have laws against interrogating an American citizen that way, you know. And besides, who the hell cares what happened on Golgotha, and especially what happened to Derrick Drake and his thugs? You do know that in the past they've killed a lot of people, don't you, ma'am?"

Slingo looked more perturbed by the minute. "I don't care what you have to do!" she yelled. "From what I understand, you two became big-time friends after that incident down in the Bahamas with Drake's father. Hell, Eldridge, you lost your sea command for saving his ass.

If I were you, I'd be angry as hell with the man. Now's your chance to get back at him for your losing your boat!"

"I would have lost her anyway, Admiral," Eldridge replied. She went directly from my command to the scrap heap, right on schedule when that patrol ended," he said, trying to change the subject.

"You're not listening to me, you thick-headed son-of-a-bitch!" she growled. "Let's understand something, Commander. I don't like you. Not one damn bit. And I'm not asking you to do this; I'm ordering you to get that information out of Callaway. And I swear to you, if you don't, I will see to it that you are shipped so far north that I'm quite sure you will literally freeze your balls off. There's a little training base, way north of Anchorage, that needs an Adjutant Officer. How'd you like to spend the remainder of your career there, big fella?"

Eldridge tensed up, the anger twisting his guts into a knot. *In my entire life, I have never, ever, thought about hitting a woman. But you've got me so pissed off, Dorcus, that I would love to knock you on your boney ass!* he thought. He tried to tune out her condescending words. *I want to belt you so badly that it hurts. But if I do, I'll end up in prison, with no pension, and no life.*

"Are you hearing me, Commander?" she screamed.

Eldridge gave her the hard look, again. "Aye-aye Ma'am, I hear you loud and clear."

Slingo now softened her tone. "However, I will reward you well if you accomplish your mission. I have some pretty good pull with command assignments in Washington. If you can get Callaway to confess to attacking Drake's island, I will bet serious money that I can convince a few people to let you go to sea again. I mean, seriously, Eldridge, you're old. How many years do you think the Navy's going to keep you around before they cashier you out?"

Seeing the creepy smile, she gave him made him tense. He realized that he had never seen his boss smile before.

"I mean, it won't be Pegasus," Slingo said. "She's already been turned into razor blades."

She looked down at the top of her desk and rubbed a smudge off the glass top with a finger, preparing to go for the throat. "But maybe… a *tin can*? A nice, fast destroyer like you used to run?" she said, almost seductively.

Eldridge tensed again. The offer was extremely tempting, since he knew retirement was imminent, and he would love nothing more than one last sea command. He already had his right hand in the slash front pocket of his jacket. He could feel the Glock magazine with Callaway's name etched on it. All he would have to do was pull it out and hand it, and his close friend Michael Callaway, over to her with one move. He thought about it for one second before he pulled his hand out of the pocket, empty.

"All right, Admiral," Eldridge said. "I'll give it a try, but I may as well start packing my long underwear, and putting a For Sale sign on my house," he said as he turned to leave.

"Just get it done! Get him drunk, get him laid, or break his damned arm, I don't care! Just get me a confession!"

It took about one hour of fighting the I-95 rush hour traffic before Eldridge pulled into a guest parking space at Callaway's condo building in Fort Lauderdale. All through the drive, Eldridge kept thinking about what Klauser, the Fort Lauderdale cop turned hit man, said about everyone having a price. He also remembered Callaway saying the same thing when they were driving to the meeting with Admiral Slingo. He put his hand on the side of his jacket, over the slash pocket, and felt the boxy shape of the Glock 9 mm magazine inside.

He had never ratted out a friend in his life, but the temptation to do so now was stronger than when Slingo was yelling at him, and he had the evidence in his hand to give her. The admiral's threat to send him to the base in northwestern Alaska was bad enough. He knew of that base as a place with no name. It was simply *TB-359*, for Training Base 359, a God-forsaken hellhole of a spot, north of Anchorage, and way up the Knik Arm waterway, that first opened when World War II began. It was a place where they sent SEAL teams to get their cold weather training, next to a little town occupied by Native Americans and some oil company people. The Navy was sending fewer and fewer teams there to train, as the base was scheduled to be closed in less than two years. Congressional budget cutbacks and the opening of a new and much better equipped training base near the North Pole, had sealed the fate of TB-359. While the new base was nick-named Santa's Toyshop by the SEALs because of all its new, high-tech equipment for them to train on, TB-359 was known as God's Waiting Room, since those who were assigned, there were near the end of their last hitch with the military. Eldridge knew the old base was the place where malcontents and those who simply pissed off high-ranking people were sent.

Eldridge pulled into the parking lot of the condo, exited the vehicle, and walked through the front entrance. *Dammit, Callaway!* he thought, as he waved to Manny sitting at the security desk in the lobby and walked into the open door of an elevator. *Why the hell did you put me in this position? I could be cruising the ocean in a real fighting ship, again. A nice, fast destroyer, ready to kick ass and take names, like the old days before I met you. And all I've got to do to get back there is hand you up to Admiral Dorcas Mae, the bitch, Slingo.* His stomach growled, reminding him he hadn't eaten since lunch, and his gut was churning out stomach acid from stress. He took the elevator up to Callaway's floor and walked to his friend's door and rang the bell.

Callaway opened the door wearing a golf shirt and a pair of old gym shorts. He had a drink in his hand, and he looked disheveled. Without a word, he turned and walked to the couch, leaving Eldridge at the door.

"You all right, Mike?" Eldridge asked, closing the door and standing in front of it.

Eldridge noticed the half-empty bottle of Crown Royal on the end table near the couch. The cap, with the torn paper sealing strips on both sides of it, sat next to it. "I see you're back drinking again," Eldridge said. "How long ago was that a *new* bottle of Crown, Mike?"

Callaway looked at him with watery, drunken eyes. "Probably about the time you left your office, if that's where you came from, he answered. "You want a glass before I kill it off?"

Eldridge looked at the table in front of the couch, seeing a framed photograph of Carrie and the half-world pendant that Mrs. Marvin had given him at the Medical Examiner's office. It was obvious that Callaway was a train about to derail again. "Yeah, I came from my office," Eldridge said. "I just had a conference with your *girlfriend,* Admiral Slingo."

Callaway sat up straight. "Let me guess. She sent you over here to talk about what happened on Golgotha, right?" Callaway laid back against the leather cushion of the couch. "So, what'd she promise you, buddy? To get me to talk," he asked.

Eldridge looked away, locking his eyes on the bare spot on the floor where a section of carpet had been cut out. The section of carpet that contained the blood of the late Alberto Cruz. Then it hit him. All the crap that Callaway had gone through, the murders of his fiancee, Cruz, and his old partner, Jorge Hidalgo, all in a very short period of time. Eldridge's right hand went into his jacket pocket, his fingers rubbing the smooth polymer edges of the magazine there. He also remembered one other thing. *If you hadn't shot that bastard Klauser, in my back yard, I wouldn't even be here today!* He looked at Callaway with no emotion at all. "A Tin Can. She also swore that she would send me to a base in the asshole of Alaska if I didn't get anything out of you," Eldridge said.

Callaway narrowed his eyes. Paranoia was setting in fast. "So, my *friend*," Callaway said sarcastically. "What are you going to do? I'm not going to tell you a thing. So, I guess you'd better do an about-face and get the hell out of here."

Eldridge was hurt by Callaway's words. He knew it was the alcohol and the circumstances talking. He turned, placing his left hand on the doorknob. He pulled the magazine out of the right pocket of his jacket, holding it up and looking at Callaway's name engraved on the side.

Callaway recognized the magazine. He instantly became sober.

Eldridge threw the magazine to him. Callaway managed to catch the object and stared at the Commander.

"Next time you pull a stunt like that, Mike, make sure you tidy up."

Eldridge walked out, glancing back at Callaway as he closed the door. He could see him holding the magazine to his chest and crying. He knew things would heal between them, but it would take some time.

Callaway knew that he wouldn't be going to jail for what he had done, but he also knew he couldn't stay in Miami, or anywhere else, for very long. A year ago, after falling back in love with Carrie, he thought his destiny was to travel the world with his love, enjoying life as the two of them found adventure everywhere they went. Now he still fully intended to travel the world, alone, trying to ease the pain of his loss, and taking some solace by dealing harshly with any low life that he came across.

*****

It was about two weeks later that Acting Special Agent-in-Charge Richard Todd was pulling into the parking lot of the United States Southern Command complex in Doral, Florida for a scheduled monthly meeting with representatives from the United States Coast Guard and Admiral D. Mae Slingo. Investigations conducted by the DEA, U.S. Navy, and Coast Guard determined that the man who previously attended these meetings, the late David Howe, had been funneling the information he received at these meetings to the late Mr. Derrick Drake. Howe had been able to provide the upcoming monthly patrol patterns for both Navy and Coast Guard vessels and aircraft. He also told them where the DEA and Customs Service boats and aircraft would be, of course, so Drake's smugglers could move their drugs into Florida without, for the most part, being detected.

God, I hate dealing with this grand bitch! Todd thought as he found a space close to the building. He saw the familiar face of Commander David Eldridge, as the big man exited the front door of the building carrying a large cardboard box.

Eldridge walked up to the government car parked next to Todd's and opened the trunk. Todd exited his vehicle and looked at the items poking out of the top of the box, one of the most prominent being Eldridge's desk name plate.

"Are you going somewhere, Commander Eldridge?"

"Yeah," he said, looking at Todd. "I joined the Navy to see the world, and it looks like I'm going to do just that, courtesy of our mutual friend, Admiral Slingo."

Todd gave him a slight, pensive smile. "I'm guessing we're not talking about Hawaii?"

Eldridge slammed the trunk lid down and shook his head. "No, Sir," he said. "I have been transferred to the armpit of the western world. A lovely little place a few hundred miles north of Anchorage, Alaska, where, if I don't freeze to death or get eaten by a bear, I will finish out my time with the United States Navy. The only good news is that I will be about as far away from that hatchet-faced bitch on wheels as I can get!"

Todd crossed his arms and looked at the ground. "Lovers' quarrel?" he asked, trying to give the man a laugh, which he immediately noticed did not happen, as Eldridge's face blazed almost as red as his hair.

"Mr. Todd, I may just take a vow of celibacy after being around that woman."

Todd chuckled at his response, changing the subject without exposing his connection with the whole Derrick Drake affair. "So, how is Mr. Callaway doing? Have you heard from him at all?"

Eldridge eyed the man suspiciously," "I think you would be the last person on earth who would care about Michael Callaway's well-being, Mr. Todd."

Todd just shrugged. "You know the old saying, Commander. Keep your friends close and your enemies closer, right?"

Eldridge seemed to relax. "I actually don't know where he is, Mr. Todd," he answered. "He said he had some business he needed to take care of offshore, and then he said he was going to cruise his shrimp boat all the way to Alaska to visit me," he said with a slight smile. "I told him that as slow as that tub of his is, he'd better get a start on the trip now, or he'll be iced-in up there for the *next* winter!"

Todd looked east, toward the Atlantic Ocean. "I wonder what he had to do offshore?" he asked.

*****

The noise of the big diesel engine almost drowned out the sound system aboard the *Orinoco Flow*. Amy Grant was softly singing "I Will Remember You," as the autopilot steered the big shrimper to a spot in the Bahamas near a small island. It was a place where Michael Callaway and Carrie Marvin had made love and professed their love for each other, in what seemed a long time ago. Callaway sat on the couch in the boat's living room, holding a half-empty glass of Crown Royal, while he listened to the lyrics of the song. He thought about the letters that he'd sent to Joseph Eagle and Mrs. Marvin before he left the dock in Eleuthera. In the letter to her, he wrote about the vacation in the Bahamas they had spoken about at the airport, and how he "caught a lot of fish." Joseph Eagle's letter contained only one sentence: "I cooked the gar fish."

As he listened to the lyrics while the boat cruised on the calm sea, Callaway imagined Joseph Eagle reading the letter and crying.

The song spoke of saying goodbye, the one thing that Callaway could never do. He wished he had died on Drake's island, after he'd killed Drake, of course, so he could be with Carrie again.

The alarm on the autopilot began to beep. Callaway got up, walked up to the helm, and pulled the throttle lever into neutral. He then shut the engine off and allowed the boat to drift in the almost motionless water. It was almost sundown, and he could hear thunder from a distant storm.

Again, the song spoke of parting, causing Callaway's eyes to well up. In the space of one year, he and Carrie had just discovered each other again. The anguish of being without her gripped his entire body.

With shaking hands, he swallowed the last of the Crown, his fourth in the last hour, and setting the glass down he walked outside to the stern of the boat. He could see lightning from the storm now, as he remembered the battle for their lives that he and Carrie had fought with Anton Drake at this exact place on the ocean. Reaching into his pocket, he pulled out two gold neck chains each with a half- world pendant attached and held them in the palm of his right hand, extended over the water as the song continued.

The song was coming to an end with the promise that the singer would be her lover's strength and he would be hers. The realization that this would never happen caused a strangling pain in his chest, far worse than he'd felt from the bomb that killed Jorge, and almost killed him.

He looked at the clouds, and all he could see was Carrie, like a cold breeze from the approaching storm hit his face. He opened his hand, letting both chains and pendants slip through his fingers and into the sea. Then he collapsed to the deck weeping, as the words of the song came to an end.

"I will remember you…"

The End.